INSIDE FBI POLYGRAPH

INSIDE FBI POLYGRAPH
(CONFESSIONS & TALES)

WILLIAM J. WARNER

TATE PUBLISHING
AND ENTERPRISES, LLC

Inside FBI Polygraph
Copyright © 2016 by William J. Warner. All rights reserved.

No part of this publication may be reproduced, stored in a retrieval system or transmitted in any way by any means, electronic, mechanical, photocopy, recording or otherwise without the prior permission of the author except as provided by USA copyright law.

This novel is a work of fiction. Names, descriptions, entities, and incidents included in the story are products of the author's imagination. Any resemblance to actual persons, events, and entities is entirely coincidental.

The opinions expressed by the author are not necessarily those of Tate Publishing, LLC.

Published by Tate Publishing & Enterprises, LLC
127 E. Trade Center Terrace | Mustang, Oklahoma 73064 USA
1.888.361.9473 | www.tatepublishing.com

Tate Publishing is committed to excellence in the publishing industry. The company reflects the philosophy established by the founders, based on Psalm 68:11,
"The Lord gave the word and great was the company of those who published it."

Book design copyright © 2016 by Tate Publishing, LLC. All rights reserved.
Cover design by Norlan Balazo
Interior design by Honeylette Pino

Published in the United States of America
ISBN: 978-1-68293-411-1
1. Fiction / General
2. Fiction / Mystery & Detective / Police Procedural
16.01.04

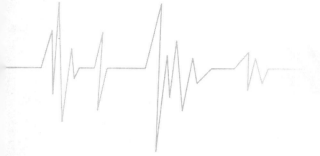

DEDICATION

This book is dedicated to all who have served as FBI polygraph examiners—those exceptional and inquisitive souls who seek truth from liars and arouse a few honest folks along the way!

ACKNOWLEDGMENTS

I gratefully acknowledge the support and assistance of many folks without which this book would never have come to fruition. First and foremost, my lovely wife, Judy, was my inspiration and role model for the past thirty-seven years and hopefully for many more to come. Her enthusiastic reviews of each chapter provided the oversight and attention to detail necessary to make the story interesting. I will always be indebted to my children, John and Alicia, as well. For without their tolerance of my absences throughout twenty-two years of service, my career would have been far less enjoyable. When it came to transfer from one state to another, they were always supportive regardless of any inconvenience and disruption it may have brought to their lives. Speaking of family, I am also very thankful for the assistance of my dear friend and close relative, Kathy Farmer. Her tireless efforts in guiding me through countless computer gymnastics were a tremendous aid in getting my manuscript through final editing.

Enough cannot be said for the exceptional staff at Tate Publishing. I am sincerely grateful to all involved to include acquisitions, photo/graphics, cover design, editing, marketing, and project management. All impressed me as top-shelf professionals.

I am most appreciative to Tom Bird whose guidance I received was most helpful. It was indeed his wisdom and instruction that motivated me to finally put my pen in my hand and start writing.

Although this book was a solo effort, it was inspired by a team—a team of exceptional FBI special agents whose fellowship as polygraph examiners formed a bond like few will ever know. It is that *bond* that sets them apart from other agents within the Bureau. The best FBI polygraph examiners are the ones who play an integral part in keeping that bond by sharing and implementing the trade secrets of their chosen specialty, interview and interrogation—a true Liars Club few can belong to and whose entry requires steadfast honesty, integrity, and a never-ending zeal to transform storytellers into truth-tellers.

CONTENTS

Author's Note 11
Preface 13
Kidnappers and Killers... 17
Sexual Misfits 67
The Storytellers... 103
Dressed For Deception 135
Red-Stained Money 173
Thugs and Thieves.. 195
Countermeasures 207
Straight Talk About Liars 226
Epilogue 255
Afterword 263
About the Author 267

AUTHOR'S NOTE

Inside FBI Polygraph (Confessions & Tales) is the second edition of *Going Knee To Knee (Confessions, Tales & Tribulations from Inside the FBI's Polygraph Program)*. Other than the title, the cover, and a few formatting adjustments, the content of the two books remains the same. Prior to the first publication, the original manuscript was submitted to the FBI for prepublication review and approval.

The events described in this book were based on actual events; however, some details and places have been altered to preserve sensitive investigative techniques. As such, historical investigative facts may differ from the stories unfolded here. All names have been replaced with pseudonyms to protect the identity and privacy of investigators, perpetrators, witnesses, and victims. The only exception is that of widely known public figures. Any name similar to any citizen is purely coincidental and unintended by the author. Displayed quotations under the chapter titles are from the author unless otherwise noted.

No recordings were made during any interrogations; therefore, the exchange in dialogue between the parties throughout this book cannot be attested to with 100 percent accuracy. However, the reader may rest assured this interplay is quite similar and, in some instances, quite precise as to what took place from story to story. No sensitive or classified information related to any pending or closed cases is revealed in this book. Any opinions expressed throughout this book are the author's and not those of the FBI.

PREFACE

Much has been written over the years about this investigative technique—this thing called a polygraph. Webster defines it as "an instrument for recording simultaneously changes in blood pressure, respiration, pulse rate, etc." It is certainly that and more. Those affiliated with the FBI polygraph program consider it an investigative tool, the utility of which belongs in the polygraph suite as opposed to the courtroom. The naysayers and the antipolygraph folks vehemently reject polygraph as voodoo-science, unreliable, and intrusive. These are the people who go to great lengths to prohibit the use of polygraph under any circumstances. One former senator even referred to it as "20th century witchcraft." If you're of the antipolygraph ilk, you can nurture your disgust with the technique any time of the day by accessing any one of a number of antipolygraph websites. Feast on the derogatory commentary and sing-along with the chorus. As is often the case however there are two sides to every story. My passion for the continued use of polygraph will become self-evident throughout the stories revealed here.

There are limitations of course. The FBI, perhaps more so than most US government agencies, abhors the admittance of polygraph into the courtroom. Why so? one might ask. It's really quite simple. Any technique not 100 percent reliable but admitted into a courtroom could be prejudicial to a jury. Add to that the opinion of an unscrupulous private examiner who operates without any real quality control, and you have a tainted product that can potentially corrupt a verdict. For these reasons and more, the use of the polygraph belongs in the hands of certified polygraph examiners who are subjected to a rigorous quality control program. Even then, the results of any such test should stay off the witness stand. More on this argument is found in one of the later chapters in the book.

Suffice it to say this book was written as a tribute to the men and women of the FBI who stepped into cases at key moments and put their training and experience on the line. These are the people who assist their fellow agents with the polygraph of a subject who often lends true direction in a case. These are the unsung heroes responsible for gaining the unknown information from reluctant witnesses that will sometimes break a case wide open. The professionalism of the FBI polygraph examiner exemplifies the highest ethical standard in the industry. The Bureau's quality control program is a program designed to overlap within itself. The results of which are unprecedented and unduplicated in the federal government.

To be a member of this elite group of investigators is a privilege sought by few and attained by even fewer. The camaraderie and memories are everlasting. It has been my pleasure and honor to have had the unique opportunity to be associated with such a group. We take the profession quite seriously. While we try to understand those physiological changes that occur in "blood pressure, respiration, pulse rate etc.," we actually take it to another level. It's called controlled confrontation. A program for social workers it is not.

So if you're one of those naysayers, a no-practical experience academician, a frustrated former investigator, a newspaper columnist who delights in espousing the sins of a good technique utilized by well-intended people, then read on. Enjoy the ride. Feast on the dessert and relish in the "up-comings" as opposed to the "shortcomings" of a tried and true method for detecting deception. Regardless of your viewpoint, continue to live a good and honorable life because you certainly do not want to find yourself sitting in the infamous black chair facing your accuser going knee to knee.

KIDNAPPERS AND KILLERS

Nobody forgets where he buried the hatchet.

—Kin Hubbard

RIGHT OF PASSAGE

The tracing climbed and leveled off as Special Agent Cyrus J. Donovan (Cy) got ready to pop the next question. He knew that Jackie's reaction to question 5 in the sequence would dictate the course of the day. She had already given him plenty of physiology to the question on the previous chart, and if the sweat ducts in the fingers of her left hand would juice up one more time, then the call would be "deception indicated" or DI. Indeed it was the galvanic skin response (GSR) Cy was most attentive to. The GSR was most reliable, and he knew it. Oh, that's not to say her cardio wasn't active. But that would stand out later. It was the GSR that took off on a climb much the way a halfback breaks out into the open field and catches your attention. Only upon replay is the right guard's block appreciated. Jackie's cardio tracing would be noticed. It had to, for it was too consistent. "Did you participate with anyone to cause the death of that woman?"

"No" was Jackie's response.

Cy quietly took his own deep breath as he watched patiently the ink on his old hand-me-down analog instrument make its move. The GSR pen shot upward, dragging a trail up eight chart divisions. There would be no need to put numbers to these charts. Any FBI polygraph examiner worth his salt would look at Jackie's charts globally and call her DI. For good measure, he ran a third chart with similar results; only this time, Jackie gave him a little pneumo action too.

The pneumograph tracing, or respiratory channel, like a center, does a lot of work with very little recognition until he fumbles a snap. In Jackie's case chart number 3 provided apnea in the pneumos at question 5. These were textbook charts for Cy, and he was quite relieved. Now, if only he could extract that confession, the allusive admission of guilt which so often finds shelter in the deep shadows of the mind. He knew he would confront her. He knew he would allow the traditional "one denial," put his hand up, and work to gain her trust. To be successful, however, he also knew he had to sell her a product—the most difficult sale any man can hope to make. The product would be *jail time*.

Cyrus James Donovan had joined the ranks of the FBI's most elite interviewers and interrogators in 1996 by completing his polygraph training at the Department of Defense Polygraph Institute (DODPI) at Ft. McClellan, Alabama. DODPI was without question the best school of its kind in the world, and he was anxious to make a name for himself. For the better part of two years, he had struggled believing his charts and going for the kill when confronting his subjects knee to knee. He didn't have a 70 percent confession rate like many of his peers, but he knew he would have. He knew that the art of interview and interrogation, or I & I, was a practice. You only get better through practice, by being in the game, by losing and getting up again. If one theme doesn't work, another one will. If not, another one, and so the practice continues.

Cy had learned from an old mentor, Rudy Mahovalich, who advised him the guilty never get up to leave—they just sit in the chair waiting for you to give them a reason to come clean, whereas the innocent tell you to pound sand rather quickly. Rudy always said, "If you're not willing to call an innocent person a liar, then you're in the wrong business." You can't let yourself get eaten up with hurting someone's feelings. Even the innocent folks have lied about something—why would they be in the polygraph chair otherwise. You make the mistake of calling a guilty person nondeceptive (NDI), and you risk a severe hit on your reputation among your peers.

Cy took Rudy's advice to heart. Not just Rudy's advice but the wisdom of so many of the other FBI polygraph examiners he had run into. There was A. J. Birdell, Billy Groom, Eddie "Snake Eyes" Simmons, Mickey Jarvis, and Tony Zarilla to name a few. He too would someday take on their role and become a beacon of guidance to younger, less experienced examiners. For now, however, it was crunch time. The moment had come for him to take control of Jackie Doolittle and bring her through the gate of salvation. The time had come for Cy Donovan to establish a reputation of his own.

Jackie was a beaten woman, and she knew it. She would not make eye contact with him. She would not acknowledge what he had to say nor would she vocalize any denial to the crime. At first, Cy was quite optimistic; he would lead this woman to righteousness sooner than he thought. After all, she had not given him that traditional first denial. *Was she implying her own guilt?* He wasn't quite sure how to cross this bridge. He told her she failed her polygraph and she had not been honest with him, but she took no issue with him on the matter. *Hey, Rudy, what do you do when they don't deny?* Don't all guilty people deny it at first? "Treat 'em the way you would want to be treated, and you'll eventually acquire their trust" was what he remembered. He pressed on not knowing what he was in for before this day expired.

Cy pulled his chair into hers knee to knee. She didn't budge. With the sincerity of a counselor, he began. He sensed she was disturbed. "Jackie, you're not a bad person. You got caught up in something you never planned. We know it wasn't your idea to bring harm to Paula. What happened here, Jackie? Is this something that started out as a good thing but got out of control? Were you with a boyfriend who lost his senses? A brother? Another family member? Jackie, you don't strike me as the type of person who would intentionally bring harm to another woman, much less a retarded woman. What happened with her?"

Jackie sat frozen in the chair.

Paula Gooden was forty-five years old and retarded. She had been that way since birth, and her family struggled to bring her along in the somewhat backward ways of rural southern Indiana. Investigators didn't know a lot about Paula, but they did know she was one of six women who had come up missing throughout central and southern Indiana over the last couple of years. Her aging mother reported her missing one Sunday afternoon after she failed to return home from an IGA grocery store just a short walk from her home. She had made this trip many times in the past. Paula was only mildly retarded but nevertheless quite vulnerable.

Normally, police are reluctant to get involved on missing person cases until at least twenty-four hours have gone by, and even then, they tend to drag themselves into the matter. This was different however. The Indiana State Police had recently got the FBI involved and a task force had been set up for previously missing women.

Special Agent Wayne Chesbro from the Bloomington office of the Indianapolis division had the ticket. Indy's front office knew if they were going to get involved with state and local authorities on this one, they had better put a bulldog in charge.

Chesbro's reputation preceded him from his days further north in Gary where he was constantly pursuing drug-related kidnapping subjects. But this one had a different flavor to it, which motivated Wayne to an even higher energy level. His relentless investigation led his task force to Jackie Doolittle.

Doolittle had been named by a couple of other poorly educated women, who, quite reluctantly, gave up her name as someone who hung out with some real troublemakers. Getting these backward people to tell him anything he could rely on was like pulling teeth for Chesbro. But now that he had a bit of a lead, he latched onto it and never let go. Subsequent investigation of Doolittle had now landed her in Cy Donovan's polygraph chair.

"Listen, Jackie, there are women out there who continue getting picked up, brutalized, and murdered, and it has to stop. You can play a big role in this. You can be a savior. If it were your loved one, you would want the killer caught, wouldn't you?"

Jackie wet her lips just a little bit.

Cy saw it and pursued. He moved his chair in slightly and cocked his head in an effort to get into her line of vision. Jackie moved her head, he moved his. Again, she moved; again, he reciprocated.

"Help me, Jackie. Let's put this behind us. You'll be a better person for it, and you know it."

Jackie's eyes met Cy's, but she didn't utter a word. She wasn't buying off on Cy's "savior" theme.

Okay, time to learn more about Jackie. I've got to get her to speak. He knew she could. He had gotten some biographical information from her in the pretest interview. If only he had spent more time with her developing rapport.

"Jackie, when you were growing up, were both parents present in the home?"

Jackie muttered something. Cy took it to be a no.

"So your mother raised you alone?"

"No, she died when I was five."

He was relieved to get a full sentence out of her. "I'm sorry, Jackie. So your father—"

"No," Jackie interrupted, "my stepfather, sort of."

"Okay, do you think he did a good job of teaching you right from wrong?"

Jackie didn't say anything.

"How old were you when—"

"He was an alcoholic," Jackie interrupted again, "he and both my brothers."

"Were you abused in the home?"

Jackie shifted her hips and elbows.

Cy picked up on the clustered movement of key body parts. He was learning in this business to ignore the tiny movements. It's the elbows, hips, and feet that are the key nonverbals to look for along with the flushing in the face, neck, or chest. He knew he had hit on a sensitive topic with her.

"Jackie, you have to trust me. What we talk about here this afternoon stays here. You had a difficult childhood, didn't you?" Before she could answer, he put his hand on the arm of her chair next to hers.

She folded her arms and took on a defensive posture.

"Jackie…"

"There ain't no need to go there. Daddy's dead, been dead, and I ain't seen my brothers for years no way. As far as I know, they're either in jail somewheres or dead too."

Cy sensed a slight watering up in her eyes, but she recovered quickly. He paused and looked at her, she at him.

She was standing her ground. Finally, she spoke. "My past ain't got nothin' to do with nothin' no way."

"It's got more to do with something than you may think, Jackie, but I'll leave it alone for now. I'm easy to get along with." *Help me, Rudy.* Jackie's eyes left him. He glanced over her shoulder to get a glimpse of the clock through a crack in the blinds. There was a clock in the hallway, and he intentionally bent a window blind and positioned his chair before the interview so he could see it.

He also had removed his watch prior to the test so he wouldn't be tempted to look at it while interviewing Doolittle. One of the fundamental rules of interrogation was not to get caught by the subject looking at your watch. They will wait you out if they sense you have a concern about time, and he was keenly aware of it. He had ignored this rule in the past and paid for it. It was now 6:30 p.m. He and Jackie had been together four hours rehashing some things but getting nowhere. He knew from his other examiners if you're going to get the confession, you will usually get it within the first four hours. He had yet to get to first base. He could throw in the towel; four hours is an admirable effort, but he couldn't let Chesbro down.

He wouldn't. The discomfort in his bladder reminded him of the rules. Any confession obtained needs to withstand the scrutiny of coercion. Cy took a moment to allow Jackie a restroom break, but just as important, he needed a break.

Cy took a moment to brief Chesbro and other interested parties in the conference room directly across the hallway. The prosecuting attorney was present along with a defense attorney claiming to represent Jackie Doolittle. Cy felt as though he may lose the opportunity to continue. "We're not getting anywhere," he was ashamed to say. "She's had a troubled childhood, but she won't go there with me. She just sits there like a worn out pillow," Cy said.

Doolittle's attorney, Rob St. Martin, spoke up, "Let me talk to her."

Cy straightened up. "She hasn't invoked," he said as he glanced at the prosecuting attorney. Max Hunter had a helluva reputation in this part of the state, and defense attorneys and judges respected him. Hunter gave Donovan a wink, and Cy knew to relent. After all, this case would ultimately be tried at the state level, and he wasn't about to make the mistake of throwing his federal weight around as other agents were known to do on occasion. He took a deep breath, fearing he may lose a confession he felt was still obtainable. He looked at St. Martin for approval, but St. Martin chose to take the lead.

It wasn't long. St. Martin spoke to Jackie and came out of the room disgusted. He knew his client was involved in something evil. What it was, he wasn't sure because Doolittle wasn't talking to him. But apparently, she had nothing derogatory to say about Cy either as St. Martin came back into the conference room bewildered. There was a long pause in the room.

Cy looked at Hunter, St. Martin, and Chesbro and said, "I'm just getting started." Donovan went back into the room with Jackie, and nobody stopped him.

He pressed on with her. Another three hours elapsed. Treating her with respect all the while, Cy once again ventured into her childhood.

"I said I ain't goin' there. It don't matter," Jackie raised her voice.

"Well, what does matter to you then?"

"I ain't a bad woman."

Cy took notice of the voluntary statement. "Tell me about it, Jackie. I know you're not a bad woman."

Her eyes were active now, not looking at him but active as if searching for a new spot on the wall to look it.

Cy waited but nothing followed. Figuring it might be time to take a bit of a gamble, he decided to lay off the "Mr. Nice Guy" stuff.

"Okay, Jackie, here's the deal. I've got all night. If you want to continue to sit there like warm dog poop, go ahead. But you've got a chance to tell your side of the story. If you don't want to tell it, someone else will. You'll end up in court with a jury never having had the opportunity to hear what you had to say. You make the decision, and you make it now. We have been more than fair with you today." Cy got up to leave and looked back at Jackie. "I'm bringing Chesbro in here," he said.

"No," Jackie shouted. "I will not speak to that man ever again."

Apparently, Chesbro's antagonistic ways were not to her liking from previous interviews.

"If you've got something to say, then say it," Cy snapped back.

First a pause; then, she spoke, "I lied on the polygraph."

It was now 10:30 p.m., and Jackie Doolittle had finally given him an opening. Although he had his foot in the door, he knew from past experience his actions from this point forward were critical. Quite confident now that he would ascertain the facts from her, he knew he had to project confidence and convey his trust that he would look out for her interests in the coming days ahead.

Cy moved his tablet aside and spoke softly, "You know, Jackie, doctors tell us it's healthy to talk about these things because it relieves the emotional pain that builds up inside you."

"I know," Jackie said tearfully.

More and more tears would follow before she was prepared to talk. This was a process, and Cy knew his patience would pay off. The watering up of her eyes and the tracks of her tears were a clear sign now that he was about to be educated on something quite heinous. He stepped out momentarily to get her a Kleenex box and give a quick thumbs up to those waiting eagerly across the hall. As he stepped back into the room, he observed that Jackie's persona had changed slightly. Other than a sniffle, there were no more tears.

She appeared fixated on a spot on the wall, almost catatonic.

He offered her the Kleenex box.

She took a tissue, blew her nose, and glanced at him.

He offered her the trash can for her tissue.

She ignored it but looked again at him.

He sensed he was about to be trusted. *Patience, patience,* he thought to himself. She will find the strength.

Gripping her soiled tissue as if it was her last link to freedom, Jackie took a deep breath and found the spot on the wall again. Several minutes passed, still nothing.

Cy placed his right hand on top of her left hand; still knee to knee looking her straight in the eye, he whispered, "Please tell me about it, Jackie, please talk to me." He couldn't have been kinder, but all he got was silence. Undeterred, he was confident it was going to come.

His patience was wearing thin however. It had been two more hours since she opened the door with her comments about having lied on the polygraph. He sat back and looked away.

"We were at an IGA grocery store…in the parking lot," she muttered. She spoke softly, but she was very clear. She didn't look at him; she was too ashamed. She would now talk to him, but she found her comfort in the wall and the soiled tissue in her hand.

"Larry and I'd been seein' each other for a while, and like a fool, I went along with him. Anyways, we and the others were in his van sittin' in this parking lot when they spotted this woman."

Cy wanted to interject something here, but he chose to listen.

"They were laughin' and makin' fun of this woman I guess because she was retarded, and they already knew it. She walked into the store, and Travis got out and went inside. Little while later, he came out and said she was in the cash line and would be out soon." Jackie paused.

"Who is Larry?"

"Larry Dill," she responded.

"The others?"

"Travis Coy and Ricky Sorrows, I think is his last name. They all know each other from the carnival, and they've all been in trouble before."

"What kind of trouble?"

"I dunno." Jackie sighed. "Somethin' to do with kids. They don't talk about it much around me."

"What happened when she came out, Jackie?"

Jackie glanced at Cy and caught his eye in a rare moment and looked back to the wall for comfort again. Her shoulders slumped like the beaten woman she was. "Larry said I had to go up to her when she came out and coax her over to the van because they had somethin' to show her. First I refused. I told Larry I wasn't gettin' involved in any of his shit today. But you see, Larry is mean and hateful, and he grabbed my arm, and when he looks at you, you just know you ain't got no choice. I jus' figured maybe they gonna' harass her, poke some fun at her, steal her groceries, somethin' like that. If I'd known what was really gonna happen, I'd never would'a brought her back to the van."

Jackie got teary eyed again, and Cy reached for the Kleenex box.

She gathered herself quickly and continued, "Anyways, she came out with but one bag, and I saw she was by herself, so I went up to her and ask her if she'd like to look at some sweaters we had, brand-new but 70 percent off. At first, she acted like she wanted me to go away, but I told her fall wasn't far off, and they'll be more expensive later. I told her to come out and jus' look. 'Doesn't hurt to jus' look. They're real cute sweaters.' She followed me back toward the van real slow like."

"Were you surprised?"

"Not really. I can be real sweet you know. Besides, she ain't all there." Jackie paused as if to catch a moment of remorse. "We got to the back of the van when Larry opened the back doors, and Ricky, well, it was like he came up from around the other side and surprised me. He got in behind her real close like, and I got a little bothered 'cuz I didn't like him no way. It was jus' a minute later when Larry grabbed her arm, and Travis grabbed the other arm. Ricky said to me, 'Get in there with her.' So I did, and Ricky went around to the front to drive, and we took off."

After a long pause, Cy intervened, "Where did Ricky drive to, Jackie?"

Jackie turned her head from one side to another avoiding eye contact with him.

He could sense more embarrassment on her part now than deception.

She fixated on another area of the wall before speaking again. "We went to Travis's house, if you could call it that. It ain't much of a place. In fact, he don't live there no more."

Cy got a brief description from her, just enough to know. He didn't want to get Jackie sidetracked on a trivial matter now.

"What happened next?"

"Larry said to get her in the upstairs bedroom, shut the doors, and for me to go in with her to calm her down." Jackie paused.

Cy got her a cup of water. "Tell me about it," he asked.

Jackie took on a dejected, defeated look and stared down at the floor with her head at an angle. "Larry said for us to take our clothes off and get to it," Jackie muttered. Another pause.

"Did you listen to him?"

"Not at first," Jackie replied. "I called him a jackass and said I was leaving."

"And?"

"He wouldn't let me. As I said, he is a very mean man. He grabbed me by the back of my neck and told me to do what I do best." Jackie glanced at Cy and added, "I'll never forget those words. He is a son of a bitch."

Jackie's eyes flooded with tears. Cy gave her a moment to gather herself before continuing. "I hate to ask you to relive the past, but for Paula's sake, you understand how important this is."

She nodded in agreement. Her demeanor took on a new dimension Cy hadn't seen yet this day. As if she was steeling herself for a tremendous challenge, she spoke further, "The woman wouldn't take her clothes off, so they ripped 'em off for her. She was pushed onto the bed, and Ricky held her down. Larry told me to go ahead and—" Jackie paused, not wanting to say.

She continued, "Travis said to the others if I had oral sex with her, then I was committed and wouldn't be able to turn any of 'em into the police. It wasn't like I had a choice."

Jackie sobbed briefly before returning to a firm demeanor. She tilted her head to the other side. She then added that Larry, Travis, and Ricky all had their way with Paula. She said the poor woman was helpless. "They didn't hurt her much, not at that point anyway. One of them slapped Paula a couple times until Larry put a stop to it."

Jackie said she got the feeling Larry wanted to keep her around awhile, and she was right. The three men had oral sex with Paula and violated her every way imaginable while Jackie was forced to watch. Jackie erupted hysterically.

Cy reached over and held her hand with his. Jackie's eyes were glued to his now as she spoke intermittently but nevertheless got it out.

"Sir, they did everything three men can do to a woman over and over, and they had no shame!"

Cy sensed she had a devil in her that needed to come out. He listened for the fiendish malignity that was to come. Sometime after midnight, she had concluded. In the end, Cy learned of the fact that Paula Gooden had been held against her will in Travis Coy's dilapidated home for fourteen days! During that time frame, Gooden was tied to box springs in the upstairs in the heat of a southern Indiana August.

On a daily basis, Larry Dill compelled Jackie to provide her with a sack lunch from one of the area's fast-food chains. This was Paula Gooden's only nourishment. According to Jackie, the mentally retarded Gooden was denied use of a bathroom. "No need for that," as Larry had said.

"We've got a bucket, and Jackie will clean her up every day," Larry said.

Jackie did so, so that Larry, Travis, and Ricky could continue to have their way with her. Finally, on the fourteenth day, Jackie went upstairs to check on her. At first, she thought Gooden was dead. She went back downstairs to tell the others.

Together, Larry, Travis, Ricky, and Jackie gathered around Paula. They poked at her as if she were an animal. There was no movement. Travis wet his finger and placed it in front of her nose. "She's alive," he said.

Larry reached into a closet and produced an aluminum baseball bat. "Who's first now? You all know what you gotta do, so just get it done," he said.

At first, nobody offered. Then Travis took a swing and cracked Gooden's skull.

She screamed violently!

The three of them took turns hitting the back of her head eight or ten times.

Jackie noted to Cy that she remembered seeing blood come down Gooden's face. Then it was Ricky who stabbed Gooden with a knife that Larry had in the glove box of his 1985 Wrecker. Jackie described the knife for Cy as having an emblem of a Texas steer on the handle with a burn mark as well.

Paula Gooden was stabbed ten times in the chest.

Ricky told Jackie to kick her. "By doing so," he said, "she too would be involved." Jackie could only manage to kick her on the foot. About this time, Travis wet his finger again and placed it in front of her nose to feel for air. There was none. Once they were satisfied the poor girl was dead, she was placed in a sleeping bag.

Together, Travis, Ricky, and Larry took Paula into Travis's shed. Once in the shed, one of them had his way with her again, Jackie believes. So she was told. In any event, after a few days in the hot shed, the smell got to be a real concern, so Larry thought it best to get rid of her.

Paula Gooden was rolled up in carpet and sprayed with perfume. The three of them put her in the van and drove her across the state line into Illinois where she was dumped into a shallow grave.

Cy and Jackie sat exhausted.

Cy knew what he had to do. He had learned a long time ago that a confession received once verbally is on weak legs. He needed it repeated, and he needed it in writing. He summoned St. Martin who came into the room. A sad time was revisited once again, but St. Martin had no issue with Cy. A plea agreement for Jackie was likely. She might see daylight again but not the others.

"The price of gas remained steady today despite the recent turn of events in the Middle East," the voice on the radio blurted.

Once satisfied that his Bucar was warmed up, Cy loosened his tie and reached for his traditional sixty-ring-size Casablanca and fired it up. He felt he had earned this cigar. He rolled down his window to take in the cool mist of an early morning fog highlighted yet by a full moon. "My goodness," he noted. *It's 4:00 a.m. I've got family arriving later today for Thanksgiving dinner. It will be a day to give thanks all right.* As he turned north on I-65, he muttered in thought to his old friend, Rudy, *So this is what this polygraph stuff is all about.*

LOSER

Dominique Diego and Orlan Pelanzio had known each other for a few days. A few days were all they would have. Although they had been in a carpool together, their relationship really began at a party with friends on a college campus. They became infatuated with each other literally over night. With the help of a little marijuana, they quickly lost their inhibitions and allowed themselves to enjoy each other in a torrid three-day love affair.

Pelanzio knew of a friend who had a place along the National Lakeshore Park of Lake Michigan east of Chicago. He convinced Dominique to join him for a romantic getaway. It was actually convenient for Dominique as her mother lived not far away in another county.

Upon arrival, near sundown, Pelanzio and Diego decided to go for a stroll along the beach as it was rather warm for mid-October. First however, Dominique telephoned her mother to report her whereabouts as she planned to visit her while in the area.

Her mother, Louisa, was delighted to hear from her and anxious for her to come by the house. Unfortunately, she would never hear from her daughter again.

"Just what kind of man are you, Terrell Wirtz?" Shawan James wasn't bashful about shouting. James was eight months pregnant with Wirtz's baby and quite outraged that Terrell would have the nerve to show up in her church with another woman. "You can't possibly do this to me, Terrell! I mean, give me a break, I'm standing here with your baby, and you walk into the house of God and shame me!"

Terrell tried to get a word in edgewise but realized it wasn't going to happen. He knew he shouldn't have come to the evening service. "Shawan, you don't understand, let me—"

"You need to leave this place!" Shawan interrupted. She was standing and shouting in front of the whole congregation, making quite a scene. It wasn't but a moment before her tears started to flow. She glanced at the other girl, known only as Tina.

Tina was surprised also. She had no knowledge of Terrell's pregnant girlfriend. She looked over at the pregnant girl and suddenly felt awkward and alienated.

The three of them, Terrell, Shawan, and Tina were intertwined in a triangular love quarrel for which Terrell was responsible.

Certainly, they were quite unprepared and uncomfortable with the situation that Terrell had created.

Terrell stood motionless for a moment. He knew he was to blame. His mind went into a whirlwind of confusion. He looked left, then right, then left again as his eye caught a door. He excused himself to the restroom and started for the door. Before leaving, he paused, glanced back again at Shawan's pregnant tummy, then bolted out of the church.

The stage was set most inappropriately for two completely unrelated human forces to meet with disaster—a tragedy neither of the parties had prepared for.

A romantic moment in time would soon rendezvous with depression and humiliation. Indeed an unfortunate mix that would bring Cy Donovan into the picture.

It was Friday, midmorning, and Cy was thinking of the weekend. His mind was on his son's Pop Warner football game that night. *How would little David perform given the fact that he had elected not to coach?*

Being an FBI special agent had its perks. One of them was a fair amount of independence, and he had stretched it to the limit during the baseball season managing a Little League team well into the all-star tournament. He didn't dare take on football too. Violent crime in northwest Indiana wouldn't allow him that much freedom. He knew his son would understand that some day.

"Hey, Cy, you got a minute?" Jake Mathers motioned him over.

Cy meandered over to Jake's desk across the bullpen area of the office. Jake was the office jokester but occasionally put together a helluva case. He knew Jake was working with the locals on a double homicide along the beach near Gary. This beach was part of the National Lakeshore of Lake Michigan and, as such, was US government property. The FBI had jurisdiction on crimes that took place there but found themselves yielding to the locals absent any organized crime nexus.

"What's up, Jake?"

"Well, do you remember that kid, Terrell Wirtz?"

"Uh, yes, I think so."

"You know, the kid who reported those dead bodies on the beach a couple of weeks ago?"

"Are you going to tell me he's a suspect?" Cy asked.

"Yep."

"You want him polygraphed, right?"

"Yep. And tonight if we can get him in," said Jake. "Are you up for it?"

Cy paused, before responding, "Absolutely."

Jake picked up on it and inquired, "Your son got a game tonight?"

Cy should have known better. Agents can't fool other agents.

"He does, but I'm not coaching. What are the facts?"

Jake kept his eye contact with Cy while he reached for the file; then, he broke into a grin. "Friday nights are hell in this outfit, aren't they?"

"As always, the bad guys dictate the hours."

"Well, it may not happen."

"Why's that?"

Jake found his way into the file. "We called him yesterday to come in for a follow-up interview, and he didn't show. You see, as it turns out, Wirtz is a troubled young man. He's twenty years old, was recently tossed out of Marine Corps boot camp, and some say he's very depressed.

"He must be a real loser if the corps let him go out of boot camp," Cy said.

"Not only that, but listen to this. He got this chick, Shawan James, pregnant. She's eight months along you see, and he had the balls to walk into her church with another girl. James happened to be there, and she saw Wirtz with this girl, and um, well, let's just say it wasn't pretty, you know?"

"And?" Cy asked.

"We don't know for sure," said Jake. "According to James and this other girl, Tina, I believe, Wirtz left the church in a huff, and neither of the girls have seen or heard from him since. Unusual to say the least, but this is the same night the couple on the beach were shot to death. Best estimate by the coroner. Wirtz reported the bodies to a resident in the neighborhood the next day. Wirtz later told investigators he was walking his dog when he discovered them lying there in this little cove. Both victims were in their early twenties, shot in the head, and might have been getting it on at the time. The male's pants were down. The female was completely naked. A semen sample was taken from the female."

"Who's is it?"

"Don't know yet. DNA takes awhile to come back."

"Warrants pending?"

"Oh yeah, blood and hair on Wirtz. He's working at a car wash over at Washington and Fifth. We're going to yank him from there about 6:00 p.m. and bring him in. This is where you come in."

Cy was already formulating relevant questions in his mind. This would be a fun one so long as Wirtz doesn't lawyer up, he thought. In any event, it will be another long night. "Where do you want him tested?" he asked.

"Olczinski, over at the PD has a decent rapport with the kid. We thought we'd let him snatch him up and bring him there. Can you set up over there?"

Cy knew the layout at the PD, and he knew he would get a room suitable for testing. "Sure," he responded. "I'll be in place by 6:00 p.m. Stop by about that time, and I'll cover the relevant questions with you."

"Sounds great," Jake said. "You're the man."

"No, you're the man. Let's just hope he sits for it. Got to read him his rights, you know, and he's got to consent."

"Understand. You'll smooth that over with him, you always do."

"Just get him in here without a preliminary interview. You've talked to him once, no need to oversensitize him. If he's good for this, he'll already be plenty hyped up."

"Gotchya."

"Looking forward to it."

"Ten four. Oh, one other thing."

"What's that?"

"The male wore a Guess watch, but we think it was stolen at the crime scene by the perp."

"Okay, see ya later."

He wore a Cleveland Indians ballcap, slightly askew, a gray hooded sweatshirt over a T-shirt and dirty jeans. Terrell Wirtz had in fact been picked up at the car wash by Detective Paul Olczinski. As he stood in the doorway, Cy extended his hand in greeting.

Wirtz returned his hand and gave a limp handshake but held his chin up high.

Cy made note of the clammy hand and the absent voice response. He detected a smugness in Wirtz, a bold attempt to disguise his anxiety so prevalent in the hand. *This will be a challenge*, he thought. *If this guy maintains an arrogant persona, even the most grandfatherly approach on this kid will be in vain.*

Detective Olczinski excused himself from the room and the game was on.

"Indians fan?" Cy asked.

"Yeah, they're all right," Wirtz replied.

"I grew up a Tigers fan myself, but I made it to a few Cleveland games over the years," Cy said. Building rapport with this kid will be essential, and he began very fundamentally. Establishing common ground and developing a willing participant is truly a skill that only comes with practice. The key is to come off sincere.

Phoniness is picked up quickly by even an inexperienced or poorly educated foe. If the foe is guilty of murder, you can bet his guard will be up, Cy figured. He was careful to maintain a lot of eye contact with Terrell. He glanced back up to the hat. It had to come off.

"Terrell, I appreciate the fact you volunteered for this polygraph. It takes a man of integrity to step up as you have. You will see how harmless this process is. I only have two rules. No hats or sunglasses, and you must sit still once testing begins. Fair enough?"

Terrell paused, held his own eye contact with Cy, and then removed his hat. Nothing was said in return.

Control established so far, Cy thought. One of the cardinal rules of interview and interrogation is to maintain control of the interview. It was far better if it can be done in a subtle fashion. Control must be accomplished early, and he was off to a reasonable start. Now for the consent form and advice of rights.

"Terrell, I'm required by policy to present you with these forms. Now you graduated from high school, right?"

"Yeah."

"So you read and understand English just fine?"

"Yeah, whatch' ya got me to sign?"

Cy presented him with the Advice of Rights form first.

Terrell looked it over and signed it with just a momentary pause.

Cy witnessed it, then handed him the consent form for the polygraph.

Terrell looked it over.

"This basically tells you that this test is voluntary. You can stop the test at any time. No one is watching us. It's not being recorded," Cy advised.

Terrell cocked his head to the right and signed the consent form without taking issue. Even though he had been taken off his job today and "encouraged" to come in for this test, he was truly sitting for this experience voluntarily. *Perhaps this Cy is a straight shooter*, he thought.

"Let me tell you what's going to happen here today," Cy started off. "I'm going to take a few minutes to get to know you. I'll cover some issues with you. I'll go over all the questions I'm going to ask you on the test. You're going to know what all the questions are ahead of time. I won't ask you any questions on this test today that you refuse to answer. How's that?"

"Fine with me. I've got nothing to hide."

"Great! Let's get started. When you were growing up, were both parents present in the home?"

"Just momma."

"Did you see your dad much?"

"Naw, man. He had a drinkin' problem. Mom couldn't have him around."

"I see. How old were you when you first learned right from wrong?"

"I don't know, man. That's hard to say. I mean, maybe six, eight. I dunno, it was early though."

"Do you think your momma did a good job teaching you right from wrong?"

"Oh yeah, definitely."

"Any brothers or sisters?"

"Got a half-brother."

"What's his name?"

"Tyrone."

"How old is he?"

"He's older than me, say, probably twenty-five now. Say, whatch'ya gotta' know all this for anyway, man?"

"Like I said earlier, I need to know a little about your background. A little about what makes Terrell tick, if you know what I mean? You want to get a fair test, don't you?"

"Well, sure, but…"

"As I have said, I'm not going to ask you any question on this test you refuse to answer. Will that work for you?"

Terrell nodded and looked away.

Cy moved on. Pretest interviews were critical for establishing that psychological focus. Generating good rapport and building trust for the eventual interrogation would be essential if Terrell were to fail his test. The first part of the interview sets the tone for the outcome of the day. Cy was aware regardless of how well the pretest interview goes, the eventual result still requires a degree of luck. He had the uneasy feeling he would need a lot of luck with Terrell.

"Now as I understand it, you found the bodies of this couple, is that right?"

Terrell shifted his elbows up to the arm of the chair.

Cy noticed.

"Yeah."

"Tell me what happened here," Cy asked.

"I was jus' walkin', you know, and there they were."

"About what time?"

"It was afternoon I guess, middle of the day."

"Was anyone with you?"

Terrell nodded as if to say no.

"Do you walk out there often?"

Terrell paused. "Well, sometimes, I mean, I like the water you know."

"Oh yeah, you're trying to get into the Coast Guard, aren't you?"

"How'd you know that, man? You sure seem to know a lot about me."

"I wouldn't be doing my job, Terrell, if I didn't make it a point to know a little about whom I am talking to. Now you said no one was with you, right?"

"Right."

"Didn't you have your dog with you?" Cy fed him back what was believed to be part of the fib he told investigators earlier.

This was a gimme. He wanted to see how he reacted to the previous fabrication.

Terrell perked up a bit, then said, "Yeah, that's right. We was takin' a walk."

Cy picked up on the subtle change in deportment. He had given Terrell a reminder, although slight, but nevertheless something for him to hang his hat on, so to speak. This in turn, gave him a false sense of security that he was consistent in his story. This was the only freebie Cy would give.

"And the couple who was murdered, did you examine them?"

Terrell's demeanor changed again. His false sense of security left him as quick as it arrived. Blankly, without emotion, he said, "Not really, but they were dead."

"You knew that with certainty?"

Terrell shifted in his chair. "Look, man, the girl looked like maybe she was shot around the head. I didn't hang around."

Ordinarily, this was an excellent time to pursue a plethora of questions with him. Many details of his activity at this crime scene needed answers or explanations. However, Cy would hold this line of questioning in abeyance until after he had collected a few polygraph charts. Although getting a pretest confession was bravado for a polygraph examiner, it was also a risky maneuver. He could lose Wirtz real quick if he were to lawyer up, and his effort would have been of little value. He could see Terrell's changing demeanor wasn't ripe for a pretest admission of guilt. In fact, he sensed it was time to run some paper. No need to oversensitize the examinee at this point.

"Terrell, before I go over the questions I'm going to ask you on this test, is there anything you have told police you would like to change?"

"No," he answered rather sheepishly.

"And you certainly didn't have anything to do with hurting those people at the beach, right?"

"Hell no!" Terrell answered.

Cy reviewed a short list of eight questions with him.

Terrell answered them all without taking issue.

"Okay, those are the questions I'll ask you here today. No surprise questions, no trick questions. You all set?"

"Yeah, this feels like an electric chair, man!"

Terrell pulled off his bulky hooded sweatshirt so Cy could attach a cardio cuff to his right arm.

As he did so, Cy couldn't help but notice a Guess watch Terrell was wearing on his wrist. He felt the hair on the back of his neck stand up. He had to inquire, "Nice watch, where'd you get it?"

"Uh, L. S. Ayres."

"L. S. Ayers, huh? Really?" Cy responded watching Terrell very carefully. Terrell had no further comment and wasn't making eye contact with him. Again, Cy felt the urge to proceed into a pretest interrogation with Terrell, but he knew he would need all the leverage he could find to persuade this maligned individual to see the light. Polygraph charts would be run. Not many however, as he was now convinced of the outcome.

Cy took his position behind his instrument. The moment of contentment had arrived. He had successfully gotten through a pretest interview of a double homicide suspect. His examinee had bitten off on the relevant questions without taking issue. Other words, Terrell Wirtz was prepared and determined to lie today. Cy knew it, and the fact that Wirtz was wearing what appeared to be the victim's watch gave him another measure of leverage in any follow-up interrogation after the test. The trick would be keeping this kid from getting too belligerent when confronted with reality in the next fifteen minutes.

Cy fired up the analog, old reliable as he preferred to call it. He had become quite comfortable with his box after tweaking it several times with new O-rings, tubing, and ink pens. While many examiners had switched to the heat-operated instruments using thermal pens, he preferred to stick with the inker due to its sharpness in clarity of the tracings it produced on the chart paper.

His only fear was that he would get a clog up, which sometimes occurred during a test when one of the ink pens would develop a blockage.

This would force him to delay the test for several minutes while he removed the troubled pen and excused himself to a restroom so that he could dislodge the clot in the plastic artery attached to the pen. This had happened to him once before, and for this reason, some examiners stayed away from the inker to the point where a few were experimenting with computerized polygraph systems (CPSs).

The CPSs were a certain eventuality for the future, but for now, the analogs continued to be the workhorse for the Bureau.

"Is your first name Terrell?" Cy spoke softly as the test began.

"Yes."

Terrell's GSR or skin response tracing was active, and his cardio was steady. *This is a good thing,* Cy thought. *Perhaps this kid will cooperate long enough to finish this test. Wow, he's even breathing well.* Cy noticed. *There shouldn't be any problem interpreting these charts,* Cy figured. Then he moved on to his primary relevant question.

"Did you shoot those people found at the beach?"

"No."

Bingo, there it is! Cy observed apnea in the pneumograph tracing, a climbing GSR through eight chart divisions and an abrupt arc in the cardio tracing. One could not ask for a more deceptive response than that. He got a bonus a minute later when he popped another relevant question.

"Do you know for sure who shot those people found at the beach?"

"No."

This was his guilty knowledge question. With nearly identical reactions, Terrell's physiology was giving him up on chart paper. Timely with the asking of the question, the perspiration channel of Cy's inker displayed two ascending steeples replicating what examiner's refer to as goalposts at the relevant questions. A clear indicator the subject in the chair is not at all content with his answer.

Shortly thereafter, Cy concluded with, "Test is over. Please remain still." He continued to study the respiration tracing for a moment longer. There was no sign of countermeasures from this guy. He came to the conclusion that Wirtz was simply rolling the dice and hoping he could beat the box.

"You can relax," Cy stated. He would give Terrell a couple of minutes to gather himself before proceeding with a second and third chart.

"So what's your machine say?" Terrell asked.

"You already know what it's saying. Let's try it again with the same questions," Cy replied. After concluding the test, he knew without question he had the killer in his chair. Terrell's reactions to the relevant questions on the charts were far too consistent to indicate anything other than deception. Terrell Wirtz had failed his polygraph, and Cy was about to accuse him of cold-blooded murder.

He took a deep breath, looked at his watch one last time, and got up to remove the components from Wirtz. He preferred to have the examinee unattached during questioning because sometimes these discussions got a little heated, and he didn't want to risk one of his components getting yanked around and possibly damaged. This would prove to be a wise decision as he was about to find out. He sat down knee to knee with Terrell.

"Terrell, you failed this test, and there's no doubt in my mind you shot those people on the beach." Cy had thrown his first punch.

"No way, man, I didn't shoot nobody," Terrell responded and looked away.

Cy ignored the denial. "What we have to do, Terrell, is find out why. I don't think this is something you planned ahead of time, and I don't think you even knew who you shot, but—

"I said I didn't shoot nobody," Terrell repeated with a slightly raised voice.

Cy put up his hand. "You already said that, but I need to hear you tell me what really happened that night."

Terrell took on a stubborn demeanor sitting grim-faced, not willing to look at his opponent.

Cy didn't need to look down at his notes. Clipboard aside, he had a few themes memorized. Not knowing how long this kid would sit, he would go to his best theme first. Primary motives for homicides included greed, revenge, anger, passion, envy, and the elimination of a witness. Theme selection for Terrell Wirtz had to focus on the specific motivation for the act of murder, double murder in fact.

"Terrell, I believe anyone who is humiliated in public is capable of losing control of their senses for a short period of time. When this happens, it's really not their fault, or in this case, your fault, is it? I mean, let's look at this for a minute—"

"What are you talkin' bout, man?"

"I'm talking about a good man here who still has a future if he can just muster up a little courage and share an experience quite similar to what many of us deal with on occasion."

"And what experience might that be?"

"Listen. Any man who is spoken to by a woman the way you were by Shawan in church that night would have every right to be upset."

"Oh, you talkin' bout that broad. Bullshit, that ho' don't run my life."

Cy put his hand up again. "She's carrying your baby, is she not?"

"Yeah, she say so. She tryin' to hang it on me. It's bullshit, man. How is it you know so much anyway? It's clear you don't believe me, man. You never did. Nobody believe me. Your machine is wrong too, man."

Cy interrupted, "Terrell, I'm absolutely certain you know a lot more about this than you're telling us. You're going to have to work with me on this. This isn't going away any time soon. What's going to happen here is this thing is going to end up in court and—"

"Well, you're wrong, man. You accused me of something I didn't do."

Again, Cy stopped him, "Just let me finish. Let me finish. This is going to end up in court, and Shawan James will testify. This pregnant girl with your baby is—"

"I said that's bullshit, man." Terrell's voice elevated. "Ain't my baby. You can't say that…you don't have no…"

"Calm down. Let me finish. If you let Shawan testify in court, in front of a jury, well, this pregnant girl is going to tell her story. The jury will see and know she is pregnant. They will be sympathetic to her story."

Terrell was fuming.

Cy caught it and gave him a slight tap on the knee. The pressure was on. Like being in the red zone and down by a touchdown, he would not let up. He knew what plays to call, and he was in his element so to speak. "I've got to give you a heads-up here to what is coming. Not only will Shawan testify to your behavior that night, but there will be one or more representatives from the Marine Corps also who will address the jury as to your disciplinary issues while in boot camp and why you got booted out."

"I didn't get booted out, man. That's unfair. You can't sit there and treat me like this. Who do you think you are, man? Some big cocky, motherfu—"

"Whoa, Terrell! No need to take it that direction. Just cool it here. Let's take this one step at a time."

"I ain't got time for this, man." He shifted vigorously in his seat, gripping the arms of the chair as if he was about to get up.

Cy knew his time was running out with Terrell Wirtz. This theme wasn't going to get him in the end zone today. By shifting the blame of these homicides to a devastating personal incident in Terrell's life, loss of a girlfriend, and a humiliating dishonorable discharge from the military, he hoped he could bring Wirtz around to rationalize his behavior. But that wasn't going to happen at least not in a way that he would ever predict. It was clear now that Terrell was attempting to take control of the interview.

Challenging the interviewer by insulting him with obscenities and displaying a complete disregard for cooperative behavior were all methods examinee's resort to when trying to take control. No one takes control of an FBI polygraph examiner, and Cy wasn't going to let it happen on this night. He squared up and got in real close to Wirtz, close enough they could smell each other's breath. Then he spoke.

"I'm telling you the facts of life right now, and you've got a choice to make." His eyes were staring a hole right through the center of Terrell's skull. "Now you can sit there and boast a pompous attitude if you want. The jury will see that too. The fact of the matter is that we have agents executing a search warrant on your car right now. If they find anything without your cooperation, you won't have much more than a prayer. If you're not willing to tell your side of the story, then the jury is only going to hear Shawan and the others. Furthermore, Terrell, when that watch you're wearing gets placed into evidence—"

"You ain't takin' my watch, man. This is bullshit. You ain't takin' nothin' of mine without talking to my attorney."

"It's called for in a search warrant."

"What search warrant? Show me so I can show it to my attorney."

"Agent Mathers has a copy of it for you, and he's standing by in the hallway. Not only does it call for a Guess watch, but it calls for your hair and blood samples also. Make it easy on yourself, Terrell."

That was all he could take. Terrell stood straight up as if to challenge Cy physically. "I ain't talkin' anymore until I see my attorney."

"You haven't got an attorney, punk, but you'll be needing one now," Cy quipped. He honored Terrell's request not to speak further without an attorney. He walked to the door to summon Jake. As Jake came down the hall, Cy made his feelings known. "I'm finished talking with this human debris. He's your shooter, and he knows it."

"We figured so. Jake responded with a chuckle. Got a little warm in there huh?"

This wasn't the way Cy envisioned this polygraph to end, but he had his pride also. He knew he had to leave the room before any physical confrontation took place. Besides, the kid did ask to speak to an attorney, and any further discussion would have been thrown out.

Terrell Wirtz was escorted out to another room where he was observed through a two-way glass.

Special Agent Mathers explained some administrative issues concerning the search warrant to Detective Olczinski in the adjacent hallway.

Cy observed Terrell through the two-way glass. Wirtz's demeanor was changing. He had a boyish look on his face. He was teary-eyed. He was searching the ceiling as if he was counting every pinhole in each ceiling tile. He proceeded to bite off each and every one of his fingernails. His shoulders had slumped. Just a few minutes earlier he was standing bold and brazen, but now Terrell Wirtz looked like a tired panther licking his wounds, done for the day.

Mathers entered the room and spoke to him.

Terrell looked at him as if he was searching for mercy.

Cy couldn't hear what was said, but he saw Terrell had managed to calm himself while Mathers briefed him on the execution of the search warrants.

Olczinski stepped into the room with Cy. "We're taking him to the hospital to draw his blood and get his hair samples."

"I see."

"After that I'm afraid we have to take him home. We don't have enough to hold him until we get lab results back."

"Well, this case will get made," Cy replied.

An hour passed, then two. Cy wasn't in a hurry to leave. He had conclusive charts, and he was quite confident Terrell Wirtz was the killer of these two innocent people—two lovers, in the prime of their life, enjoying a romantic get-together at the beach when their life was suddenly taken from them without rhyme or reason.

Cy sat and pondered why this interrogation took the direction it did. *Could I have done this any differently?* He had no admission or confession to show for his work. He packed his instrument and started for the door. Then the phone rang.

"Is Donovan still around?" a police dispatcher hollered from inside the radio room.

"He's just getting in his car," Olczinski answered back. He had just returned from dropping Wirtz off at his grandmother's house. "What do you need?"

"This guy on the phone wants to talk to him."

"Hold on, I'll get him. Who is it?"

"Don't know for sure, but he sounds shook up. I think it's the kid he polygraphed."

"Hey, Cy, don't leave yet. You've got a call from, Terrell, we think."

The police dispatcher cupped the answering piece to the phone and looked at Olczinski as Cy entered the dispatcher's office. "He says he has a gun, and he's gonna shoot himself."

Olczinski motioned for a uniformed officer. "Get all available units started immediately for Wirtz at his grandmother's house. I'll advise further on the radio. We have Wirtz with a gun threatening suicide."

"Hello, Terrell?" Olczinski picked up the phone motioning for Cy to listen in. The sobbing and trembling voice of Terrell took Cy and Olczinski by surprise. The detective was smooth and attempted to calm Wirtz down. A three-way connection was set up so that Shawan James could talk to Terrell. Before any significant conversation could be established, Terrell Wirtz spoke his last words, "Tell that polygraph dude he was right. His machine didn't lie. I did. The gun I used is in my car tucked between the seats. I admit I did it."

Before Cy could respond…*bang!*

Mathers dropped a copy of the *Sunday Times* on Cy Donovan's desk. It was a rainy Monday morning, and Cy was nursing a lukewarm cup of coffee. Front page headlines with a lengthy script.

Cy glanced at the article and looked up at Jake.

"It's really a shame. Who would have thought it would turn out this way?"

"Right, but you did your job."

"Yeah, but let me tell you, if this kid would have had the good fortune to have some fatherly guidance along the way, this might not have happened."

"He grew up in the hood, Cy."

"True, but if he had had the opportunity to be influenced by a Little League baseball coach, you know? Positive influences can work wonders on young boys."

"You're right. Suffice it to say he didn't have that opportunity. Remember what your motto for special agents has always been, Cy?"

"Remind me, Jake."

"'We ruin people's lives for ruining others.' Does that ring a bell?"

"Right, Jake. Cy looked away with a tear in his eye. Let's just call this one…a validated polygraph test."

NO CORPUS DELICTI

"Look what we have here!" Cy pulled down a package from the top shelf of the closet.

"Well, I'll be," said Johnny Keill, team leader for the Evidence Response Team (ERT). "Do you suppose he used it on her?"

"We may never know. I'll let you handle it since you seem to have a passion for this sort of thing."

Agent Keill reached up for the package Donovan was referring to. With his latex gloves on, he dropped the dildo into a paper sack. "I'd say we better enter it into evidence."

"You bet. What time is it anyway? It's hot as hell in this house."

"About 4 a.m.," Keill said.

"Thanks a lot for calling me out on this one. I was just about to go to bed, but no, none other than my buddy Johnny Keill rings me up for another ERT call out."

"Be grateful you get to work with me again. Besides, it's a good change from driving all over the countryside doing polys, isn't it?"

"I guess so. Hey, there's an attic door in this closet. Actually, it's a drop ladder. Has anyone been up there yet?"

"Nope. That's where we're going next. Then hopefully, we're outta here."

"Any luck on the arrest?" Cy inquired as he struggled with the drop ladder.

"Actually, I'm hearing that the county boys picked him up about ten this evening over near Illinois. They brought him back and have been interviewing him ever since."

"Really? Hasn't given anything up yet, I take it?"

"Too early to tell," Keill said.

"Well, I'm getting plenty tired."

"Yeah, we all are, but we've got some good stuff. You know we got quite a break on this thing when his wife gave him up."

"Ten four to that. What's her name?"

"Josie, I believe."

Josie and Pete Michaelis had been married about five years. Their marriage had been strained recently. Pete worked as a physical therapist for cardiac patients at a local hospital in northwest Indiana. It was no secret he developed a fondness for a coworker. Her name was Lynn Majors.

Majors was happily married, and her reputation at the hospital was that of a good Christian girl.

Early in 1999, Michaelis began taking his liking of Majors to another level. He began stalking her and coming onto her at work. One day in February, he reached into her purse, got her keys, and drove to her residence over his lunch hour. She had no alarm, and her husband worked about an hour away. While in the house, Michaelis helped himself to her dresser drawers and picked out a few of her underclothes that suited his fetish. He was in and out quickly and back to work. He returned the keys to her purse; she never knew the difference. It wasn't long, however, before Josie discovered the items taken from the Majors's home.

Josie was aware of her husband's special room he had built in the attic. She seldom ventured up there until one day her curiosity got the best of her. She had seen Pete going up into the attic more frequently than what appeared necessary. After all, there was no problem with the roof or the ceiling for that matter, and whenever she asked why he was up there, she never seemed to get a plausible answer.

As Josie dropped down the attic ladder and clambered up, she took notice of the disturbance in the insulation and more or less tracked her way over to a wall. She could not understand why the disturbance in the insulation stopped at the wall. She looked around and studied how the rafters and support beams came together. She wasn't particularly keen on how homes are framed, but something struck her as odd. The wall she stood in front of didn't seem to have a purpose. At least not a supportive purpose as all the rest of the lumber up there had. She placed her hands on the two-by-four partition and noticed it was a bit unsteady. *Strange*, she thought. She stood among the rafters momentarily looking at it. *So this is what he used the lumber for*, she guessed.

Over a month ago, Pete had come home with a carload of two-by-four boards. She remembered how evasive Pete had been when she asked about the materials stacked up in the driveway one afternoon. Now it all came together. She was able to move the partition inward a bit but left it go at that. Perhaps Pete had concluded this area of the attic needed additional support; hence, he took it upon himself to shore it up a bit.

Probably so. Well, I've got better things to do today, she thought and headed back toward the drop ladder. Josie placed her foot on the top rung of the ladder. She stopped herself. *No, sir, that's not why he built that wall, just can't be.* She stepped back up and carefully made her way back over to the wall to inspect further.

The fact that it wasn't quite secure was odd. This time, she pressed against the end two-by-four with more pressure and discovered it actually moved the entire partition on one side. Further inspection revealed it was hinged on the other side. She was able to move the partition just enough for her body to pass through. She stepped; then she stopped.

Overcome by bewildering sadness, she was quite disappointed at what she saw. A small desk occupied one side of the small area. On the desk were scissors and tape and cutout pictures of nude women from various magazines Pete had accumulated. Taped to the walls were centerfolds from *Playboy* and other popular men's magazines.

What concerned Josie the most were the collection of items on the floor in the corner of the room. They were not Josie's items, a necklace and a couple of panties. *Where did Pete get these, and whom did they belong to?* Alarmed by her husband's eccentricities, she chose to let them lay.

It was 6:00 a.m. Cy wiped his brow and removed the latex gloves. The ERT was cleaning up and preparing to leave the Michaelis residence. One vehicle had already departed with evidence collected at the scene. Cy was exhausted. He hadn't pulled an all-nighter since finals week his last semester of law school. He planned on dropping by the office to clear up a few administrative details and have the remainder of the day to himself or so he thought.

"Hey, Cy, the county boys want to know if you would like to pick up on the interview of Michaelis." It was Agent Keill.

Before he turned to respond, Cy closed his eyes for two seconds. He needed those two seconds at least because he knew he could not say no, and he knew he wouldn't get a chance for some shut-eye for quite some time. This would be a career experience he would not let get past him.

"Absolutely," Cy responded.

"He hasn't lawyered up yet, and the county stopped the interview about 4:00 a.m. to give him some sleep. They want someone fresh to get after him before he does ask for counsel. Actually, they would like him polygraphed. The ball's in your court Cy," Keill said.

"I'll be right over, Johnny. Have I got time for a cup of coffee?"

"Fresh pot has already been brewed for you. They knew you couldn't say no. Doughnuts too!"

"Sounds like a healthy way to start the day. Absolutely no sleep, lots of caffeine, cholesterol bombs, and a high-stress interview."

"You can handle it."

"Ten-four," Cy shouted as he threw his car into drive. *Polygraph? They can't be serious. Michaelis has had practically no sleep, I haven't had any, and he's way oversensitized at this point to have any chance of getting a fair test. Besides, by the time I get to the office to pick up the analog and get back to the county, this guy may ask for counsel,* he thought. He knew the polygraph examiner from the county used the same type of instrument as he did. He knew he could probably use that instrument if necessary. It would be convenient since the examiner's room was next to the room Michaelis would be interviewed in. However, given the circumstances, Cy wasn't too excited about trying to interpret charts with poor physiology. Polygraph results today would likely be INC (inconclusive) at best. He had a better idea.

Special Agent Doug Burlstein met him at the front door.

"Hey, Doug, guess you guys have been humpin' it on this one, huh?" Cy said.

"The same can be said for you. We really appreciate your help on this," Burlstein replied.

"Not a problem, but I better get started on the coffee. Is he here yet?"

"Jailers will bring him down whenever you say. Did you bring the box?"

"No. I'll use the county's if necessary. Actually, I've got an idea. With your crisis negotiation skills, you can help me, Doug."

"Be glad to."

SA Burlstein had a reputation of his own, and Cy fully intended to utilize his talent in this interview. After all, he was well informed on the case after having assisted the county with the Michaelis interview to this point. Running paper on Michaelis is a little pointless.

"How's that?" Doug asked.

"Well, let me put it to you this way. If you were accused of a brutal murder in which you were innocent but were interrogated for six hours all the while agents were going through your house, would you trust your ability to do well on a polygraph? Especially with little or no sleep?"

"But we know he did it."

"Sure we do, that's my point. Reliability of this box for a guy in his condition diminishes with lack of sleep and overexposure to the central issue."

"I see."

"But that doesn't mean we're not going to use it. I want you to walk Michaelis over to me all the while explaining you want him to take a polygraph. Introduce me to him as the examiner. He'll see the box, the chair, and all the components. I'll explain to him our interest in getting a polygraph test from him today. However, before we conduct any test, we're going to go over a few things. From that point, we'll start the interview together. You'll play hardball with him for a while. There will come a time when you will leave. I'll take it from there."

"How will I know…"

"You will know, trust me."

"It's your show from here, Cy."

"I'm ready when you are."

"Good morning, Pete. Cy Donovan, FBI."

Pete Michaelis nodded.

"Pete, I'm a polygraph examiner. Have you ever had a polygraph?"

Michaelis glanced over the shoulder of Donovan at the instrument on the desk and said no.

"Well, we'll get to that later, but before we do, Agent Burlstein and myself would like to cover some things with you. Did you get any rest?"

Michaelis shook his head but said, "Yes, couple hours."

"Great! That's more than I've had."

Together, Cy and Doug escorted the shackled Michaelis into an interview room directly across from the polygraph room. Michaelis was seated in such a way as to be able to see the instrument sitting on the desk in the room across the hall through a window in the door. The interview began.

"Now, Pete, as I understand it, you've spoken to the county detectives earlier this morning, is that correct?" Cy asked.

"Yeah," Pete replied.

"And as it turns out, you've known and worked with Lynn Majors for about four years, is that about right?"

"Yeah, about."

"You're quite fond of her, right?"

"We loved each other," Michaelis piped up. He had been looking down, but after a pause, surprised Donovan and Burlstein with that comment. Over the last two hours since his discussions with the county officials, he had put together a story he was about to unload piece by piece with Donovan or whoever else would listen. A fabricated tale of abject bullshit he hoped would suffice to render him innocent of any murder charge. He made one big mistake with that comment—he had spoken in past tense, and Cy picked up on it.

"So she's no longer with us?" Cy asked.

Michaelis did not respond.

"Pete, we need to know where Lynn is at, and we need to know it right now," Burlstein chipped in rather impatiently.

There was no response.

"Pete—" Cy started but was interrupted by Burlstein.

"Look, Pete, this has gone on long enough. We know you're involved with her disappearance. Have the courage and decency to give her up."

Michaelis looked in the direction of Burlstein but not in his eye, sighed, and remained neutral.

Cy Donovan took up his familiar position, directly in front of the defendant, hands folded with a serious but somewhat compassionate look on his face, observing every glance, every twitch made by Michaelis.

"You've got to talk to us," he asked. "We can help you here today, but you've got to help us. Where is Lynn?"

After another pause, Pete said, "She wouldn't want you to know."

"Oh stop with the crap, Pete," chimed Burlstein. "He made it clear to you that you can help yourself, and that's not going to get it done."

Michaelis didn't take issue with Burlstein, not initially. As is often the case with fabricators, his mind was busy spinning a web of deceit.

Donovan had no clue as to what he was in for on this day. With absolutely no sleep, no breakfast, very little leverage to use on Michaelis, and mounting expectations outside the room, he trudged on. "Pete, if you truly loved Lynn, you would—"

"He didn't love her," Burlstein interrupted once again. "He just wants you to believe that."

Cy put up his hand to halt Burlstein and continued, "What harm has been done to Lynn?" he asked.

Michaelis's response came rather quickly. He looked up at Cy and very boldly stated, "None, we had a plan."

Once again, Cy picked up on the past tense. "Tell me about it, Pete." He had to get Michaelis talking. They had already been in the room forty minutes, going nowhere.

"She wanted out of her marriage, and we started having sex."

"Oh really? For how long?" Cy asked.

"I dunno. Better part of four years."

"Doubt it," added Burlstein.

"Tell us more," Cy said.

"We worked together. We talked a lot. We once did it in a back room while patients were undergoing therapy at the center."

"In your mind!" shouted Burlstein.

"We used to ride bicycles together. She enjoyed that. Getting away from her husband is what she enjoyed. We had sex, lots of it."

"You're not being truthful, Pete," stated Burlstein. "He asked you some time ago where Lynn is now. Now where the hell is she? What did you do to her?"

57

Again, Michaelis provided another facet to the tale. "She's waiting for me somewhere in the Great Smoky Mountains in North Carolina. That was our plan."

Burlstein could not resist taking the lead on that note. "Oh, she's waiting all right, but not for you. She's waiting in a place where you'll never go. You see, Pete, you're going straight to hell."

Michaelis shifted in his seat with his eyes fixated on the floor. "Can I smoke?" he asked.

Cy reached for a cigarette from Burlstein's pack sitting on the desk.

Burlstein groaned. "Cater to him, go ahead, cater to him. He's a bullshit artist."

"I don't, um, I don't think I want to talk to you anymore," Michaelis said while glancing in the direction of Burlstein but again avoiding eye contact.

"Don't worry, Pete, you won't have to. The next time you hear me speak will be at your trial," Burlstein responded.

Cy gave Doug a look, and Doug got up to leave. He had done his part, played out his role. The "good cop, bad cop" scenario had run its course. Now Cy would go solo. His stomach growled.

Midmorning approached. Cy had allowed Pete to feed him a story so that he could flip it on him eventually.

Over a period of about four hours and what remained of Burlstein's cigarettes, Michaelis laid out a fantasy he hoped Cy would buy off on—a twisted tale of sex with neither of their spouses knowing, an affair that encompassed numerous bike rides in the country and intimate liaisons in both of their homes. This was part of the deception Michaelis employed.

Cy was getting tired of Pete's gasconading demeanor. He would have to turn this interrogation around soon. "So, Pete, are you willing to take a polygraph on what you've told me so far?"

Pete looked startled. Slightly shaken, he said, "Well, they're not reliable though, right?"

"Need to talk to you, Cy," a voice shouted following a knock on the door.

Annoyingly, Cy excused himself leaving Pete alone for a few minutes. It was Johnny Keill and one of the county detectives.

"Josie got him an attorney, Cy, and he wants to talk to Pete."

"So? He hasn't invoked his rights. When he invokes, the attorney can have him. Until then, he's mine. You know that."

"Yeah, but it's the county's case now, and I think they are getting a little—"

"Whoa," Cy interrupted. "This is a kidnapping until her fate is determined. Now, I've been asked to talk to this guy, and I'd like to finish the job."

"Are you making any headway?"

"If I didn't think I was, I would tell you so."

"Just to remind you," Keill added, "it was Josie who gave him up. She was at an in-service out of state when she heard the news from a friend who read about Majors's disappearance in the newspaper. She left her in-service early, came straight home, recovered Pete's handgun from his toolbox, and got him the attorney. Together, they came to the county and told of Pete's previous burglary of the Majors's home. You know, the underwear and the necklace. This is why we're here."

"Really? Thanks for the update. Is there anything else I should know?"

"There is," Keill responded. "One of the county bloodhounds tracked the whereabouts, the scent rather, of Michaelis to a pond a few miles from his home. The dog first circled the pond, then ventured down a disappearing trail. Along that trail the dog took a keen interest in a large tree. It was like they could not pull the bloodhound away from the tree."

"And?"

"Well, nothing." Keill came back, "Nothing yet, certainly no shallow grave in the area."

"Anything else?"

"No. We do have agents talking with his cellmate though. The cellmate asked to talk."

"Okay, keep me informed, Johnny."

"I think you should…"

Cy ignored Keill's subsequent request and slipped back into the room. He knew he would forge ahead now in a full attempt to get a pretest confession. There would be no polygraph today. Time would not allow. The county would come knocking again and soon.

"Can I get a cup of coffee?" Pete asked.

"When you start telling me the truth, you can have all the coffee you want," Cy remarked.

Michaelis slumped his shoulders.

"I want the details of her disappearance, and I want them now."

There was silence.

"You're gonna need to talk to me if you're going to get through this day, Pete."

"Can I speak with my wife?"

"You'll get that opportunity. Now square with me, and square with your God. Help us locate Lynn."

"I told you she's waiting for me somewhere in the Smokies."

"Bull!" Cy began losing patience. "Details, son. You're our only chance. Work with me, and I'll get you all the help you need."

After a long pause, Michaelis belched out some facts. "She told me she and her husband were moving away. When I saw the For Sale sign in their yard, I figured it was true. Then Josie's in-service came up, and I decided this was the best time for Lynn and me to make our move."

"Okay, you're making progress, but your still fabricating a so-called plan the two of you had."

"It's true, we—"

Cy held up his hand. "No, it isn't. Come clean with me. I've been fair with you, so be fair with me."

Without looking back at Cy, he mumbled.

"What was that?"

"I drove to her house at lunchtime. I had her garage door opener from her car."

"By way of the keys from her purse?"

"Right."

"You put the keys back in the purse in case she would miss them?"

Michaelis nodded.

"Then what?"

"I left early from work, drove home, got my bike, and rode out to her house." Pete paused.

"Go on."

"She knew I would be there."

"No, she didn't," Cy said, "but tell me what happened."

"I placed a sign on the wall just as you enter the door from inside the garage."

"What did it say?"

"'Don't look at the shotgun.' Something like that. I just waited for her to come home. I just wanted her to pause and read the sign."

"Long enough for you to—"

"It's not what you think," Pete interrupted. "It was part of our plan."

"Stop with the 'our' plan bit. It's time you start telling me about your plan."

Pete hung his head and sobbed.

Cy sensed a breakthrough. He had been in this room five hours, and the strain of the last twelve had been wearing on him. Suddenly, Pete lifted his head, looked over Cy's shoulder, and, with dry eyes, stated, "She's alive."

Cy kept his disappointment inside and came back with, "Where is she, Pete, please tell me?"

There was silence again. Cy was losing his patience and broke first. He knew he was running out of time. "What happened after she came home, Pete?"

"I cut her on the gum first just inside her lip with a bread knife. Just enough to draw blood. I'm sure you found the knife. It was left in the kitchen purposely. This didn't really hurt her. I never wanted to hurt her."

"Where else did you cut her, Pete?"

Pete avoided the question but offered the fact that Lynn's glasses were broken and left on the kitchen floor. "You see this was a staged event," he added. "It was made to look like—"

Cy stopped him in midsentence. "Where is Lynn now, Pete? Tell me. Then we'll get you some help." *Help,* Cy thought, *this bastard's gonna fry.*

"I put my bike in her car, and we went to my house."

Cy stopped him again. "No, Pete, you're leaving out pieces of the puzzle. You started to tell me about the knife. What happened in the kitchen?"

"I told you. We made it look like a struggle." Before he could continue, he hung his head again.

"How did she die? Just tell me please." Cy never liked to ask his perpetrators for a confession. Using the word "please" with these monsters was akin to accepting a position of subordination, a willingness to give up control of the interview. However, recalling a bit of advice from his old friend, Rudy, he remembered one thing: "When all else fails, ask them for the confession. Sometimes, all you have to do is ask." So he asked…again and again.

"We had sex at my house—in every room. For me, it was all about sex. For her, she wanted me to elope with her. She wanted out of her marriage."

Wrong again, Cy thought. However, he let him talk. He let him fabricate a story that encompassed felonious admissions. Then came a knock on the door again. It was Johnny Keill.

"Cy, Josie's attorney has a court order to speak with him. You gotta give it up, man."

"Johnny, you went to the same FBI academy I went to. When he invokes for counsel, he'll have his counsel. You know that."

Cy shut the door. Pete's head was on the table. Cy was up against a very short clock now. It was crunch time. If he didn't get a confession from Michaelis right now, he knew someone would drag him out of the room. Resorting to one last theme, he began with a theory based on sexual motivation.

Pete raised his head once again and stated, "She's alive." He then dropped his head on Cy's shoulder.

Cy embraced him. He whispered into his ear, "Pete, pornography can ruin a person, can't it?"

Pete responded with a muffled "yeah."

"Just tell me where she is, Pete. Where is Lynn?"

Michaelis wouldn't give her up. Another long pause ensued. His pauses were now about ten minutes apart. Michaelis broke from the embrace and fumbled for another cigarette.

Cy took back the cigarette. "Not any more, Pete. Game is over without your cooperation."

"I told you the plan," he responded.

"Not hardly. You lied to me about what happened in the kitchen, what happened at your house, and by the way, how did Lynn's car end up in a cornfield?"

"I took it there. I put my bike in it and drove it out in the country, set it afire with gasoline, and rode my bike back home."

"There's more to it than that."

"Whaddya mean? I told you—"

"Details!" Cy raised his voice. "Where the hell was Lynn when you did this?"

"She waited for me at the house."

"I'm not buying it. There was never a plan between the two of you. It was only your plan. Your plan was to kidnap her, rape her, kill her, dispose of her car and any evidence found in the car. Furthermore, you had been formulating this plan for some time. Your plan went terribly wrong."

Pete Michaelis dropped his head in his hands and sobbed. Cy embraced him once again and pleaded one more time.

"Where is she, Pete? Just tell me. Give her the respect of a decent burial."

The sobbing continued. The shoulder of Cy's shirt was soaked with Pete's tears. Cy whispered again, "Pornography perverts our soul, Pete. We're all subject to it. It just got the best of you. It controlled you, didn't it?"

Cy felt the tears subsiding as Pete raised his head, sat straight up in his chair, looked Cy straight in the eye, and repeated once again, "She's alive!"

At that point, Cy knew the game was over. He indeed had a monster in his presence. Pete Michaelis was likely responsible for more than one missing woman. There would be no confession today to the brutal killing of Lynn Majors. Cy was bitterly disappointed and was about to give Pete Michaelis a real piece of his mind when Johnny Keill walked in.

"Sheriff needs a tape-recorded statement, and he needs it now."

"You got it. Just get me a county dic' in here for a witness."

An hour later, Cy had the recorded statement of Pete Michaelis. It included admissions to stalking, kidnapping, aggravated battery, rape, and the theft and arson of her vehicle. It did not include a confession to her murder. It did conclude Cy Donovan's longest day in his law enforcement career.

"Nice job, Cy," Keill offered.

"Not really, I'm going home."

A few days later, Cy got a call from a task force member looking into the Majors case. He responded and drove over to the county where he met the detective at the evidence room.

"Would you look at that," Cy murmured in disbelief. "Where did you get these?"

"Michaelis's cellmate, remember?"

"Yeah so?"

"You remember the bloodhound, right?"

"Go ahead."

"Well, as it turns out, Michaelis gave it up to his cellmate that if we ever found these polaroids, he would be toast. He mentioned he had them hid in plastic under a tuft of grass near a tree."

"The same tree the bloodhound hit on?"

"Same tree."

"My God, that's one fabulous dog!"

"You bet."

Their excitement waned a little as they perused over the photographs of Lynn Majors. Michaelis had taken the polaroids as souvenirs and hid them under the grass near the tree. The same tree just down the trail adjacent to the pond, the same pond that Michaelis frequented with his boat.

"These may shock the jury. Can we get them in?" Cy asked.

"Prosecutor sees no problem with how we got them. There was no entrapment issue with the cellmate."

"This is great! Unfortunately, we still don't have a body. No corpus delicti," Cy muttered to himself.

"What was that?" the detective asked.

"Oh never mind. Without a body in evidence, it gets tough to prosecute is all I was referring to."

"We'll have her someday."

"Have the divers scanned the pond?"

"Oh yeah. Six times, other ponds too. No luck. We're sixty days out from trial."

The sixty turned into ninety, but the day finally came. Cy Donovan walked into a packed courtroom as opening statements from the prosecution were about to begin. He was stunned at what he saw on the big screen set up by the prosecutor.

There she was, a back view of the poor, beaten, sexually abused Lynn Majors. Her nude body compressed together with boat straps so tight you could see the folds of her skin erupting between straps. *Was that the unfortunate dildo I had discovered in Michaelis's closet inserted into her anally? This would get the jury's attention in a hurry. What a way to open a trial,* he thought. *Perhaps the only way if you don't have the body.*

There was little defense put up for Pete Michaelis. Cy's testimony was crippling, but it was the work of the bloodhound the jury found most intriguing. After a few hours, Pete Michaelis's fate was sealed.

As the jury returned, Cy sat in the back of the courtroom. He was lost in thought as to why he had not gotten a confession and the location of Lynn's body. He was so wrapped up in thought over the matter that he failed to hear the jury foreman read the guilty verdict.

Pete Michaelis was later sentenced to 155 years in a state penitentiary. He would eventually give up the burial site to a prison chaplain six years after his trial. Lynn Majors was recovered with the help of Michaelis from deep in the ground on the property of Michaelis's father in an adjacent county.

Michaelis had wrapped Majors so well in plastic that her body was fairly well preserved. As the courtroom drama concluded, Cy raced down the courthouse steps in a hurry to get to his car.

It was a cold day in late January, and Cy had left his coat in the backseat. Just as he was about to get to it, he noticed a head sticking out of a window of a marked county cruiser just a few spaces ahead of his. Forgetting the chill in the air, he walked up to the cruiser to have a look at this beautiful creature of a bloodhound. The canine handler sat in the front seat having a smoke.

"I've got to have one of these someday," Cy said while fondling the dog's big droopy ears.

"You might want to think twice about that. They stink, you know?"

"I don't care. These dogs are heroes."

"Yeah."

SEXUAL MISFITS

They ruin lives; we ruin theirs.

POOLSIDE PROWLER

Richard Cardwell Jr. appeared for his polygraph with the FBI in the summer of 1996. He presented well. So well in fact that Cy Donovan mistook him for the assistant US attorney accompanying him along with his own attorney.

Cardwell stood out between the two at 6'4", 220 lbs., clean cut, articulate, and wearing a suit from Hart, Shaffner & Marks. Certainly not the profile of your typical pedophile which is exactly what Cardwell was.

He had been charged a month earlier with violations of Title 18, US Code 2252, to-wit: transporting or shipping in interstate commerce a visual depiction of a minor engaging in sexually explicit conduct. Cardwell utilized his home computer to nurture his unforgiving and despicable habit of trading child erotica and pornography with individuals throughout the country.

Bringing Cardwell to justice was Special Agent Al Royster who had been assigned the distasteful task of pursuing the kiddie porn violators in southern Indiana. Cardwell's case was part and parcel to the Bureau's major case widely known as "Magic-Makers." Stats in this case were on the increase and didn't speak well of a society inundated with sexual deviants. SA Royster took on the chore of rooting out these people with a determination and resolve like nothing Cy had experienced before. In mid-August, Royster invited Donovan into his world of investigation—the world of the pedophile.

"Cy, these four shelves contain video cassette tapes I have seized from other sickos in the region. Several came from across the country."

"You have to view every one of these?"

"Unfortunately, yes. If I expect to make a case on these guys, I have no choice. Furthermore, I document in writing what is depicted if it's in violation of Section 2252."

"Better you than me."

"Well, someone has to do it, and I'm not sure how much longer I can do this."

"How's that?"

"Let me show you something."

Royster inserted a tape into his VCR for Cy. After about ten minutes of viewing an adult male grooming and fondling a four-year-old girl, Cy interrupted before the scene reached it's obvious conclusion.

"That's enough, Al. I can't watch that anymore. I don't know how you do it. This is one violation I wouldn't want to work. I see exactly what you mean."

"This has been my world for the last two years. I've got my share of these toads off the street, and with your help, maybe we can get another."

"More than happy to help, sort of."

"Great. Now this guy, Cardwell, has agreed to plead to two counts of trading child erotica, kiddie porn, over the Internet. This is a deal for him. No previous trouble with the law. No angry parents coming forth with allegations of unwarranted touching, fondling, or molesting their children, none of that. However, we suspect him of doing just that. We know he's a molester. Got to be. Too many tapes. Too much erotica found in his possession. And he was too quick to plead."

"What do you have specific?" Cy asked.

"Look at this." Royster inserted a copy of another video cassette seized in the search of Cardwell's home. The two of them studied it carefully. Featured on the film was an adult male wearing a well-pressed knit shirt, with manicured fingernails. His face was not apparent in the film. The unknown male was playfully bouncing a young girl, age three or four, on a bed. The girl had what appeared to be a Sunday dress with panties. Each time the child landed on the mattress, she giggled as the unknown male grabbed her and again tossed her gently in the air. Unsettling in the film was the fact that the unknown male placed his thumb on the little girl's vagina each time he tossed her. In fact, near the end of the film, he can be seen hovering over the girl while he ran his fingers inside the lining of her panties eventually inserting his thumb into her, forcing vaginal penetration. The look on the little girl's face turned from a giggle into a blank stare as the tape ends.

"You think it's Cardwell?"

"Has to be," responded Al. "He denies it. There's another tape we found in his camcorder. We had some trouble with it, but we're still working with it. Not sure what it could reveal."

"So enter polygraph to determine if he's actually had contact for sexual gratification?" Cy asked.

"You got it. It's part of his plea agreement. He passes your poly, he does little time. Chester the molester fails it, and well…"

"Do you really think his attorney is going to let me go after this guy in post-test?"

"It's worth a try. It's all we can do at this point."

"I'm up for it. He'll fail, you know."

"What makes you so sure?" Royster asked.

"The odds are stacked against the pedophile. It's an emotionally charged issue—sex, that is. The deviancy of it all permeates their thinking so much they cannot separate it from what you and I would consider normal adult male aspirations."

"What about testifying against Cardwell should he fail?"

"Don't worry. Polygraph results don't come into federal court over objection of the defense, very rarely anyway. However, whatever he tells me throughout the interview is fair game."

"Knowing what you just told me, are the odds stacked against Cardwell and he just doesn't know it?"

"Most likely yes. But this isn't postconviction monitoring. We're at the federal level. He is not yet a convicted sex offender, and we have an obligation to society to root out any victims of this guy that we can. We use polygraph as an investigative tool to do just that. Imagine for one moment, if you will, that you accept Cardwell's plea without threat of polygraph, without further inquiry into his past or into his criminal mind and consider what a disservice you do, if indeed there are victims out there for whom justice is never sought."

"I couldn't agree more."

"Indeed. Now if we could just convince the naysayers out there who see polygraph as nothing more than Ouija board illusionism."

"Really?"

"That's right. That's another chapter for another time. Let's put a set of questions together for this guy."

"Do you understand these rights?"

"I do," Richard Cardwell Jr. responded. With pen in hand and not so much as a glance at his attorney, Cardwell inked his signature to the polygraph consent form. His attorney then left, as was protocol, and Cardwell was on his own with Cy.

For just a moment, Donovan was rather awestruck. Richard Cardwell epitomized the all-American male. *This man, a pedophile?*

He got a grip on himself in a hurry after seeing Cardwell's face blush when he asked, "You don't fondle young children, do you?"

With confident denials, Cardwell provided Cy with a convincing nondeceptive demeanor throughout his pretest interview. Aside from his initial blushing, there was little Cy could hang his hat on in terms of body language.

Cy took his time probing the childhood of Cardwell, exploring his family upbringing and then onto adolescence. After about forty-five minutes of getting to know him, he dove into the meat of the matter.

"Now tell me, Rick, tell me about your sexual experiences with minors." He was not at all bashful about assuming Cardwell indeed had such experiences to share.

"Actually, I have only one such experience, but I don't suppose it will have a bearing on my immediate future."

"Tell me about it," Cy said.

"You see, I was twenty-four years of age when I met my wife. She was sixteen at the time. We had consensual sex quite often prior to our marriage. I hardly consider that under the purview of the court in my present case, however."

"I'll let you speculate on that, Rick. What you're telling me is, aside from your wife, you've never had sexual contact with a minor, is that right?"

"Aside from her, right."

He didn't actually say no, Cy thought. *He said, right. Funny how they struggle with telling lies.* He had him pegged. This will be the bald-faced liar. There were terms for all of them. This is the guy who will hide the first lie as he had done; then, after confrontation, he'll go bald-faced with the flat out no.

True to form, performing as a cool customer, Cardwell followed along in the remaining pretest interview. Admitting his thoughtless transgressions on the computer for which he had already agreed to plead to, Cardwell was quick to answer no to questions that might incriminate him further.

Rather than banter back and forth with him, Cy decided to run his paper and get Cardwell's responses as a matter of record. Discussing the issue any further in pretest would only lead Cardwell to quarrel about Cy's predisposition of him, which he chose to avoid.

"Are you ready for your test, Rick?"

"That's what I'm here for."

Cy made a couple adjustments to the components he had attached to Cardwell. His subject sat straight in the chair and followed his instructions.

"Regarding sexual contact with minor children, do you intend to lie to me today?"

"No."

Cy observed skyrocketing reactions to the galvanic skin response as much as nine chart divisions high with accompanying cardio elevations timely with the question onset.

"Are you afraid I will ask you a surprise question even though I said I would not?"

"No."

Another hit, this time, in all channels to include suppression in the upper pneumograph tracing. Cy made a sensitivity adjustment just prior to the next question. Further adjustments after that were not allowed. Hoping Cardwell would settle down a bit, Cy dropped the GSR from 2.5 to 1.0. Another question, another hit in GSR and cardio.

Finally, the issue was posed: "Other than what you told me, have you ever had sex with a minor?" Cy had altered the question to accommodate Cardwell's admission concerning sex with his wife when she was a minor. *Gee wiz, that's what I call rising cardio!*

Cardwell's cardio cuff had been set at seventy-four in an effort to reduce any possibility of a vegas roll. By doing so, the examiner hoped to achieve a tracing that was easily interpreted even though it meant a snugger fit to the examinee's arm. The end result was usually appreciated. Cy finished his series of questions and was perplexed at what he saw. Reaction versus reaction to nearly every question with no one question greater than the other but all hitting the pen stops. He ran another chart with the same result and then another. Cardwell reacted to every question every time in such a way as to render the whole test numerically inconclusive. Cy didn't have to study Cardwell's charts for long before he realized that reaction versus reaction on a child molester's charts indicate deception. Although academically inconclusive, from a law enforcement perspective and from the FBI's prior experience with sex offender testing, these charts were to be treated as deceptive.

Cy knew if he called them anything other than deceptive, he would be viewed by quality control as a social worker, too timid to confront, and his call would likely be reversed. Deceptive would be the call.

Cardwell's face froze after Cy advised him he had failed. The denial Cy expected did not come as anticipated. Instead, Cardwell listened while Cy appealed to the love and affection Cardwell had for children. He would withhold discussing Cardwell's need for sexual gratification. By showing respect, Cy hoped to get some respect in return. His tactic brought results.

"Now, Rick, we both know you love your wife and you're children, but tell me about your habits." Cy paused and waited for the argument that didn't come.

"Well, I don't molest children, but I love to watch them, and I video them," Cardwell offered.

"That's a nice start, but that too is a lie. Why do you video them?"

"It's just something I like to do."

"Where do you do this?"

"Usually at swimming pools and parks. You see, I'm not violating anyone's rights, and most don't know I'm even doing it."

"What age group are we talking about here, Rick?"

"I usually find young girls under the age of six as they are the most fun to watch."

Cy let him go on for awhile as was his style to give the examinee a chance to reveal some half-twisted truths before turning the table on him. After about thirty minutes, he had noted several different swimming pools in the area Cardwell had mentioned to include an elementary school yard before he felt he had heard enough. Finally, Cy interrupted. "Where are all the tapes you recorded, Rick?"

"The FBI has them all, but they've all been erased. I was careful to erase them for fear of Janet finding them."

Janet Cardwell was completely oblivious to her husband's poolside manners. Apparently, he did most of his "prowling around" when she was at work or away somewhere.

"Weren't you concerned someone would confront you sometime?"

"Not really. I'm good at what I do. When you want something bad enough you figure out a way to get it." Cardwell's voice dropped off. He had given up a part of his personality he wished he had kept to himself.

An eerie comment, Cy thought. He sensed that Cardwell might clam up. "That's all right," he said. "Listen, I'm not here to work against you today. You've come to your agreement with the government. What I want to do, Rick, with your help, is find a way to make this agreement work best for you."

Cardwell listened.

"Are you confident in your ability to lead a normal life once this term gets behind you? I mean, it's not a lengthy term. You will have your freedom again. What I am saying is, are you confident you can lead a productive life, untangled from desires of the flesh that lead you to satisfy any fetish you have with young children?"

"I think so. I mean I hope—"

"You're not confident, are you, Rick?" Cy interrupted. "Rick, you will need counseling, continuous monitoring, not by the government necessarily but by psychologists and social workers. You will need help whether you think so or not."

Cardwell continued to listen. This guy wasn't badgering him. He actually seemed to care. Rick pondered.

"Rick, I've seen it happen again and again. A man like yourself gets out, goes right back to his old habits. Unfortunately, the next time, the court isn't so lenient. Before you know it, your life, your freedom is gone."

"So what are you saying? What do you need from me?"

"The truth, Rick, the truth."

"But I've told you—"

Cy stopped him. "If you want me to work for you and try to get you the counseling you need without fear of permanent loss of freedom, you will need to be 100 percent forthcoming about the tape found in your camcorder."

"What? Which tape are you referring to?"

Before Cy responded, Rick's eye contact with him had drifted off into thought. He knew he had erased everything he ever taped, but did he forget the last one?

"The girl in the yellow dress—a member of the family?" Cy searched for a breakthrough.

"I don't know what you're—"

Cy interrupted again. "A tape was recovered from inside your camcorder, Rick. I need you to tell me where it was filmed."

Cardwell's thought processes were racing now. He had not counted on this. Had he really forgotten about the tape in the camcorder? Or was Donovan bluffing him?

"We have it, Rick, and we know it's you. I just need you to confirm where it was filmed at?"

Cardwell knew he had filmed the girl, but he was fairly confident he had not filmed his own face. His actions in the film would spell his doom however. He just couldn't give in. Perhaps he had filmed his face. Perhaps Donovan was genuine in that he could avoid further internment if he cooperated. *No, I'm being bamboozled.* But was he? He just didn't know.

Cy sensed the vulnerability of the moment. He locked on to Cardwell with a look of concern waiting for Cardwell's next move.

There was none.

"Well, that settles it."

"Settles what?" Cardwell asked.

"Look, you failed your polygraph here today. I've asked for your cooperation. I haven't got it. We have the tape. As such, your plea agreement hangs in the balance. I'll see you at trial." Cy got up to leave.

"She's my niece."

Cy paused at the door not looking at Cardwell. "And?" he asked.

"I had the camcorder hidden on top of a chest of drawers at my sister's home. I left the bedroom door open while my sister visited in the other room with her grandmother. The girl had been napping but was awakened by the dog. I went in to check on her, and we began playing around. It started out as a harmless frolic as I tossed her up and down on the bed." Cardwell paused.

"Keep going, Rick. You don't want that tape viewed by anyone." Cy was implying the tape would be played in front of a jury if he chose to go to trial.

"She was enjoying it," he said. "Look, I never harmed her. I love that little girl. She is so fragile," he said.

"I need details. If we're going to make this work out, I need your unequivocal cooperation. Then you'll never have to look back."

"I understand."

A few minutes later, Cy Donovan had his story to include molestation of his five-year-old niece.

"Could you be so bold?" Cy asked, referring to the mother and grandmother being present in the other room while Cardwell conducted his sin.

"Yes, I could be, and I was."

"This is a shocker, Cy!"

"Why's that, Al?"

"His attorney didn't expect this. He'll probably think twice before he let's his client sit for a polygraph the next time."

"And perhaps he won't think twice."

"Yeah, right. I'm surprised. I didn't think this guy would give it up to anyone."

"I doubt he would have had it not been for that tape you told me about. Once I played that card, he started singing like a bird."

"Wow! That tape doesn't incriminate him so much without his face on it."

"No, but the one in the camcorder must."

"I see. Looks like you got it out of him by bluffing him." Al laughed.

"Believe me, Al, this isn't something I make a practice of doing. In fact, I don't recall the last time I ever attempted a real bluff. They just don't work, and you risk losing all credibility."

"That's all right. It worked this time, and that's all that counts."

"Well, sometimes you just get lucky."

"Are you saying you just roll the dice on occasion?"

"Right. There comes a time when that is all you're left with."

KIDDIE DIDDLER

Rain, rain, and more rain. It was about time, Cy thought. Nearly an entire summer without it in Knoxville, and Cy was beginning to wonder why he had chosen a transfer south. He had had his fill of the dreary dark days in northwest Indiana, and he yearned for the Sun Belt again. He had processed into the FBI fifteen years earlier through Atlanta and was sent north to the garden spot of Gary. He often thought he would once again end up south of the Mason-Dixon line.

Knoxville was a small office, as FBI offices go, and was not an easy office to get assigned. However, after doing a five-year stint in quality control at FBIHQ in the nation's capitol, Cy opted for the examiner's job in "orange" town. This would be an opportunity to once again work with street agents and mix it up in the exam room with local derelicts of east Tennessee. Upon arrival, he didn't have to wait long.

"Hey, Cy, little wet?"

"Yeah, but it feels good. You know, Eric, I was beginning to think it never rains in Knoxville."

"You have to go up into the Smokies to get wet most of the time," said Dristoll. Eric Dristoll was a first office agent and a good one. He was in his third year in the Bureau and was awaiting orders for a top-seventeen office assignment. Bright and aggressive, he had established a reputation for himself as someone who didn't bellyache about the administrative minutia the Bureau burdens it's agents with in such a way as to make it difficult to actually bring people to justice. Eric Dristoll took the bad seeds of the area off the street and into the federal building usually in leg irons and always with a smile on his face.

"I may have some business for you, Cy."

"Great! Sexual misfit, I presume?" Kiddie porn was Dristoll's specialty.

"You got it. This one's a baseball umpire."

"Is that right? Oh, wait a minute, Cleo Briggs?"

"He's the one."

"Yeah, I read about it in the paper, nice job, Eric."

"Thanks."

"Ex-con, right?"

"Thirteen years in state prison in Colorado. Diddled three boys out there before one finally complained to his mother. The dominoes fell on him from there."

"He's lucky to have survived thirteen years in a state system. Cons are pretty tough on perverts," Cy said.

"Right. He's willing to plead to a federal rap. He knows he's got a problem, and he'll do anything to avoid going back to a state prison. He's a self-acclaimed 'scum-of-the-earth monster.' Those are his words."

"Really?"

"That's right. Listen to this. I got a lead to do a knock and talk at his residence."

"Spin-off from the magic-makers major case?"

"Right. Typical webcam thing you know. He's not only trading images of kiddie porn over the Internet, but he's producing live, with boys ages ten to sixteen using a webcam. Mostly hand jobs, oral, and one or two anal shows that we know of."

"Geez, a real sicko right here in K-town. At what level does he umpire?"

"Up through high school and he loves teenage boys. Can't get enough of them," Dristoll said.

"So what happened?"

"Briggs comes to the door. We announce, show our creds, and he invites us in. We didn't have to say much. He figures he's toast already. Takes us to a room where his computer is. Pulls up a screen. There it is."

"Kiddie porn?"

"Yep. He was actually viewing when we knocked! At that point, we asked him for consent to search his computer. Only then did he balk. However, he did consent. In the spirit of fairness, we got a search warrant anyway."

"You didn't have to do that," Cy said.

"I know. But this guy wasn't going anywhere. He was quite cooperative. While we waited for the search warrant, he volunteered his own sickness."

"That's when he told you he was the—"

"Right. And he really is a monster. As forthcoming as he has been, I just know he's withholding."

"Sure he is. Child predators will never tell you everything."

"He'll tell you," Dristoll said.

"How's that? What makes you so sure?"

"Because you're the polygraph examiner. You've done it before, and you'll do it again. You'll break him."

"Sounds like he's already confessed a lot to you."

"He's given up enough to get a plea in hopes we'll take what he's given and go away. You see, Briggs knows he has to go back to prison because he cannot control his desire to fondle young boys. He's afraid of himself. He's concerned he may do more than diddle with them. And he expects to see daylight before he's seventy."

"How old is he now?"

"Fifty-one."

"Do you think he's capable of killing?"

"No evidence of that, not yet anyway."

"Trust me, Eric, he probably is."

"All the more reason I want him tested."

"No problem. Did the SAC approve it?"

"Yes. I've met with the assistant US attorney and Briggs's attorney too. It's expected as part of the plea agreement."

"Ten-four. You're a bulldog, Eric. You've already got a stat from him. He's going to prison for a long time, and you want more!"

"That's right. I want you to mess with his mind. Anyone who goes around destroying the minds of our youth doesn't get an inch of forgiveness from me. Did I tell you he groped one boy just a week out of prison?"

"Wow! What have you got him charged with?" Cy asked.

"Indicted him for receipt, attempted receipt, and possession of child pornography. I have debriefed him twice for details of victimization of other children as well as other sex offenders he may have knowledge of."

"Other umpires?"

"You bet. You know when it involves a Catholic priest, it makes all the headlines. People don't realize how prevalent this in other professions, i.e. umpires, referees, and coaches."

"So sad."

"It really is. After you work this stuff a couple years, you feel as though you can't trust anyone around your kids."

"What has he owned up to besides the three in Colorado?"

"He's confessed to molesting three male children in Knoxville including one during a webcam."

"So we're talking six altogether, three of which are now irrelevant victims for whom he's done his time for?"

"Exactly."

"Cooperation as to other sex offenders?"

"None. Won't admit to knowing any. You can test him on that, right?"

"Can do. It'll be a two series test. First, I'll cover the issue concerning his knowledge of other sex offenders. Following that, I'll cover identities of additional victims he may be withholding."

"That's what I want."

"That's what you'll get."

Prior to his polygraph, Cleo Briggs had given Agent Dristoll what appeared to be his full cooperation. After all, he was willing to plead guilty and go back to prison for a long time. He owned up to the molestation of three boys in Knoxville, and the government already knew of his three previous victims from Colorado. Additionally, he had confessed to downloading child pornography. In fact, it could certainly be said he had cooperated from the very instant the FBI had knocked on his door.

Cy Donovan didn't have to question Dristoll's real motive for wanting Briggs tested. It wasn't just to "mess with his mind." Dristoll knew wherever there's smoke, there's fire. Briggs had been too cooperative and too willing to go back to the joint. No, it wasn't about playing with someone's mind when he's down just for kicks. It was far deeper and more important than that. There was a much bigger picture that Briggs could paint for investigators.

There was a demon in Briggs that had yet to be exposed. Dristoll was determined to find that demon, and he counted on Donovan to do the dirty work. And dirty work it was.

Whenever a man sits knee to knee with another man, the better part of eight hours discussing child molestation, a wretched filth can grip the soul. Cy had been in this situation before but not to the extent he was about to experience.

Getting admissions from the perverted kiddie diddler was always more difficult in his opinion than say, a killer, robber, or thief. Obtaining that confession is a difficult task in and of itself. The real devil is in the details.

Getting a judge or a jury to understand child molestation is one thing, but *selling* a judge or a jury on the true nature of the crime is another if you want to put the guy away forever. Donovan knew he had to get those details, and he also knew he would feel cleaner after spending eight hours in a coal mine than with Cleo Briggs.

"Cy, this is Cleo Briggs," said Dristoll.

Briggs, in handcuffs and leg irons, held out his hand.

Cy reached and shook it. The last thing he wanted to do was shake this guy's hand, but he knew if he was going to have any luck today he had to get over touching this man.

"Cy is our polygraph examiner, Cleo."

"Before we get down to business, I'm going to need him out of the hardware," Cy instructed, all the while looking Briggs in the eye.

Dristoll acknowledged and complied by removing the handcuffs from Briggs.

"Leg irons too, Eric."

"Um, you sure you…"

"Leg irons come off. Maybe you'd like to shuffle around in 'em for a day or so," Cy quipped, winking at Eric out of sight of Briggs.

"Will do," Eric groaned.

With the consent forms signed, it was just Cy and Cleo. He sat across from Cleo with his legs crossed, not directly in front but at an angle. Cy would counsel himself about this later. Sitting at an angle was less personable, but he would get away with it on this day. He did enough of everything else right. He laid his clipboard aside. The clock had just struck 9:00 a.m. before Cy had come into the room.

"What time did you have breakfast, Cleo?"

"It was around seven thirty."

"Feeling all right today?"

"As good as can be expected I guess."

"Given the circumstances, huh?"

"Yeah. This thing makes me a little nervous." Cleo glanced over at the polygraph instrument sitting on the desk behind him.

"That's a good thing, Cleo. It's the people who aren't nervous that I worry about."

With half a chuckle, Cleo asked how reliable he could expect this thing to be.

"Cleo, I'm going to be real honest with you today," Cy spoke with his hands folded in his lap. "In return, I'm going to need you to be equally honest. Fair enough?"

"Sure, I have no intention of being anything less than honest."

"Eighty-five percent."

Cleo cocked his head and squinted, asking, "Eighty five percent?"

"Right 85 percent. You asked about the reliability of the polygraph, and I'm telling you, 85 percent."

"Oh, okay."

"Can you live with those odds?"

"Well, of course I'd prefer 100 percent, but I suppose I haven't much choice."

"It's like this, Cleo. I've been living with 85 percent for the past twelve years testing people like you, and I'm rather fond of the results."

"Well, if you are, then I guess I will be too. Hopefully."

"Do you think for one minute that a law enforcement agency with the reputation of the FBI would spend the time, effort, and money fooling with an instrument if we couldn't trust the results?"

"No, I don't suppose. But what if I'm one of those 15 percenters?"

"Then, I'll tell you if you are, and you'll just have to trust me. Do you think you can trust me?"

"You haven't given me any reason to think not."

"I'm going to explain this instrument to you today. I'm going to take some time to get to know you. Together, we'll cover some issues, and then I'll go over the questions I'm going to ask you on the test. You're going to know what all the questions are before we start the test. Does that sound easy enough?"

"I think so, yes."

"Furthermore, I'm not going to ask you any questions on this test that you would refuse to answer. And there won't be any surprise questions. No trick questions."

"Okay, fine."

"Now tell me about Cleo Briggs."

"Where do you want me to start?"

"Childhood. I assume you enjoyed sports?"

"Yes, mostly baseball and basketball, but I was never really very good at either."

"I see, tell me about your father." Cy wanted to probe into Cleo's childrearing years for a reason. Sex offenders who have been subjected to sexual abuse by a parent sometimes have an unconscious need to pass on the humiliation they experienced themselves to others—revenge, if you will, for the pain they suffered themselves as a child.

"What do you want to know?"

"What kind of influence was he on you?"

"Mostly good, I guess. Probably not as actively engaged with me though as other fathers, but I can't fault him."

"Did he ever—"

"No sexual abuse," Cleo interrupted. "None of that if that's where you're going."

Cy nodded.

"I've been down that road many times with therapists and such. Seems they always think it's the parent's fault, but that's not the case with me."

"Who is to fault?"

"Myself. I am to blame for my indiscretions."

Cy felt encouraged by Cleo's apparent willingness to accept responsibility. "Am I to believe then that you were never sexually abused at any time as a child?"

"That's right, never."

"Abuser but not a victim?"

Cleo just looked at Cy with no response. His teeth tugged slightly on the corner of his lip. It was a micromovement that Cy would have to observe often during his time with Cleo, a movement that would eventually sicken him.

Cy knew he had hit a chord with Cleo. "I'm going to tell you, if you want to pass any polygraph here today, you will need to be forthcoming with me from the start."

"I intend to be."

"So other than the three boys in Knoxville and the three previous boys in Colorado, there are no other victims you're responsible for?"

"No." Cleo responded shaking his head rather weakly.

"Well, if you weren't abused as a child, then when did you have your first homosexual experience?"

"I don't consider myself to be a homosexual," Cleo responded.

"That's not quite what I asked, is it?"

"Well, you asked—"

"Listen, Cleo," Cy stopped him. "Don't sit here today and insult my intelligence. I won't insult yours, but you're the one facing another tenure in prison. You're the one who needs to pass this test if you expect anyone to have any sympathy for you in the justice system."

"I'm not looking for sympathy," Cleo interjected.

"What are you looking for?"

"Just…just…just help. I know I'm not a good man."

"Well, Cleo, help starts with straight answers. When I ask you a question, I need a straight answer. Do you understand?"

"Yes."

"I need a straight answer, Cleo. Truthful responses. You need to be forthcoming. I don't want just the answer that settles the question. Other words, I need to know those things you think I would need to hear but that you're too embarrassed to share. You know what I mean?"

"Yes, I think so."

"Forthcoming, Cleo. Don't omit the obvious. Tell me more than I ask for. Not side stories that deviate from the issue. I'm talking about pertinent relevant detail of your victims and your acquaintances you know to be involved in child molestation."

"I'll do the best I can."

"The best you can may not be enough. You'll need to surrender your soul if you expect to get anywhere with a judge."

"I suppose you're right."

Cy leaned in close to Cleo. "You can paint the picture, Cleo, but unless you provide detail for that picture and capture it with the proper frame, no one is going to buy it."

Cleo nodded and bit his lip again.

Cy cocked his head and looked again at Cleo. "You still don't fully understand, do you?"

Cleo looked down, then up, then down again.

Cy recognized what Cleo was thinking. Would he try to placate the polygrapher by admitting to a previously undisclosed molestation, hoping this would satisfy the interviewer resulting in a discontinuance of further inquiry? Or would he choose to unshoulder the burden of all his victims and seek a cleansing of his guilt through Cy?

Cy was confident an admission would be forthcoming but was unsure of how much of the real picture he would get.

"I am compelled to touch young boys," Cleo admitted.

The disgust of the comment thwarted Cy's response momentarily. "Well, would you say your work as an umpire helps you form a bond with young boys?"

"Yes, I suppose so. But I love sports."

"And young boys?"

Cleo slumped his shoulders in resignation.

"If you'll share with me the identity of these boys and the identity of other men who have your same problem, then together, we can put together a test today that should enable you to succeed."

Cleo nodded affirmatively.

"So we know of Charles, Alex, and Darin, but who are the others?"

"There was the Richter brothers, Barry, age thirteen and Dustin, age eleven."

"How were they victimized Cleo?"

"I had oral sex and masturbation with them twice at the same time. I've had sex with them four to five times all total," he spoke without hesitation opening the door for Cy.

Cy took advantage. "Were they you're first Tennessee victims?"

"No, that was Alex."

"We know about Alex. Have you disclosed to investigators everything you can about him?"

"I think so."

Just to be sure, Cy reviewed the matter further knowing they always withhold 25 percent of the complete truth.

"The first time I had sex with Alex was at his father's house. He was twelve at the time, and I was living at his house for a short time. Alex was in his shorts, and I began rubbing on his stomach."

"Where was his father?"

"In the next room."

"You mean to tell me you had the nerve to molest him with his father just around the corner? How was it you were able to handle that kind of risk?"

Cleo thought for a moment, then replied, "I just compartmentalized the risk."

"I guess you couldn't help yourself, right?"

"Well, as I said, I feel compelled—"

"Yeah, I know," Cy interrupted. He didn't care to hear it again. "Were you straight with them about what you did with Alex?"

"I suppose I had sex with him a couple of dozen times, most of which occurred after I moved out of their house and into my own."

"Are we talking about oral sex and masturbation, Cleo?"

"I fingered him too, but he was the only one I did that to."

"At your house?"

"Yes, but he traveled with me also. He is the only one I had sex with while traveling."

"His father let him go with you?"

"Yes, actually it was his mother who let him go. She trusted me. His father couldn't do much with him due to a lung disease of sorts. He was frequently on an oxygen apparatus."

"I see."

"I masturbated Alex in Cincinnati, Memphis, and Atlanta," he said rather casually. He had reached a comfort zone with Cy.

"And you were going to tell me of the others," Cy reminded him.

"After Alex came Randy. This was on New Year's Eve."

"How old was Randy?"

"Eleven."

"Go on."

"I had oral sex with him twice. Once while he was on the telephone with his girlfriend," Cleo added with a chuckle.

Cy just glared at Cleo, then looked away.

"Did you tell them everything about Charles?"

"Charles is the only boy I had anal sex with."

"How often?"

"I had oral sex with Charles a couple of dozen times. I was able to get him to masturbate me as well. I've told them this," he added.

"How about Darin?"

"I was straight with them about him. He was the one I did a live webcam with."

"The depravity of it all," Cy mumbled.

"What did you say?"

Cy looked up at Cleo who was biting his lip again. "Never mind. Let's move on. Who don't we know about?"

"Another fifteen-year-old, Louis, was present during the webcam. And Charles had another friend also whom I fondled, um, his penis, but nothing else occurred with him."

"What was his name?"

"I don't remember."

"Next?"

"Did I mention Kibbet?"

"No, tell me."

"Kibbet had a father out of state. His mother encouraged me to get with him because he was lonely."

"How old was Kibbet?"

"I would say he was fourteen at the time."

"What happened with him?"

"I had oral sex with him twice and masturbated him four or five times—once while a friend was with him."

"So tell me, Cleo, how did you get these boys to play along with your desires?" Cy was well aware that sex offenders are well supplied with toys and books that are of interest to a child. In many ways, they can relate to them better than their own parents because they have the patience to talk to them and listen to what they have to say. Often they present the child with a gift as a reward for their sexual acts carried out. The abuser will sometimes even take nude pictures of them for blackmail.

"Oftentimes I would let them watch a porn video. This would get them in the mood and allow them to feel that what we do together is a normal activity commonly practiced by others. I just enjoyed their company too. It wasn't all about sex. I had a pool table, so we played pool, watched ballgames, and such."

"But the primary motive was sex, Cleo. We both know that."

There was no response.

"It's like I said earlier, Cleo, you need to come clean. I know you spent time in Texas. Tell me about your Texas boys."

Cleo was taken back. He hadn't counted on this. Did Cy really know there were victims in Texas? He bit his lip again while looking back at Cy. His eyes were blinking, but he could not give a response.

I knew it, Cy thought. *Likely deception. The innocent person would have had a timely negative response.* "Cleo, I really don't want to keep reminding you here today. This isn't a game we are playing. You're fifty-one years old. Let's face it, your activities as an adult have robbed you of ever having a normal life. However, your revelations of past deeds will contribute to our understanding of what makes people like you tick. Therein lies your contribution to society. Yes, you can contribute to society despite your shortcomings in the past. Are you with me?"

Cleo dropped his chin slightly and nodded in the affirmative.

"The Texas boys?"

"I lived in Texas from 1996 to 2000."

"Where in Texas?"

"Dustin—at an apartment complex."

"And?"

Cleo took a deep breath. "There was a girl who lived upstairs who had two boys ages five and six. I wrestled around with them making every effort I could to grab them in the crotch area. I made it a point to touch them there. It was part of my warped mindset. That is all I did with them however. They were younger than I preferred."

"Their names?"

"I cannot recall."

"Go on."

"There were the Hockmann brothers. Jonas Hockmann, age fourteen and—"

"Wait a minute, how did you become acquainted with the Hockmanns?"

"Their dad was a coach who I had become friends with. All total, there were six brothers in the Hockmann family."

"Did you molest all six?"

"Only four. I masturbated Jonas and had oral sex with him twice. Later on came AG, age fourteen and his friend, Brad Forrest, also age fourteen. Both AG and Brad were present when I was with Jonas."

"So you're telling me of a group thing here, Cleo?"

"These were not orgies. I molested these boys separately. I masturbated AG and had oral sex with him twice. Then I masturbated Brad."

Cy just listened. Cleo seemed to be on a roll.

Cleo paused.

"The other Hockmann?"

"Jeremy Hockmann was ten or eleven when I rubbed his crotch at his house. He wasn't comfortable with me, so I discontinued. His younger brother Averill Hockmann let me touch him once. That was it for the Hockmanns."

"Okay, now what about the other Texas boys?"

Cleo took another deep breath and thought for a long minute. Finally, with a look of resignation, he raised his head and spoke, not looking at Cy, "There was a boy named Merrill, but I do not remember his last name."

Cy took notes.

"I had oral sex with Merrill and masturbated him. He was fourteen years old. I must have done him ten times. There came a time when I was taking him home, and he was in the backseat. He told me to stop the car. I asked him why. I could hear him masturbating himself. I stopped and got into the backseat with him." Cleo paused again.

"What happened next?"

Cleo started chuckling. He looked at Cy. "What do you think?"

It was all he could do to keep from bolting out of his chair at Cleo. "He's alive to tell us about it, I presume?"

Cleo frowned. "Oh yeah. I never hurt anyone. Well, psychologically I suppose I have."

"Any more?" Cy wasn't sure if he really wanted to know of anymore, but he dare not quit.

"There is. My former boss's son Blair Wellington."

"Tell me about him."

"He was a baseball player, fifteen years old. I took him to games. I had oral sex with him, and I masturbated him also. He had a friend with him once. Don't recall the name. He just watched. There was also another friend of the Hockmanns. His name was Paul. We masturbated each other." Cleo laughed again. "I can't recall any others in Texas. I really can't."

"We'll see. The day isn't over. Have we covered all your victims here today?"

Cleo thought for a moment before responding. "I believe we have. I think so."

"Let's talk about other umpires for a moment."

"Other umpires?"

"Yes. Other child molesters whether they be umpires, referees, or other guys you know."

"I've had this discussion before with Eric. I don't know of any."

"What are you afraid of here? You're not going to be in a place where these guys can bring about problems for you."

"That's not the point. As I have said, I don't know of any."

"Sure you do. Remember what I said about making a contribution to society?"

"Yes."

"Well, it's time to get it done."

Cleo shook his head no.

Cy was quiet.

Cleo sat perplexed and uneasy. "I'm telling you. I don't know of any other guys out there doing what I did. It's not something we talk about."

Cy took note of how he said *we* as he thought, *Is this like a secret club or something where they know each other but don't talk?*

"You know, talk to me."

"I don't know."

"It's like a little click, isn't it?"

"I do not know."

"Who are they?"

"How many times have I said, I don't—"

Cy interrupted, "The boys talk, Cleo. The boys talk."

Cleo paused.

"You learn from the boys. You learn from the boys, do you not?" Cy asked.

Cleo again started a denial before Cy raised his hand.

"Don't fuck with me, Cleo. Don't fuck with me, or you'll never get a chance at the box."

Cleo sat slumped in his chair.

Cy started with the boys he knew who played baseball. When he mentioned Charles, there was a definite change in Cleo's demeanor. It was like a peak of tension polygraph test without the components attached. He didn't miss it. He probed immediately.

Irritated and flustered, Cleo confirmed the identity of a fellow named Glen. Glen was another umpire who had molested Charles. Cleo denied, however, knowing anyone else.

Nearly four hours had passed. This had been an unusually long pretest interview. Cy had his questions prepared. He was ready to bet his paycheck that Cleo wouldn't pass his polygraph. He had a two-series test prepared just as he had advised Eric.

"We're done with our preliminary discussion. Are you ready for this test?"

"Let's go."

He already had Cleo in the chair. He wasted no time draping the convoluted tubes around him, attaching the fingerplates, and sliding the cardio cuff into position. After his customary instructions, Cy took up his position in his seat behind old reliable. He noted Cleo looking about with that worried look so many have just prior to commencing with the test.

"How long will this take?" Cleo asked.

"Not long. If you've been straight with me, we'll be out of here in less than thirty minutes."

A few minutes later came the questions: "Do you have more information of other child molesters you have not told me about?"

"No."

"Are you now withholding the name of any man whom you know to be molesting young children?"

"No."

As to this series, Cy's official report would read "indicative of deception." Onto series 2.

"Are you deliberately withholding from investigators the names of any boys you molested?"

"No."

"Other than what we discussed, are there any other victims you have molested that you have not named?"

"No."

Without question, Cy's report would reflect "indicative of deception" to this series also. It didn't take Cy long to evaluate the charts. He didn't need to. He took the components off Cleo all the while maintaining a blank look on his face.

Cleo couldn't stand the suspense and quipped, "How did I do?"

"You know how you did."

"I'd like to think that I know, but—"

"You failed the test. Both series, you're off the charts."

"Oh no, now this is just what I knew was going to happen. I was afraid of this."

"You should have been. You haven't disclosed the truth today."

"Yes, I have!"

"Not completely, that much is obvious." Having been through this before, Cy was well aware it was time for direct positive confrontation. He would challenge Briggs the rest of the way. The time had come to do some real soul-searching. He touched Cleo slightly on the knee and looked him straight in the eye.

"Remember what I said about contributing to society? This is your opportunity, your chance. You won't get another. Now think this through for a few minutes. We need to know who all of the victims are. Don't leave any out, none. I'll be right back." Contrary to his usual approach, Cy left the room momentarily.

"We're making progress, Eric," Cy spoke into his cell phone down the hall from the polygraph suite.

"Really, how much?"

"He gave up several more victims prior to the test. He failed the test. I told him to think about his sole opportunity to contribute to society. I'll go back in on him in a minute with a bogus file."

"I like it. Ruin his day."

"For ruining others."

"Right. That's your motto."

"So, Cleo, are we ready for a come-to-Jesus meeting?"

"You know, there may be others, but I can't for the life of me think—"

"Let's start with Florida," Cy cut in. He reached around the desk for a three-volume file and flipped to a tab labeled "Florida Victims" in full view of Briggs.

Cleo glanced at him and back to the file, then back at him again.

Cy leaned back in the chair holding the file in front of him. He flipped through numerous pages of administrative memos he had pulled out of the confidential trash that pertained to anything but the Cleo Briggs matter. "Do I need to jar your memory?"

After a long pause, Cleo opened. I moved to Florida in 1972 and attended Florida Tech. That is now the University of Central Florida. While there, I had a ten-year-old cousin, Stephen, spend the night with me. I masturbated him twice. Another boy, Brett, lived close by. He was also ten, between age ten and sixteen I should say. I violated him about seventy-two times. Then there was Harold, age eleven. I did him seventy-five times." Cleo stopped and asked for a drink of water.

Cy provided him a small glass of water. "Go on."

"Dennis."

"Dennis who?"

"I don't remember their last names."

"How old?"

"Eleven also. And his brother Sammy, perhaps fourteen."

"How often?"

"Constantly for about a month. Then there was another set of brothers whose names I don't recall, but I masturbated both of them." Cleo went on, and Cy took notes, more and more notes. By the time eight hours had passed, Cleo Briggs had admitted to molesting forty-eight boys. Four of them between seventy-two and one hundred times each. *Especially odd*, thought Cy, *that he was capable of remembering precise numbers for a few of them, but he could not remember their last names.*

To make matters more interesting, in a statement of complete resignation and fatigue, Briggs concluded by telling Cy that there were twice as many more boys that he attempted to molest. He could not, or would not, remember their last names either. His victims ranged in age from five to sixteen. He stalked and lured victims in New Jersey, Florida, Texas, Colorado, and Tennessee.

Cleo Briggs steadfastly denied ever hurting any of his victims other than the irrecoverable and life-lasting psychological damage he imposed upon them, not to mention the domino affect his victims will parlay on to victims of their own—immeasurable damages to an innocent generation of youth.

When he was finished, Cy thought he should recap everything with Briggs to be sure he got it all down accurately. He looked at Briggs. Briggs looked back while biting his lip.

Cy started. "Cleo, let's review..."

Cleo chuckled, interrupting.

Cy paused and looked at Briggs in disbelief. *How could this man possibly find humor in the debauchery of what he had revealed today?*

"Where do you want to start?"

"With the end."

Nauseated by now, Cy figured he'd heard enough and left the room.

Down the hall was Dristoll who responded on cue.

"I've heard all I need to hear from this sick bastard," Cy said.

"Anything further out of him?"

"We'll talk about it. Let's get him back to jail. C'mon I'll give you a hand."

Once they had Briggs reshackled, Donovan and Dristoll transported him over to the county lockup where he would wait further disposition of his case. There were no pleasantries exchanged among the three of them.

A couple of months later, Briggs sat in a courtroom eagerly awaiting his fate. He appeared optimistic despite his criminal history as a sex offender. He felt he had been cooperative with investigators and that the judge would see it that way. Indeed he had come forth with disgusting details of how he had preyed upon the youth he had come into contact with. He had given up his soul to Cy Donovan.

Contrary to what Briggs had hoped for, this would not be his day. Having read Donovan's report, perhaps the judge also felt soiled and betrayed. He passed sentence onto Briggs. A sentence Cleo Briggs would find virtually impossible to outlive.

Score one for the kids.

CROSSDRESSER

"Mahovolich here."

"Hey, Rudy, Donovan here. Catch ya' at a bad time?"

"No, not really, just tryin' to get wired up with a caffeine fix before I get too far into another day. What's up?"

"I tested a special agent applicant yesterday, and you're not going to believe it."

"Hey, nothing surprises me anymore. Tell me about it."

"Have you ever had one of these jokers who gets a little too obsessed with their honesty and tells you a little bit more than you counted on hearing?"

"Oh yeah, I get it every day from Zip Lynch who doesn't know when to retire." Rudy chuckled.

"Hey stick it, will ya?" Cy could overhear Zip in the background.

"Thankfully for the Bureau, this guy didn't shut up," Cy said.

"How's that?" Rudy asked.

"I had him plus four, plus four on foreign contacts and passing classified, right?"

"Okay."

"So I know he's not a security risk."

"Go on."

"He's a lawyer by trade and never even had a clearance but a cool dresser. You know the type? Cuff links, pink shirt, mousse in the hair, cute little tie tack."

"I got him pictured. So you got NDI charts, but he's DI to somethin'?"

"Listen to this. In the pretest interview, I covered the typical issues—you know the drill, lying, cheating, and stealing."

"Right."

"So he comes out with this thing he did in college about stealing a girl's underwear from the laundry room at the dorm. Okay, I'm thinking, typical college prank kind of thing, so I set it aside in my mind, although I didn't dismiss it of course, and I continued on with other matters."

"Right, right, a clue for post-test."

"Exactly, but I didn't expect to have to go there again."

"Yeah."

"Anyway, we cover the application, his background, education, law school, employment, etcetera. All's good."

"But he's not?"

"Right."

"Deer in the headlights?"

"Right, how did you—"

"Been there, Cy."

"Well, I run my charts, and like I said, not so much as a whisper at foreign contacts and passing classified. Rudy, he doesn't even tickle the drug questions, but my theft questions…"

"Pen-stopping?"

"Absolutely! So I'm thinking, rock solid applicant but for a college prank which he can't let go of in his head. I've got no choice but to confront him on it."

"Got to."

"I pull my chair around, and I say, 'Look, Tony.' Tony Bancher was his name. 'You've got to get this stolen underwear issue out of your head.'"

"What'd he say?"

"He comes back with, 'You didn't let me finish.' So I say, 'What do you mean?' He says to me, 'After I took the girl's underwear, I went back to my dorm room, masturbated in them, and then returned them without washing them.'"

"Oh Christ!" Rudy chuckled. "Send him to Quantico!"

"It gets better. My follow-up question concerned additional thievery. I say to the guy, 'Okay, Tony, you're applying to be a special agent with the FBI. Certainly you must understand the necessity of candor and how important that is in the selection process of new agents.' 'I do,' he says to me. I come back with, 'So, Tony, what else have you stolen?' He tells me, nylon stockings from a base exchange in Europe. I ask why. He tells me, 'I wanted to wear them.'"

"And did he?" Rudy tried to control his laughter on the other end.

"Oh yeah, he told me so."

"Dear Lord, what else?"

"He tells me before he stole the nylons, he stole his sister's swimsuit, her underwear and nylon stockings also."

"Holy crap, give me a break."

"So I asked him, 'Tony, did you wear these things to see what it would feel like to be a woman?' He says to me, 'Well, sort of.' I asked him what else he stole. He goes on admitting to stealing a girl's skating dress from a coed locker room. I ask him why. He tells me he wanted to wear it."

"This is too much for me to envision," interjected Rudy.

"Oh, he wore the dress too, Rudy. He told me so without hesitation."

"Spare me," laughed Rudy. "Hold on. Hey, Zip, listen to this stuff."

"Just put it on speaker," Cy said.

"Yeah, right, hold on," Rudy replied.

"There, go ahead, Cy."

"Hear me?"

"Yeah, we hear ya go ahead."

"I figure the guy isn't through. He's got more to tell me, and he's coming out with it, like maybe he thinks we'd still hire him, you know?"

"Well, let me stop you right there, Cy. This Bureau would you know!"

"That's another story for another day. I'm listening to what he has to say, like a counselor. After all, nothing unusual here, right? Ha!"

"Right, Zip wacks off in girls shorts at least once a week." Rudy laughed.

Cy kept going irrespective of any reply Zip had to Rudy's sarcasm.

"Next, he tells me about his neighbor. His neighbor lady has a cat, and she had asked this Bancher fellow to baby sit the cat while she was gone. She gave him the keys to her house. So what do you think he does?"

"I can only guess," said Zip.

"He rifles through her dresser drawers, tries on an assortment of her underthings and decides the girdle fits just right. He steals the girdle!"

Rudy roars in laughter. "You've got to be kidding me! The kid doesn't know when to shut up."

"Actually, he did shut up at that point. I think he finally figured out that he had revealed enough perversions that he wasn't likely to get a job with the FBI."

"Let's hope not," Rudy replied.

"Needless to say, I felt compelled to probe a little further with him to be sure he wasn't into kiddie porn or some similar activity. He adamantly denied it."

"Now that would have made for an interesting polygraph, wouldn't it have?" Rudy said.

"You bet. Not one he likely would have done well on either with all his sexual baggage."

"I appreciate the call, Cy. Lovely tale to start my day off with. Where is he from?"

"Orlando. Thought you guys would get a charge out of it."

"Interesting, yeah, good to hear from you, Cy."

"Yeah, take care, Rudy. Be good Zip. Later."

THE STORYTELLERS

The problem with the storytellers is that only 90 percent of them are telling tales.

HATCHBACK MAN

"Hey, Cy."

"Hey, Brenda, what's up?"

"Oh, I'm just frustrated, that's all."

"About what?"

"I got assigned this twenty-six matter concerning a woman who claims to have been raped in her car by a guy she didn't know was in the car until she gets about a mile down the road. He apparently forces her at knifepoint to a construction site and has intercourse with her in the driver's seat of her old Gremlin."

"Wait a minute did you say Gremlin?"

"Right."

"Those are hatchbacks. Are they still around?"

"Apparently so. She owns one."

"How is this a twenty-six matter?" Cy asked knowing the propensity that Brenda Rivens had to get in over her head as a first office agent. "Does he steal her car?"

"They end up in Illinois. She worked at a rehab center in Gary. Been in the area most of her life. As I said, she claims this guy was laying in wait for her in the back of her Gremlin for when she got off work. She says she didn't see him in the rear compartment of the hatchback. As she is headed home to Crown Point, he pops up behind her with a jackknife, puts it to her throat and threatens to kill her if she doesn't do exactly as he tells her."

"Really?"

"Yeah. It gets good. He directs her into Illinois to a construction site and tells her to stop the car. He then positions himself in front of her and has intercourse with her."

"While she's still in the driver's seat?"

"I presume."

"I'd like to know how that's done. C'mon, Brenda, she's making this up, don't you think?"

"She sounds like an excellent candidate for you, Cy."

"Sure. When do you want her tested?"

"I know tomorrow is New Year's Eve. She's available, and I'm out at a conference the following week."

"You're never one for convenience."

"I know."

"What time?"

"She can't make it until four in the afternoon," Brenda said, wincing.

"Why not just make it midnight and start the New Year off right?"

"Sorry, can you?"

"Anything for you. Four o'clock it is."

"I have an idea as to what the relevant issue would be."

"Oh really? Gee, I bet that took some thought," Cy came back with his sarcasm. "How about these questions: 'Did that man in your car have intercourse with you?' And 'Did that man in your car force you to have sex against your will?' Assuming that rape in the car is the issue here?"

"Right, exactly."

"However, if I get a pretest admission that there was no man in the car to begin with, even better, right?"

"Right, good luck with that," Rivens replied.

Sheila Boyles was late for her scheduled polygraph with Cy. This didn't surprise him nor did it please him. It didn't please Agent Rivens or the squad supervisor, Bill Lamens, either with the holiday looming. With an office of unhappy campers, Donovan figured it might be a good time to press for a pretest confession especially given the absurdity of the case facts. Little did he know the facts were about to become a little more bizarre.

"You're late, Sheila," Rivens said as she greeted Boyles thirty minutes beyond her appointed time.

"My babysitter was late," Boyles replied.

"Well, you're here, and this is Special Agent Cy Donovan. He'll be your polygraph examiner."

"Hello," Sheila said as she took a short glance at Cy.

"Hi, Sheila. He extended his hand and shook hers. We're in this room over here. Do you need to use the restroom before we get started?"

"No, I'm okay."

"Sure?"

"Yes."

"Okay. He opened the door to a dark room."

Boyles hesitated, then walked in slowly.

After a moment, Cy flicked on the light switch.

Sitting abruptly before her was a stark black chair with arms raised slightly. Draped over the back of it were two convoluted tubes with black cables and steel chains that ran behind the chair to the bronze-plated instrument sitting snugly into the desk. At the end of each tube was a steel prong forked so as to accommodate the fitting on the chain as it was wrapped around the upper torso of its voluntary participant.

The purpose of each tube was to capture changes in respiration during the onset of a stimulus or question when posed by the examiner to the examinee. The respiratory channel had been measured for years now. Originally, it consisted of only one tube, a much larger tube proposed by Leonard Keelor in what was known as the Keelor polygraph or box back in 1930.

Dangling peacefully across the left arm of the chair were a set of steel fingerplates, curved in design, attached to yet another black cord, which also ran behind the chair and attached to the bronze instrument. An intimidating component, these electrodes were designed to measure changes in the galvanic skin response (GSR) during the onset of a question. If all you had was one component, the GSR would suffice to assist in detection of deception. It is the fingerplates that capture the soul of a person's physiology. It is indeed the fingerplates that prompt the participant to wipe their hands profusely on their trousers prior to the examiner placing them on their fingers. And it is the fingerplates that always bring on the comment "I feel like I'm getting into an electric chair."

Finally, the cardio cuff sits ready to be placed on the examinee's arm. "This is the only thing you will feel today, Sheila," Cy mentioned as he unfolded it. The cuff was attached with black Velcro snugly around Boyle's upper right arm. Donovan wasted no time. He got her right into the components during the pretest interview hoping the intimidation of the moment might prompt a more forthcoming, accurate account of the facts.

Brenda Rivens took a seat next to Cy to witness the signing of the consent forms to include the Advice of Rights waived by Boyles. Sheila Boyles wasn't being accused of anything; she wasn't a suspect in a crime, except perhaps telling a tall tale to the FBI, which is a federal offense but rarely charged and prosecuted. However, FBI policy requires the administration of the Miranda warnings to polygraph examinees in a criminal case regardless of whether or not the subject is in custody. Due in part to the fact that once examinees are strapped into the chair, they have a tendency to feel restrained even though they sign a consent form that clearly spells out the fact they can stop the test any time. They can also refuse to answer any question at any time. They can demand to leave any time they wish, and they will be allowed to do so. It is quite rare that examinees balk at the signing of these forms, and Sheila Boyles was no exception.

"Thanks, Brenda, see you in a little bit," Cy said.

"She's all yours." Rivens left the room.

"Can I assume you've never had a polygraph before, Sheila?"

"No, never," Boyles replied.

"Do you want to take one today?"

"Not really, but I said I would, and I'm not lying."

Cy studied her. Within seconds, he knew what he was about to deal with. Sheila Boyles was 5'5" tall, weighed 250 pounds, and barely squeezed into his chair. When Cy placed the pneumograph tubes around her and connected the chains, he had but two links left in the upper chain and one link remaining in the lower chain. Boyles was single, depressed, twenty-nine years of age, dealing with a sinus infection and in dire need of attention, fond attention at that. She was a prime candidate for a *storyteller*.

Cy looked her straight in the eye and moved in close right away. "Sheila, you don't have to sit for this test. If there is anything in your previous statement to Agent Rivens you feel you need to change, you can do that with me now, and we can avoid all of this. You're not in any trouble. We can all go home, and all is forgotten."

"I ain't changin' nothin'. You mean you ain't goin' after these guys? I was raped and humiliated you know. You've got to know—"

"Wait a minute, Sheila," Cy said as he raised his hand. "Did you say 'these guys'?"

"Yeah, that's right. There was two of 'em."

"In the car?"

"No, one in the car. One showed up later."

"Later? Where later?"

"At the site."

"Construction site?"

"Yeah, right. He was the one that tried to get in the car, but the guy wouldn't let him in."

"Okay, this is new information to me. Have you told Agent Rivens this?"

"She didn't ask."

"And you didn't think to make her aware of it? Is this second man not part and parcel to the act?"

"Well, he tried to be."

"Okay, Sheila, let's start from the beginning here. I need 100 percent of the facts from you before we do any testing."

Boyles's shoulders fell into a slump.

"You own a purple Gremlin, is that correct?"

"Yes."

"Hatchback, right?"

"Yes."

"Rear compartment exposed, closed, or filled with anything?"

"I have stuff in there, but I don't recall if it was secure."

"Where was your car parked?"

"Where it always is, in the parking lot near the middle."

"Did you do anything unusual before leaving work?"

"No."

"Tell me what happened."

"I drove out of the parking lot out onto Highway 30."

"Westbound?"

"Yes, west."

"So this took at least ten minutes or so for you to get to Highway 30, right?"

"Probably. It was nearly a half hour before he popped up."

"Popped up?"

"Yes, this man just popped up from behind me. I never knew he was even in my car."

"Didn't see him in the backseat?"

"No, he had to come from my hatchback area."

"Little guy, then huh?"

"Oh no, he was, I mean he was, well, good size," Boyles said as she spread her arms out.

"Oh really!" Cy expressed his surprise. This was getting good. "What happened next?" he asked with renewed enthusiasm like a child eagerly awaiting a grandfather's tale. "Did he threaten you?"

"As a matter a fact he did."

"How so?"

"With a knife, like a jackknife."

"Can you describe the knife?"

"Just a jackknife."

"What did he do with the jackknife?"

"He put it beside my neck."

"Did he say anything when he put the jackknife up to your neck?"

"Just to keep driving and I wouldn't get hurt."

"Did you say anything else to him?"

"No, just asked him not to hurt me."

"Where did you drive to?"

"We got off of Highway 30, and he directed me to a construction site."

"How long was the drive?"

"Total, probably forty-five minutes."

"Then what happened?"

"I've already told the other agent what he did."

"And that is?"

"He got into the front and had sex with me." Boyles looked away.

"Tell me, Sheila, your car has bucket seats, right?"

"Yes."

"And if I recall reading the report, this all occurred during a pretty violent rainstorm, right?"

"Yes."
"So it was a pretty messy affair out there at that site, right?"
"Probably."
"Probably? Did he get out of the backseat, out of the car, and into the front, or did he climb over the front?"
"I don't know. He was just there." Boyles seemingly began to pout.
"Okay, and he's a big boy, right?"
"Um, um."
"Bigger than I?"
"'Bout the same."
"Which seat were you in when he had sex with you?"
"I never got out of my seat."
"Tilt wheel?"
"No."
"So you're telling me he straddled you and had sexual intercourse with you while you remained in the driver's seat?"
"Yes."
"And the other man, Sheila?"
"He wouldn't let him in the car."
"Explain."
"The other guy was waiting in a gray pickup truck. When we got there, he just sat in the truck and watched us for a few minutes. When the man in my, in my…"
"You mean the 'the hatchback man'?"
"Yes, the man in my car, when he got on me, the guy in the truck came up to my window and wanted to get in the car too, but the guy on me locked the door and wouldn't let him in. This made the other guy mad."
"How do you know?"
"I could tell."
"Then what happened?"
"The guy on me just forced his way with me."
"The big guy between you and the steering wheel, right?"

"Oh yeah."

"Wow! Did you try to do anything to help yourself?"

"How could I?"

"Tell me, Sheila, what was the hatchback man doing with his hands while he was having intercourse with you?"

"He had the jackknife in his right hand and a bottle of beer in his left hand."

"A bottle of beer? Really?"

"Yeah."

"Had you seen the beer before?"

"No. Don't know where he got it."

"Is it still raining outside at this time?"

"Yes, hard."

"What is the other guy doing?"

Sheila paused.

"Sheila, what was the other guy doing? You know, the guy from the truck?"

"Yeah, I know. He had unzipped his pants."

"Is that right? In the rain?"

"Yes. He masturbated on my windshield."

"Okay, then what did he do?"

"He got back in his truck."

"And the hatchback man?"

"He got in the truck also, and they left."

"So as I understand it, Sheila, not only are you not changing your story, you're adding to it here today, is that right?"

"I can't help what happened."

"And you're willing to take a polygraph here tonight based on what you've just told me?"

Boyles nodded.

Cy wasted no further time. He would run three charts. It didn't matter that she could barely fit behind the wheel herself let alone two her size. The scene she depicted was so preposterous, it was all he could do to keep from laughing, but he assumed she suffered from some sort of depressive disorder, probably *dysthymic disorder* characterized by a depressed mood for most of her day over a period of time longer than two years. Furthermore, with her obese condition, one could easily add-in overeating and low energy, low self-esteem, feelings of hopelessness as symptoms of such a condition. He would simply need to employ some patience with her and be willing to show some empathy. However, he wasn't in an empathetic mood.

After reviewing the test questions with her, Cy was ready to go. He ran one chart, pulled it off the kymograph, and got what he expected—erratic tracings in respiration and a rolling tracing in the blood channel despite his efforts to keep the cardio cuff up and away from her abdomen. However, the galvanic skin response was as reliable as it could be.

The sweat gland is the mechanism Cy relied on time and time again in determining detection of deception. It is the sweat gland by which the human body is responsible for thermoregulation or temperature control. When the body gets too hot, this gland activates and releases a fluid intended to cool the skin much like a thermostat would turn on the air conditioner in a building.

In physiological detection of deception, the sweat gland plays another role. Besides thermoregulatory functions, sweat glands respond to external stimuli, especially those found in the palmar surfaces of the hand that include the fingers. These sweat glands, also known as eccrine sweat glands, play against the individual whose goal is to deceive. As such, it is critical the examiner obtain scoreable tracings from the galvanic skin response channel. He does so through proper placement of the fingerplates (electrodes) on the fingers where the incidence of electrodermal activity is highest.

There was little question as to proper placement of the electrodes with Sheila Boyles. When the relevant questions were presented to her, the GSR tracing rose from five to eight chart divisions each time repeatedly throughout the three charts Cy ran. He set the charts aside, took a deep breath, and moved his chair around in front of Boyles.

"Listen, Sheila," he spoke softly, "you failed this test. There is a far bigger issue going on here today, isn't there?"

"What do you mean?"

"Tell me about your family, Sheila."

"My family?"

"You're family upbringing."

"I don't understand."

"I know you have had experiences in your life that are troubling for you, and I just want you to know you can talk to me here tonight. You're not in any trouble with the FBI. What I am asking you is, is there anything in your background, in your family history, or early adult history that you have had to seek counseling for? Anything for which you have been referred for counseling for but didn't pursue?"

"So what you're asking me is, am I a nut?"

"No, that's not what I am asking you, Sheila."

Boyles crossed her arms in a defensive posture, her feet firmly planted shoulder length apart. She was dug in, prepared for battle.

"Brothers or sisters?"

"Three brothers, one sister, all older, much older. I's a mistake."

"Did you graduate high school?"

"GED, 1985."

"Active in school?"

"I worked. Fast-food places mostly. What's all this got to do with what happened to me anyway?"

"Everything."

"Well, you better explain it to me then 'cuz I'm confused."

"You seem firmly set in your ways here tonight, so I'll be fair with you and very straight forward. After that, if you care to explore it further, I'll be happy to."

"Okay," Sheila said while peering into Cy with curiosity.

"It is physically impossible for a man the size you describe to position himself between the steering wheel of your car and your body and have sexual intercourse with you, Sheila."

"I just knew it, I just knew—"

"Hold on. Let me finish. You have taken it upon yourself to occupy the time and effort of law enforcement in this circus act, so I'm going to take the time and effort to lay it out for you. Actually, I may have said enough. I will not sit here and entertain the folly of the so-called second man ejaculating on your windshield during a rainstorm."

Sheila Boyles was reduced to a red-faced, teary-eyed, apologetic whimper. She did not expect to have her tale spun back to her so quickly. Her eyes found a spot on the wall well beyond Cy's left shoulder, and she fixated on it. Her chubby fists we're clenched inside her folded arms, and she sat frozen to the chair. Her breathing was slow but deep. She contemplated her next move.

Cy remained firm, insisting her story was fraught with error. He asked for clarification on numerous points but received no cooperation from Boyles. Sheila had chosen to revert back into her shell. After about an hour of hopeless attempts to get the missing details of her story put into a believable perspective, Cy chose once again to probe her childhood and early adulthood.

He knew she was likely a victim of abuse at some point in her past or a product of neglect, perhaps a combination of the two. In any event, she never received much-needed attention, and he was at a quandary as to whether he wanted to be her psychologist, caregiver, or disciplinarian. At some point in the evening, he chose to leave the room.

"Take a shot at her if you like," Cy said.

"I assume she failed," Brenda replied as she bit into a sandwich.

"Oh yeah. Sitting there stone-cold too. This gal's got a real circus act going. Take some time with her. Ask her why she didn't tell you about the second man."

"Second man?"

"Yeah, it gets messy, have fun. I'm going to check in with Lamens."

"Hey, Cy, how's it going, did you get anywhere with her?" Bill Lamens asked.

"We're at a standstill. She failed her test."

"Figures. Preposterous story."

"There are actually two men involved, or so she says."

"Two? Really?"

"Yeah. I'll let Rivens tell you the details of the second man." Cy chuckled.

"How much longer?"

"Not long. This is a waste of time, Bill. She needs counseling."

"Perhaps we should put a wrap on it?"

"I thought I'd give Brenda awhile to work with her. She clammed up on me."

"I see."

"I'm going to get a Coke, need anything?"

"No, I'm good."

Cy headed down the hallway for the vending machine. Just before turning the corner, he hollered back at Lamens. "Hey, Bill?"

"Yeah?"

"Brenda did run NCIC checks on Boyles, right?"

"Pretty sure. She mentioned how long it was taking to get the printouts yesterday."

"I was just wondering. Would you mind checking the radio room to see if they've come in?"

"Yeah, sure, I'll let you know."

Cy gave Rivens another thirty minutes before coming back into the room. As he opened the door, she sat squarely in front of Boyles with a look of frustration. He was surprised to see that Boyles had not appeared to have moved at all since he left the room an hour earlier. He took a chair next to Brenda and opened conversation again with Boyles.

"Is there anything further you want to share with us tonight?"

No response was forthcoming other than a sigh.

"Sheila, with your cooperation, I would like to propose we get you a counselor. Would you be receptive to that?" Cy asked.

Again, there was no response.

Just then there was a short knock on the door as Bill Lamens interrupted and asked for Cy.

Cy stepped out of the room.

Lamens handed him a criminal history printout. "You need to be aware of this. She's been down this road before. Also, take a look at the message left for Brenda from Boyles's employer. Apparently, on the day of the alleged incident, Boyles turned off the cameras to the parking lot twenty minutes before she left the building to get into her car."

"Wow! This figures right in. Thanks, Bill."

Cy stepped back into the room and confronted Boyles face-to-face. "Sheila, perhaps you would like to tell me what happened in another southern Indiana town when you filed a rape allegation that supposedly took place in a vehicle about five years ago?" He handed the printout to Rivens along with the employer's note.

"I believe I'll leave now," Boyles mumbled. She maneuvered her way out of the chair not once looking at Cy or Brenda.

"Your prerogative," Cy replied as he opened the door. Rivens sat mesmerized as she read the NCIC report.

Cy watched along with Lamens as Sheila Boyles made her way to the elevator. She never looked back.

Cy and Bill stood looking at each other.

"Well, the night is still young, Cy."

"That it is. Where's Brenda?"

Brenda Rivens came walking down the hall from the polygraph room.

"Hey, Brenda," Bill asked, "what's this I hear about a second man?"

"I don't know. Cy knows about him. She wouldn't talk to me. Cy?"

"Let's just say it was a rainy day and leave it at that."

CEILING SEX AND POPCORN

In the previous story, we came to understand how an individual, Sheila Boyles, compensated for her low self-esteem and feelings of inadequacy by seeking attention through the reporting of an utterly ridiculous act that never happened. She attempted to validate her self-worth by drawing people of authority into her circle, if only for a short time, in an effort to obtain some sort of favorable outcome. It is often unclear as to what result people like Sheila actually hope to achieve.

With others, there *is* a motive for the story they assemble. There is a reason, albeit a poor reason, yet understandable as to why they choose to concoct their fable. One such fable was craftily put together by a young lady from France, Maryann Bobely.

Ms. Bobely was born in the Comoros Islands located in the Indian Ocean, 1974. She was raised in France where she was educated and emigrated to England. Her credentials were strong enough for her to obtain employment as a teacher of the French language in a London middle school.

There came upon a time in 2002 when Maryann Bobely visited the United States and met Henry Salazar from North Carolina. She became romantically attached to Salazar, and shortly after arriving back in London, she discovered she was pregnant with Salazar's child. This would be her second as she already had a two-year-old son from a previous foiled marriage.

After a period of commuting back and forth with Salazar, Ms. Bobley elected to leave her employment in London and sought to reposition herself in the United States along with her son and recently born daughter. She made arrangements with Salazar to pick her up at the airport in Charlotte, North Carolina, in January 2003. FBI Special Agent Cy Donovan had the unique opportunity of unraveling her story from that point forward.

"So tell me, Maryann, you arrived at Charlotte, and Henry picked you up, correct?" Cy asked.
"That's right?"
"Your son was with you?"
"Yes."
"Where was he?"
"In the backseat."
"And you had had the baby?"
"Yes."
"Backseat also?"
"Umm, yes. No, I had the baby in my arms."
"You don't remember?"
"I had the baby."
"I believe babies are supposed to be secure in the backseat up to a certain age, are they not?"
"Right. He didn't have a baby seat."
"I see. So, according to the report, he drove you to his home in the mountains?"
"Yes, but…"
"But?"
"Well, while we were driving, he wanted me to give him oral sex."
"While he was driving?"
"Yes."
"And did you?"

"No."
"What did he do?"
"He beat me."
"How did he beat you?"
"With his fist."
"So while he was driving. Let me get this right, Maryann, he hasn't seen you in ten months?"
"About."
"It's all been good?"
"Yes."
"You quit your job, come to America with his baby, you trust him well enough to do this, and you're telling me the first thing he asks you for is oral sex, then basically greets you with a fist?"
"Basically, that's it."

Cy had been briefed by his case agent about what to expect. Fortunately, it was early in the day he was up for it and willing to sit through a new moon rising if necessary to get Maryann Bobely to admit to her falsehood.

"Not a very friendly man was he, Maryann?"
"No."
"Now, as I understand it, you lived with him in his house trailer in the North Carolina mountains from January 2003 to July of 2005, is that correct?"
"Yes."
"And during that time, you were confined and denied access to the outside world?"
"I didn't have a car. I wasn't sure where I was."
"But didn't Henry work?"
"Yes, he went to work and threatened me not to leave."
"Where did he work?"
"I don't know."
"What kind of work did he do?"
"I don't know for sure, deliveries, maybe?"
"I see. How did he threaten you?"

"Said he would kill me. There were snakes."

"There were snakes? What do you mean, Maryann?"

"There were snakes and rodents that came in through the floor of the trailer."

"Did you feel threatened by these snakes and rodents?"

"Yes."

"You're telling me, then, the floor had holes in it or was rotten in places?"

"Very much so, and he wouldn't repair it. I was forced to live in this environment with my son and daughter."

"What did you do to help yourself?"

"There was nothing I could do. I didn't know where I was. If I left, I knew he would find me, or I would get lost. Plus, I had the two children, don't you see?"

"Did he hurt you in any way?"

"Oh yes."

"Can you tell me about it?"

Maryann looked away and was quiet. Then she spoke, "He forced my right breast nipple onto a hot plate and burned me."

"What prompted him to do that?"

"Nothing. That is just how he was. He was very mean."

"What else did he do?"

"He took a shotgun and put it to my head and pulled the trigger so I could hear it go click just to frighten the hell out of me. Then he laughed about it. It was all a game to him."

"Was he this way with your son and the baby as well?"

"He mistreated them by not providing them with food or water when they needed it."

"Sexual abuse?"

"Just with me."

"Can you describe what he did with you?"

Maryann paused and asked for some water. Cy stepped out and retrieved a glass of water for her. As he came back into the room, he observed that Maryann seemed to be very well composed.

"Thank you," she said as she took the glass he offered.

"No problem." He waited patiently.

Within a minute, she continued, "He constructed this, what you would call a human bondage apparatus in his bedroom which hung from the ceiling with chains." She paused, then spoke again, "You see, he forced me to perform sexual favors for him all the time, so I guess he got bored and built this *thing* he wanted me to get into. I would climb up into this—"

"Like a harness?"

"Yeah, that's it, a harness. I would get up in that. It was not so bad at first, but then he started inviting numerous black males and females over wearing clown masks and disguises and such, and I was forced to engage in various sex acts while hanging from the ceiling. All kinds of sex to include lesbianism and homosexual acts, you know. And I was handcuffed to this apparatus the whole time."

"Go on."

"Well, they would use various sex tools too. It was awful."

"Was Henry a participant with them?"

"Actually no. You want to know what he would do?"

"Sure."

"He would sit back in the corner and watch while eating a bowl of popcorn. Oh, occasionally, he would join in."

"Is that right?" Cy acted amused. He had heard some stories in his day, but this one was a frontrunner. "Tell me, how often did this type of activity go on?"

"I would say he had these people over as many as eight at a time, from December 2004 to June. Yes, June 2005 at a frequency of three to four times a week. When they finished, he took money from the couples, but I don't know how much they paid him to participate."

"Very well, anything further?"

"Well, I don't recall." She paused. She looked at Cy as if to say, "Do I need to say anymore?"

Cy really didn't want any more details. He saw no point in collecting anymore lascivious fiction. He did want to hear her conclusion however. So he asked for it.

"How did you end up at a homeless shelter in Newport, Tennessee?"

"You see, I found the nerve to escape one day while Henry was working. I left with my children, and we hitchhiked out of North Carolina. We were picked up by a couple from Sevierville, Tennessee, who allowed us to live with them from July 2005 through February 2006. Although they were kind to me, I felt I needed to move on. So I left and ended up here."

"There is a lot more to it than that isn't there, Maryann?"

"That's really it."

"Okay, we've talked a good bit this morning. You've been asked to sit for a polygraph examination today, right?"

"Yes."

"Are you still up for it?"

"Yes. I have nothing to lie about. I want to get this behind me."

"Let me just ask you one question before we get started if you don't mind."

"Go ahead."

"Have you made up any part of your story about the sexual abuse you suffered from Henry Salazar or the physical abuse you or your children received from Salazar?"

"No, I have not," Bobely insisted.

"Very well. If that is the case, then you shouldn't have any problem with this test." Cy proceeded with the usual instructions he gave everyone else just prior to their test. He noticed her attentiveness. Her eyes grew wide as she looked curiously at the components he was attaching to her. Although she was thirty-two years old, he got the impression her maturity level was that of a young teenager.

"Nothing hurts today, Maryann. Just keep both feet flat on the floor, look straight ahead during the test, and breathe as you normally breathe. Try to refrain from any unnecessary movements during the test such as smacking your lips, nodding your head, clearing your throat, and that sort of thing. Do you understand?"

She sat motionless with no response.

"Maryann?"

"Oh, yes, I understand."

"Okay, give me a moment, and we'll get started." He hoped she was listening to his instructions and that he would get conclusive charts during the test. One never knows what to expect with people so caught up with the weaving of a tale. The focus of their thoughts continually shifts throughout the administration of the examination to the point where it becomes quite frustrating for the examiner.

"Regarding any sexual or physical abuse you received from Henry Salazar, do you intend to lie to me on this test?"

"No."

Cy had asked his sacrifice relevant—the preparatory question that is asked early and designed to give the examiner a clue as to whether the examinee will react to the additional relevant questions later on in the test.

Of particular peculiarity was Bobely's first chart. He observed little reaction in the galvanic skin response, which was at first a surprise to him. However, upon further review of the chart's conclusion, it was clear that she was not going to be a responder in the GSR channel. She was going to give him all the deception he needed to see from within the pneumograph or respiratory tracings. He took interest in what he was seeing.

Although she exhibited poor GSR physiology, she saw fit to be troubled in the breathing channel as evidenced by the baseline change in the pneumograph tracing at each asking of the relevant questions. He rolled into chart number 2.

"Have you made up any part of your story about the sexual abuse you suffered from Henry Salazar?"

"No."

A minute later, Cy asked, "Have you lied to authorities about the physical abuse you and your children received from Henry Salazar?"

"No."

Clear again, he observed. She was unable to maintain her baseline in respiration when presented with the relevant questions. A third chart will seal the deal.

From the beginning of the third chart, her focus was lost. *Typical,* Cy thought. *She isn't even touching the relevant questions this time. It's as if she didn't even hear me ask them.* Somewhat frustrated, he came around in front of her.

"Are you feeling all right?"

"Yes."

"One of these questions seems to be bothering you more than any of the others. I'm not going to tell you which one it is, but we'll go through them one more time. Then we'll talk about it, okay?"

"Okay."

An old ploy he used many times in an effort to get his examinees focused. Fair and ethical, it was not designed to oversensitize them in any one direction. It was simply an effort to get the guilty person focused on guilt, and the innocent person focused on innocence. It worked more often than not.

It worked well with Maryann Bobely as her fourth chart was a clear indication of deception. Cy wondered what sort of afternoon he was in for.

"Maryann, I'm afraid you've told me a tall tale here today, and we need to come to an understanding as to why?" Cy asked.

"Why?" she responded as if she didn't understand.

"Yes, you've told me a series of fibs."

No further response came forth with the exception of watery eyes.

Cy could see her weakness, and he was glad of it. *Patience, be gentle. Be kind, be caring, and be cautious.* She would tell him what he wanted to hear if he could convey trust.

"It concerns your children, doesn't it, Maryann?"

She looked down. She looked to the side. She sniffled; she sniffled again.

Cy paused and waited.

Maryann continued to sniffle and took some deep breaths but held back.

"Are you concerned you will lose them?"

She nodded as a tear rolled from her right cheek onto her right knee. She touched the wet spot with her finger and stared at it blankly while taking another deep breath. Without looking at Cy, she spoke, "He never sold me for sex to anyone. He never beat me with his fist in the car because I would not perform oral sex. He never built any device that hung from his bedroom ceiling nor did he ever force me to have sex with anyone while hanging from any such an apparatus. He never put a shotgun to my head and pulled the trigger. I accidentally burned my nipple while losing my balance at the stove." She looked up at Cy for the first time in the eye and said, "I'm sorry. I was just afraid I would lose custody of my kids."

"I understand," he responded. "Listen, Department of Human Services will deal with you fairly on this. They will appreciate your cooperation and your situation."

The strange truth of the matter was there were some details of her story that were validated as truthful. There were indeed holes in the floor of the trailer, and Salazar himself admitted to the fact it wasn't unusual for snakes or mice to find their way into his trailer. The unsanitary living conditions that Bobely described were also confirmed and would play in her favor in a subsequent child custody hearing.

Cy took her signed, sworn statement and calmed her fears. "It isn't unusual, Maryann, for someone who, out of no fault of his or her own, find themselves in a situation so bizarre that they exaggerate their circumstances for their own self-survival."

"I wasted a lot of people's time, didn't I?"

Cy mustered a grin. He had simply run out of words.

SPOOK IN MY GARAGE

"I just had this feeling the night before when I took the garbage out to the street, came back into my garage, shut my garage door, and started into my house that there was a spook in my garage. Do you know what I mean?"

Cy nodded.

"Anyway, I paused for a moment, you know, to be sure the garage door closed as it should. I glanced around the garage over the two cars and didn't really hear or see anything unusual. I went on into the house and forgot about it."

"Did you lock the door to your house?"

"Always, yes."

Cy Donovan's services had been requested once again from an old friend, Special Agent Wayne Chesbro. Chesbro refused to buy into the story relayed to him by Tom Huddlesbury, a sixty-two-year old branch manager for the Bank of Detroit. After all, Huddlesbury was on the short list of managers the bank was looking to let go in the near future for reasons not made clear to Chesbro. In any event, after hearing his story, one began to understand why.

"Did anything unusual happen at your house during the night?" Cy asked.

"No, no, sir, can't say that there was anything different about that night as opposed to any other night," Huddlesbury said.

He was an articulate man who thought before he spoke. When he spoke, the words rolled off his tongue like a craftsman well schooled in his trade. Not only was he well spoken, but he looked like what a bank vice president should look like. A well-pressed conservative gray suit captured a navy blue tie highlighted ever so slightly with a diagonal white stripe back-dropped against a plain white shirt. Of course, his gray hair was well groomed. His steely blue eyes had no reservations about looking Cy straight in the eye while conveying his story.

"As I understand it, you were confronted in the morning, is that right?"

"Yes, that is correct."

"Tell me what happened."

"I make it a point to be up by 6:00 a.m. I normally rise before then however. After all these years, you see, I don't need an alarm, and I didn't need one this day. I went about my usual routine, you know, daily hygiene and such. I prepared a pot of coffee and got dressed."

"Did your wife get up with you?"

"No. Betty doesn't normally get up until after I leave. That is why I make the pot of coffee. There is plenty for her. She is a heavy coffee drinker." He paused.

"You were saying?" Cy asked.

"I'm just gathering my thoughts here because I do remember going into the garage to get into the truck, but for some reason, I went back into the house…and…well, I guess I went back in for something. I'm not sure what."

Cy wanted to intervene, but he sensed Tom was determined to regain his thought. Finally, he offered, "Perhaps it will come to you. Now you eventually went back into the garage, right?"

"Oh yes. Right. I sat my coffee on the rail of the truck, you know, the truck bed rail by the driver's door. That's it!"

"What?"

"I went back in the house to get my cup of coffee. Of course, I never leave the house without it. I also went out the front door first to get the newspaper off the driveway. I remember this now, Cy. You don't mind me calling you Cy, do you?"

127

"No, no, go ahead."

"I picked up the paper for Betty, brought it in the house, and laid it on the table. I pulled out the classifieds to take with me to work. I remember now because both of my hands were occupied when he surprised me in the garage, and this is what caused me to spill my coffee."

"You said you had placed it on the rail of your truck bed?"

"Yes, I did, what was left of it. He startled me so, half of it ended up on the floor and down the side of the truck."

"All right, Tom. You're going to have to take me through this. It's not every day we run into someone in our garage, a locked garage at that."

"He was a real spook, I tell you. I never really saw much of him."

"Was he alone?"

"Yes, as far as I know, he was. I mean I didn't see or hear anyone else."

"Tell me what happened next."

"I went to place my coffee on the rail of the truck bed so I could reach my keys in my pocket. I had the classifieds in my left hand. Before I could even set my coffee down, this guy produces a silver handgun from behind me. I tried to look back at him. He pushed my face against the windshield of the driver's door with my head turned toward my mirror. I remember this because this is all I saw of him. I mean through the mirror, you see?"

Cy nodded.

"He had on a camouflage ski mask, black gloves, shorts I believe."

"How was it that you saw this gun?"

"First, in my peripheral vision, I guess. I know it was shiny-like, because he pushed my head up sideways to the window, and I felt the gun against part of my head as he was talking. I could see just part of it."

"What did he say to you?"

"What did he say? Do you expect me to remember everything?"

"Did he give you any instructions?" Cy asked.

"Plenty. He was a man with a purpose let me tell you. He threw a black plastic bag into the cab of my truck and told me I was going to fill it with money when I got to the bank. You see, I was to drive directly to the bank, open up, open the vault, fill the bag, place the bag back in my truck, and drive to an intersection and leave the truck unlocked and unattended about a mile from the bank. I was to walk back to the bank like nothing happened."

"And what did you do to carry out those instructions?"

"Well, let me finish. Before I got in the truck, this guy had a satchel with him. He pulled out a black device that I didn't see until later."

"Device?"

"Right. I'm tellin' ya."

"Okay, go on."

"He stuck this thing like a transistor radio into the small of my back with silicone and duct tape."

"Really?"

"That's right. Places it right there"—Tom reached behind himself to show Cy—"Tells me it's a bomb that can be activated by radio transmission. Tells me further if I fail in any way to drive straight to the bank, he will blow it. Or if I call police, he will hear my voice and blow it."

"So he wraps the duct tape around you securing this device, is that right?"

"Along with the silicone, yes."

"You saw a caulking tube?"

"Oh yes, that's what he had, like contractors use."

"So let me see if I get this picture, Tom. You are standing there in your garage and allowing this stranger to place a device on your back with silicone and duct tape..."

"I didn't allow, wasn't my choice, he..."

"Hold on here. It took him two hands to do this, right?"

"Well, yeah."

"What happened to his gun while he's getting this device on you?"

"Well, I'm not sure, he's behind me, you know?"

"Uh-huh."

"And like I said, I wasn't positive there wasn't another man with him. It all happened so fast. Almost like he had done this before or had rehearsed it."

"Okay, and you didn't open the garage when you went out to get the paper?"

"No, like I said, I went out the front door."

"There was no evidence of any forced entry into your garage, Tom. Your back door was locked. Your window was locked."

"It baffles me as much as you. All I can figure, and I've gone over this many times, believe me, is that he was waiting for me the night before and followed me in unbeknown to me as I drove the car in. He must have spent the night in the garage."

"If he did that, he must have pissed in a bottle because there was no indication he had urinated anywhere in your garage."

"I know. I looked for that too. I didn't see any."

"So what happened next?"

"I did as he told me. I got in the truck, pulled out, and drove straight to the bank."

"Which is about—?"

"Which is about a mile away. I went into the bank, turned off the alarms, looked around, and paused. I made a decision. I called bank security in Chicago. Soon thereafter, police arrived. I met them in the parking lot."

"And the device on your back?"

"I began to have doubts about that, so I untaped it myself, took it off, set it down in the parking lot. I don't know what the police did with it. I heard it was an empty box."

"Tom, tell me something here. Why is it, you called bank security? You cooperated with police throughout the day, but at no time did you call your wife to check on her? Tell me that, Tom. You left your garage with an intruder still in it, is that right?"

"I had no reason to think he was there to bring harm to her."

"Is that so? You were real confident about that?"

"It was me and the bank's money he was after. His instructions were clear."

"Okay. I'm going to give you some clear instructions today for this polygraph. Are you still willing to sit for it?"

"Absolutely."

Cy gave Huddlesbury a few moments to use the restroom while he prepared his questions. He understood why Wayne Chesbro doubted his story. Bank robbers don't hang out in people's garages the night before, and they don't strap make-believe bombs on people and give them the freedom to drive away. If this did happen as Huddlesbury described, he certainly took a chance calling bank security and removing the device himself unless of course he put it on himself. *And why didn't he call his wife?* This is what really bothered Cy.

Tom's wife had been interviewed and stated she neither heard nor saw anything unusual that morning. *Where was Tom's concern for what may have been going on at his house after he left for the bank?* Finally, no suspects were identified and no suspicious vehicles were noticed at the intersection described by Huddlesbury where he was to deliver his truck.

Nevertheless, Cy recognized that Huddlesbury was straightforward with him so far this morning. He had displayed no deceptive body language commonly associated with those who are fabricating their facts. However, he also knew Huddlesbury had had plenty of time to review his own set of facts. He had had time to prepare for this discussion today, and he had found out through a source that Huddlesbury had jokingly told his son the day of the event to watch the evening news because he (Huddlesbury) would be on it, and it would be good stuff. With that in mind, Cy chose a couple of strong, relevant questions for him.

"Are you all set?"

"I'm ready when you are."

"Have a seat in the black chair. He presented Huddlesbury with the customary consent forms and reviewed the questions. Huddlesbury took no issue with them. Following the attachment and short discussion of the polygraph components, Cy was sitting comfortably behind old reliable. Huddlesbury sat still like a model examinee.

"Did you lie to the police about that man in your garage?"

"No."

Cy observed little if no reaction to the question. *There was no motive to tell this story, and he got nothing out of it.* Soon he popped the next relevant question. "Did you lie to police about anything concerning that man in your garage?"

"No."

Again, very little reaction to the question in any of the channels. Even the GSR was nondramatic. *Interesting.* Cy ran through it twice more with similar results. Even if his examinee was lying and had the conscious will to pass this test, his autonomic nervous system operates independently from his conscious will, and as such, his own physiology would give him up in terms of deception with significant reactions to these relevant questions. But where were the significant reactions?

After an extended pause that grew to be uncomfortable, Cy gathered himself. He knew he dare not even call it inconclusive. Huddlesbury had passed this test, and he had to accept it.

"Well?" Huddlesbury asked impatiently.

"You have some reactions here," Cy quizzed him.

Tom cocked his head and squinted his eyes.

"But I must say I don't think it's anything you need to lose any sleep over."

"Listen, I've lost plenty of sleep over this. The bank thinks I'm a nut, the police think I'm some sort of attention seeker, hell, I'm not even sure my wife believes me, and now this machine? Are you gonna square with me or not?"

"Have you got anything else to share with us you haven't told anyone about?"

"No, sir, I've been over this and over it. You have the facts as I know them to the best of my recollection."

"We're done here today, Tom."

"I guess that's good news?"

Cy nodded. "Stay out of trouble," he said as he escorted Tom out the door.

"I'll do that."

"Oh, and one more thing, Tom."

"I'm still disappointed you didn't find a moment that day to call your wife."

"I know."

Cy went back to his testing room only to find Wayne Chesbro standing there peering back at him.

"Wayne, you're not going to believe this."

"Don't you tell me he passed this test."

"Crystal clear, Wayne."

"No way! Cy, that's a phony story if I ever heard one. That's crap! Don't you think?"

"Wayne, I gave him a tough test to pass. We went over this thing at length, and I have to tell you he was straight up with me."

"Yeah, well he's been 'straight up' with a lot of folks, but no one believes him. They don't believe him because this kind of robbery doesn't happen. Think about it. I've been in law enforcement twenty-eight years, and I'm telling you, this didn't happen!"

"You know, if I even dared to call it inconclusive, quality control would turn it around."

"No, you call it as you see it. We'll live with it. He's a con, that's all."

Cy packed up his equipment and headed home. *Maybe he was lying, and I just got a false negative today. No, don't get those thoughts.* He began second-guessing himself as examiners tend to do in these situations. *Just forget it and move on. There will be more tests, more liars, and more confessions in the future. Or will there? Wayne Chesbro wasn't happy with the results. It is hard to say what impact this test will have on my reputation,* he wondered.

This was a troubling thought that would permeate within him as he debated staying in the polygraph program. A few weeks later, it became an issue that was no longer up for debate. His problem evaporated with a telephone call.

"Cy?"

"Hey, Wayne, what's up?"

"You're not gonna believe this."

"What?"

"I'm going to be using your services quite a bit in the future I believe."

"Really? That's good news. Got something else pending?"

"Not right at this moment, but remember Tom Huddlesbury?"

"Yes."

"You were right. He told you the truth. They caught the joker trying the same scam on the owner of a car dealership the other day."

"You're kidding?"

"That's right, can you believe it? Same kind of deal, hid in the guy's garage, but he got caught."

"Wow! That is good news."

"Yeah. He admitted to the bank job involving Huddlesbury. I want to thank you again."

"That's what I call a validation."

"What did you say?"

"Oh, never mind just poly talk."

DRESSED FOR DECEPTION

Beware of the mannequin who comes draped in deceit.

CRUSADER FOR CHRIST

Mickey Stafford wasn't a bad kid, just nineteen years old and trying to find his way as a struggling college student at a small college in northern Illinois. Not unlike many collegians, Mickey liked to party and did his share to fit in with fellow frat members. Unfortunately, doing one's share to fit in often meant drinking to excess that was and still is considered a virtue among many on college campuses throughout America. Be that as it may, boys will be boys, and young new frat members like Mickey Stafford are oftentimes subject to the influence of their peers, be it good or evil.

Evil prevailed one evening in the spring of 1998. Stafford, accompanied by others, attended a party at a neighboring fraternity house. There were some old friends who were going to the party, and Mickey wanted to see them. As was typical at these parties, frivolity ensued, and alcohol ruled the evening, lots of it. Mickey found his niche on an old card table chair situated between a radiator heater and a makeshift bar tended by the house's social director, a senior frat member.

"Who's the chick dancing with Lee?" Stafford inquired.

"I don't know," the bar tender replied, "but Lee's getting awfully close to her, probably too close. So is the other guy, Ellsberry, I think."

"Why do you say that?"

"Because they're black. She's white, and the others aren't going to like that."

"Others? You mean the other frat members?"

"Yeah. Especially Connor. He's got this thing about mixing races. I mean he can be very, um…"

"Overbearing?"

"Right. Intolerant too. Throw in the fact that he has a thing for this girl, and well, it just isn't good."

"Yeah, I remember Lee from last year. He was in my dorm. Nice guy."

"But Connor thinks he's too nice, if you know what I mean?"

"Yeah, he comes across a little gay, both of them actually."

"Maybe. You want another?"

"Keep 'em coming."

The blue lights on the runway were just visible through the fog. Cy Donovan peered through the window of the American Eagle prop jet as it lumbered onto the pavement in a less than gentle landing. It had been a turbulent flight from Washington to Chicago, but he was happy to be on the ground once again following yet another trip to FBIHQ to assist his fellow examiners in the testing of new special agent applicants. Cy had conducted twelve polygraphs over the week, and as was usual, one in four failed these exams usually due to drug use issues.

As the plane taxied into the gate, Cy's mind shifted to the weekend trip he had planned with his wife. Actually, it was a four-day trip around the Great Lakes taking in the thumb of Wisconsin and the upper peninsula of Michigan. The trip would conclude following a drive down the eastern shore of Lake Michigan with several stops along the way.

As he unbuckled his seat belt, he felt the vibration of his pager. Great, it was 7:00 p.m. on a Friday, and the senior resident agent (SRA) was paging him. He picked up his baggage and phoned in.

"Hey, Cy, you back in town?"

It was Bill Lamens from the Gary office over in Indiana. "Yeah, I just got into Midway, what's up?"

"Give Chief Gene Wisler a call over at the college. He has a suspect he would like polygraphed."

"Okay, what's this about?" Cy asked.

"We've been working a hate crime matter this week, Cy. While you were gone, someone over there left a threatening and hateful message on the answering machine of a couple of black male students. We have the recording. These guys were pretty upset. It's all over the school now, and the chief would like to put it to rest soon."

"When does he want this done?"

"As soon as possible."

"I'll get right on it, Bill." *So much for a trip through the U-P*, Cy thought. He dialed up Chief Wisler hoping not to catch him this late on a Friday. No such luck.

"Chief Wisler here."

"Hey, Chief, Cy Donovan, FBI."

"Hello, Cy. Appreciate you getting back with me."

"No problem. I'm in Chicago just getting in from Washington. Understand you may have a polygraph matter for me?"

"Yes, indeed."

"Tell me about it."

"Someone, actually a young man whom we believe is Mickey Stafford, left a horrible message on the answering machine of a couple of black students here last Saturday night. Cy, this message, well, you'll just have to listen to it, is very disturbing. Never in my thirty years of law enforcement have I heard anyone voice so much racial hate. To say it is vulgar is an understatement."

"Is this Stafford fellow a student also?"

"Yes, if it's him, and we think so. His voice is familiar to one of our officers."

"Has he been interviewed?"

"Yes, in fact, he has. Two of my detectives spent a couple hours with him Thursday. He wasn't real comfortable with them, but he has agreed to a polygraph."

"Denies it all I presume?"

"Oh, yes. Adamant about his denial and his whereabouts Saturday night."

"Do you know where the call emanated from?"

"We've determined it came from another student's room at one of the fraternities. Fellow's room is occupied by Connor Reich. He's been interviewed also, and he too denies involvement."

"Polygraph?"

"He's willing also. What do you suggest?"

"Your hottest suspect first. If that is Mickey, when do you want him tested?"

"He is available Monday."

"He'll go to an attorney by then, Chief."

"Yeah, that's what I'm afraid of. Could you test him tomorrow?"

"Sure. How about 1:00 p.m.? That way I have all morning to familiarize myself with the facts."

"We'll make contact with him and set him up for one."

"Now he'll probably give you an excuse for Saturday."

"Well, Monday is our first day of registration for summer classes. He'll be told to cooperate, or he won't register."

"Ten-four, gotta like that. I'll come by your office, say about 9:00 a.m.?"

"Great! See you then, Cy."

Cy wasted no time the following morning. After a quick breakfast, he sped over to meet with Chief Wisler. The chief was discussing the matter with Detective Zeke Bickler when Cy appeared at his door fifteen minutes early.

"Hey, Cy, good to see you."

"Morning, Chief, you're holding up well these days."

"I try to keep it together. This is Zeke Bickler, Cy. He interviewed Stafford on Thursday."

"Nice to meet you, Cy," Zeke said.

Cy shook hands. "Nice to meet you, Zeke."

"I'll let you guys chat awhile. Zeke has the file. I've got to run out a few minutes, Cy. Everything is arranged as we discussed. I'll be back soon."

"Thanks, Chief."

"It's not a real thick file. Just a few interviews so far. However, we have the tape of the call here. You'll want to listen to that," Bickler advised.

"Okay. Why don't I go through it, formulate some questions, then I'll get back with you," Cy said.

"All right. Would you like some coffee?"

"Sure."

"Take cream?"

"No, black is fine."

"I'll be right back. Oh, the tape recorder is in the drawer of the corner desk."

"Thanks." Cy went straight to the desk, pulled out the recorder, and inserted the tape Zeke had provided. *Hey you faggot niggers. You fucking monkeys from hell....you're not going to live to see another...!*

Wow! Cy was taken back by what he heard. It went on and on with obscenities and threats. He had never heard anything quite that graphic and hateful. *This is disgusting. How could anyone come up with such vulgarity? I can see why we have a case opened*, he thought. He continued to listen, rewound it, and listened again.

He thought he heard the caller slur his words. He definitely heard someone else in the background laughing. He listened a little longer, then began writing. Within a few minutes, he had his questions formatted.

"We're all set, Zeke."

Zeke Bickler sat down, and together, he and Cy listened to the tape once again.

"This is a prank. No real threat intended, just a very nasty prank," Cy said.

"You really think so."

"Yes. I may be wrong, but listen carefully. The caller is drunk. His partner is laughing."

"Let's hope that's all it is."

"We'll find out. He's coming at one, right?"

"Said he was."

"Are you the polygraph guy?"

"I am, and you must be Mickey?" Cy was slightly startled. He was making some adjustments on his instrument and hadn't noticed the young man standing in his door.

"Yeah."

"Cy Donovan, FBI, come on in." Cy studied Stafford for a moment as the nineteen-year-old kid came into his room and took a seat in the polygraph chair. Mickey Stafford appeared to be an all-American college kid, a nice-looking boy, the very kind of student one would want their daughter to bring home for dinner.

Of particular note, Cy observed that Stafford had on a white knit collared shirt, fairly new, with a Christian logo that read "Crusaders for Christ." Stafford also sported a sharp-looking ball cap with a cross pinned to the front. *He's dressed for the occasion*, Cy figured.

Cy wore a cardigan sweater with a light-blue shirt, tie slightly loose as he sat down in front of Stafford. He engaged Stafford in conversation while he wiped his reading glasses clean with his tie. Additionally, Cy sipped his coffee rather sloppily from a well-used Styrofoam cup during his pretest interview all in an effort to appear less rigid and formal and to perhaps convey a relaxed atmosphere for an obviously nervous nineteen-year-old. This was all part of establishing rapport and enabling his subject to trust his examiner as an easy-going guy. At least this was part of his strategy on this Saturday afternoon.

Mickey Stafford was cooperative and provided Cy with the cursory information such as date and place of birth, marital status, employment history, current address, social security account number, etcetera. However, the manner in which he provided this information led Cy to believe his decision to sit for a polygraph was, at best, tentative. As such, Cy felt it was necessary to make an introductory statement. Experience taught him that by making such a statement, it would greatly increase behavior symptoms often displayed by both truthful and deceptive persons.

There were additional reasons for making an introductory statement as well. First of all, Cy wanted to clearly identify the issue under investigation. Secondly, he needed to establish his own objectivity concerning Stafford's truthfulness or deception. And finally, such a statement may persuade Stafford that if he lies, his deception will be detected.

With this in mind, he offered the following: "Mickey, during our interview and throughout this test today, we will be discussing the racially hateful and harassing telephone call made to Lee and Ellsbury. Some of the questions I'll be asking you I already know the answer to. What is important for you is that you be completely truthful with me. If you are not involved in making this call, this test will indicate that. However, if you are involved, in any way, this test will validate that as well. Do you understand?"

"Yes."

"Mickey, did you make that call?"

"No."

Cy picked up on a very unconvincing, subdued no. Not the kind of no he would expect out of an innocent person wrongfully suspected. "Did you participate in any way in making that call?"

Again, Mickey denied it.

"So can I assume you don't know who made that call?"

Stafford shook his head.

"No?"

"No," Stafford said.

"If I ask you questions like this on the polygraph, you'll do all right with them?"

"I should, yes," replied Mickey.

"Great. We shouldn't have a problem then." Cy spent some additional time confirming Stafford's background and upbringing. "I see where your parents sent you to a Christian high school, is that right?"

"Yes, they did."

"Does it go without saying they are paying your tuition here?"

"Yes, unless I get a scholarship."

"Do you feel you are living a life they would be proud of?"

"Yes, for the most part."

"For the most part? Do you feel you are living a life that would sit well with God?"

"Well, nobody's perfect you know."

"I know. We're all sinners. But for the most part, you're doing what you need to do to succeed here, right?"

"Yes, I think so."

"Good." Cy would leave religion out of any further discussion until later if necessary. He had planted the seed he wanted to.

After a few more questions, he felt Stafford was ready for the test. "I'll need you to remove your cap."

"Sure," replied Mickey as he took his cap off and set it on his lap.

Cy took the cap and sat it on the desk next to Mickey with the cross in full view. He then gave Mickey the perfunctory instructions before starting the test. He had Stafford's chair positioned sideways in front of him so that he could monitor any movements throughout the exam. Once the test started, he soon discovered he need not be concerned over movements on the part of Stafford.

Mickey sat stone-cold in the chair. He remained that way through three runnings of polygraph charts. The only thing moving during the test was a bead of sweat falling from behind his ear down the side of his neck. Cy saw the perspiration and realized the room was actually quite cool. *This kid is obviously up tight.* The polygraph charts told a similar story. Clearly deceptive on two out of three charts.

Only one thing concerned Cy. During the running of the third chart, he had heard someone outside the room. This room, while located in a basement, had a set of stairs leading down to it with a landing separating another flight of stairs up to the next level.

Cy was certain he had heard someone coming down the stairs in hard-heeled shoes during the test; however, the individual did not complete the journey past the landing. Odd, but he dismissed the thought as he was compelled to concentrate on the administration of the test with Stafford.

As the test concluded, Cy gathered himself for the accusation and follow-up interrogation of Mickey Stafford. Without question, Stafford had significant physiological difficulty when presented with the relevant question, "Did you make that racially harassing telephone call to those black students?"

Cy started off by handing Stafford a paper towel. By giving him the paper towel, he was highlighting the fact for Stafford that he was fully aware of Stafford's uneasiness with the questions sort of like rubbing salt in a wound.

Somewhat surprised, Mickey took the towel and wiped his neck and brow then mumbled, "Are we finished?"

Ignoring the question, Cy responded with a question, "This wasn't your idea, was it, Mickey?"

"What do you mean? I volunteered for this test."

"No, you know what I mean. Connor is very influential, isn't he? Or was this your idea?"

"Oh God," Mickey sighed. "Are you saying I failed this test?"

"Miserably."

"But I didn't—"

"Hold it," Cy interrupted. "Remember what I told you, Mickey, before we got started. I already know the answer to some of these questions. What we need now is your cooperation." Cy moved in closer. With a softer voice, he stated, "Mickey, I'll make your cooperation known to Chief Wisler. He is not a vindictive man. He's raised a couple boys himself you know. As have I. Mickey, we all make mistakes in life. In the overall scheme of things, this is not an unforgiveable act. We have killers and rapists out there. You're neither. You've committed a youthful prank. One you regret, I know."

Stafford shook his head.

"Yes, you have," Cy intervened again. "This is not going away any time soon, Mick. Not unless you step forward and man up. Now I need the details of what went on that night and I need them now."

Stafford slumped in the chair with a long shallow sigh. No eye contact was forthcoming. Mickey dropped his chin, looked left and right, and then glanced at Donovan. "This isn't right," he said.

Cy didn't respond.

"This isn't right," Mickey repeated. He wanted more out of Cy.

Cy knew he had said enough.

Mickey fell silent.

After a few moments, Cy picked up the ball cap and toyed with the silver cross attached to the front. "What does this mean to you, Mickey?"

"It's just a cross."

"But it's more than just a cross, isn't it?"

Mickey half-nodded.

"Sure it is." After a few more minutes of silence, Cy added, "Mickey, you're obviously a Christian. You're family raised you that way, and they're paying your tuition, am I right?"

"Yes."

"And you want to continue here, right?"

"Yes."

"Well, I'm confident, with your cooperation, I mean Chief Wisler is not a ruthless man. I've already mentioned that to you."

Stafford looked away as tears began swelling up in his eyes.

Cy watched and waited before continuing, "Mick, you want to talk to me, but something is holding you back. What is it?"

Mickey grabbed the ball cap and fumbled with it before putting it on his head with the bill pulled down low.

"Are you afraid of something? Are you in fear of something or somebody?" Cy asked.

Mickey could not respond.

"If we can erase that fear, can we resolve this today? Can we put this issue to bed? I know we can, but I need your help."

Stafford was not responding; however, his tears we're making tracks down both his cheeks now.

"Mick, are you concerned these guys you called are going to seek some kind of revenge? Are you afraid of perhaps being harmed by them? Because if that is the case, I will bet you right now we can get past that issue."

"How?"

Cy reasoned with him. "Have you ever done something really hard but after it was done you felt really good about it?"

"Yeah, I suppose."

"Sure you have. And I am asking you here today to be the Christian I know you are. Be true to the symbol on your cap. Be true to your God. Be straight with me. Can you do that, Mick?"

"I don't know."

"I will bet you if I went to Chief Wisler and asked him to get in touch with Lee and Ellsbury and asked them to come down here today for the sole purpose of hearing your apology, they would do it, and they would accept your explanation. I will bet if you sat down with these guys, face-to-face, and come across with a sincere apology, they will respect your courage. In fact, they will shake your hand when this day is over, Mick. You will not have to be looking over your shoulder for what you did."

Stafford sat still with a dazed look, deep in thought.

"We can get this done. You can do this. I will help you. I will be there along with the chief. We will all sit down together. Lee and Ellsberry will know if there is any vengeful act perpetrated against you, and we will know who is responsible. But you won't have to worry about that. It won't happen. In fact, the opposite will happen. Can we get this done and get it behind us?"

"Okay," Mickey whispered.

"Fine, now I need to hear how this whole thing got started so I can advise the chief."

Mickey Stafford owned up to the deed. He spoke of how Connor was quite upset about a black man dancing with a white girl and that a price needed to be paid for such an act. He spoke of how much he had had to drink and as such, was easily influenced by Connor to do something he wouldn't normally do. Finally, Stafford shared with Cy how he and Connor discussed the text of the call and that he, Stafford, actually made the call from Connor's room at the frat house. He provided a full statement to Donovan.

"Mickey, it took some courage for you to tell me that. You'll be glad you did. I'm going to walk down the hall to get Chief Wisler, and he will reach out to these guys and get them down here, okay?"

"Right," Mickey said.

"Just sit tight for a minute, and I'll be right back." Cy removed the polygraph components from Stafford and headed out the door of the room.

As he did so, Stafford asked a question, "Do you mind if I have a cigarette?"

"That's fine, but you'll have to smoke it in the hallway."

"Thanks."

Cy turned right outside the door away from the direction of the stairs. As he walked down the hallway, he heard a voice in his head telling him, *Hey, dummy, you never give them a cigarette break, no cigarettes, no sodas until you get it all.* It was Rudy's advice coming back to him. Cy knew he had erred, but he trusted Stafford. Or did he?

Chief Wisler was on the phone but concluded quickly with Cy in his doorway. "Any luck?"

"Oh yeah. I have his statement. He did it."

"I knew it."

"I told him he needed to apologize to these guys, and he is willing to."

"Okay."

Chief, can we get Lee and Ellsberry down here? Stafford is very concerned about his safety. In an effort to assuage his concerns, I told him that a face-to-face apology in our presence would likely alleviate that."

"That's good thinking. Let me get my day officer on it. We'll locate them and get it done."

"That would be great, Chief."

"Cy, can we get a recorded statement from him as well?"

"Shouldn't be a problem. I'll go get him."

Cy headed back down the hallway, made the turn to the office he had been testing in, but Stafford was nowhere in sight.

"Great!" Cy said to himself. He had made a mistake, and he knew better. Cy stood in the hallway just outside the door of the testing room where he had left Stafford. Disgusted, he contemplated what to do next. He could smell cigarette smoke, and then he heard a couple voices muttering from up on the stairway next to the room. As he looked up, he saw Mickey coming down the stairs.

"Who are you talking to, Mick?"

Stafford came all the way down and threw his smoke on the floor. "Let's just say my sister tells me I need an attorney."

"And what does Mickey Stafford say to that?"

"Well, she normally gives me good advice."

"Chief Wisler is reaching out to these guys. They'll be here soon. You can confront the issue, or you can run from it. Whatever you do, Mickey, know that your cooperation has been made known and—"

"Never mind," Stafford interrupted. "You don't have to say anymore. Let's get it over with."

Cy half-grinned.

Mickey gave a half-grin back.

It was a long Saturday.

Mickey Stafford was forgiven, by Lee and Ellsbury that is. They bought into his apology and urged that all charges be dropped. The school's board of regents intervened in the matter. In lieu of dropped charges, another price had to be paid. Unfortunately for Mickey Stafford, he was suspended indefinitely from the college.

THOSE JEANS ARE REALLY STARCHED

Winter had not left yet in March of 1998 in Gary, Indiana. But it wanted to. The dirty remnants of the last snowfall were still on the ground. When it snows in Gary, it comes down the color of pewter due in large part to the steel mills along the shore of Lake Michigan. Once the snow settles on the ground, it appears as though someone sprinkled it with pepper. Again, a result of the soot that arises from the belching smoke stacks and mixes with the cold north wind.

The main drag in Gary, Broadway, got plowed this winter, but little effort went into clearing the side streets in the nineties. Lack of money or perhaps a redistribution of available funds created this dilemma—a mystery never quite understood as the city suffered during the winter season.

Penny Littleton, a sixty-year-old black female, lived on one of those side streets. A distinguished-looking lady, she had retired from a bank in neighboring East Chicago where she had been a head teller but continued in the banking business as a cashier with a currency exchange. Divorced, with a son in college, she had little choice but to work.

It was shortly after 9:00 p.m. when Penny stepped out of her car onto her driveway. She had just closed up a late night at the currency exchange and was contemplating what she would prepare for dinner while sidestepping some leftover slush near her walkway. A dimly lit streetlight provided just enough visibility for her to recognize a pistol in the hand of an unknown subject who surprised her by stepping out from around the corner of her house. He was accompanied by another individual as well.

"It all happened so fast," she told Cy. Although she had been a resident of Gary for most of her life, she did not recognize her abductors. The description she had provided investigators was vague at best—two black males, late teens or early twenties, one with a dark skull cap, one with a hooded sweatshirt. No outstanding features and very little for police to go on.

"Penny, we appreciate your cooperation and the fact you volunteered for the polygraph today," Cy said.

"Anything I can do to help," she replied. "But I've really told the police about everything I know."

"Right, right. Tell me, Penny, before we get started here, could you once again relay the facts to me? I mean this is really an unusual way for a bank to be robbed, or, in your case, a currency exchange."

"Yes, I know, and they really startled me, but they were dead serious, and when you have a gun pointed at you, well, I just figured I would follow along."

"I see. Tell me what happened when you got home."

"Let's see. I had just stepped out of my car, headed for the house when these two guys came out from around the corner. One of them had a gun."

"Can you describe the gun?"

"I wasn't sure at first, but I got a closer look at it when we got in the car. It was a black pistol."

"Not a revolver?"

"No, a pistol. I am sure of that. You see my former husband worked security. He carried a gun, and he had explained to me the difference a long time ago."

"Okay, good, go on."

"They were very mean. Called me a fucking bitch and a few other choice words I don't care to repeat. Now as I think back, they really were not bad kids, just trying to scare me and take control of me."

"Which they did, I presume?"

"Oh, they did that. I was told to get in the car and I wouldn't get hurt."

"In the driver's seat?"

"Yes."

"Where did they sit?"

"They both got in the back at first. Then the one with the gun told the other to get in the front seat. Just in case I needed some coaxing, I suppose. Anyway, he didn't like that and didn't want to show his face to me much."

"You mean the one that got in the front?"

"Yes, he was a bit put off at the other guy. It was about this time I could see the type of gun the other guy in the back had was a pistol."

"How could you see that?"

"He kept the gun up close to my ear, and I could see it through the rearview mirror."

"What did they tell you to do?"

"They wanted me to drive to the currency exchange and open up. I told them it was alarmed and all monies are locked up."

"Did they threaten you in any way?"

"Well, I would say the gun was certainly a threat now, wasn't it?"

Cy nodded realizing he had just asked a stupid question.

"Look," Penny added, "they never really said they were going to hurt me. It was all so stupid. Almost like a prank, but they did mean business. And I have to say I believe they have been in the currency exchange before."

"You've seen them before?"

"Maybe just the one."

"Which one?"

"The one with the gun, but I can't be sure. He was good at staying behind me most of the time. He seemed to know about the safe."

"How's that?"

"When I told him it was alarmed and the monies were locked up, he said, 'That's right, and you're gonna shut the alarm off and open the safe.' It rolled right off his tongue. Then I knew he had been in before."

"How soon before?"

"Not sure. Couple of weeks maybe. Maybe he was in more than once. I'm not always in there you see."

"I understand. What happened next?"

"They had me pull up right in front. We walked up just like it was routine business, you know?"

"Okay, go on."

"I unlocked the door, one followed me in, while the other, the one without the gun, stayed in the car. I shut off the alarm as I was told."

"What was he doing at this time?"

"Which one?"

"The one who followed you in—the one with the gun."

"He was kinda all over me. We have this revolving door, have you been there?"

"No."

"Okay, see there is this revolving door with bulletproof glass you have to go through to get behind the cashier's counter and get to the safe. Only one person can go through this door at a time. I told him this, but he didn't listen. He tried to go in with me, but it just doesn't work that way. This made him nervous. I guess because he felt like he would lose control of me if I got out of his reach."

"But he would have known this had he been in there before, right?"

"You would think so, yes. Again, I'm not 100 percent certain he was in before, but he seemed confident, you know what I mean?"

"Okay, so you went through?"

"I did, and the safe is like, right there. I opened it up like he told me."

"The alarm?"

"Actually, I hadn't alarmed it when I closed. Bad habit, I know."

"Did he come through the door too?"

"No, actually, he stood on the other side."

"Did you feel like you had any options at this point?"

"Not really. I mean there is a way to freeze the door, and the glass is supposed to be bulletproof, but being there by myself, I wasn't about to play games with this guy. A man with a gun is just too unpredictable."

"So you emptied out the safe?"

"Not completely but around $50,000, I believe. He came through and grabbed it immediately and yelled at me to get out. We left."

"Wait a minute. Did you shut the safe?"

"I don't think so. He came through real quick like I said. It was fast."

"So he was all the way through the revolving door at that time with you?"

"Yes."

"Who went out first?"

"First, he did, no, uh…it was confusing. He was yelling at me. He pushed me. That's what happened. He pushed me through first. Then he came through. I think, I can't swear to that."

"So you're both through. Then what?"

"I locked up again, and he told me to get in the car and drive. I said, 'Where to?' The guy with the gun directed me to an intersection southeast of Broadway. The both of them got out of the car and let me go."

"Who had the money?"

"The guy who came in with me, he kept hold of it."

"Did he have a bag or something?"

"Yeah, like a laundry bag. Army green like."

"What intersection did you let them out at?"

"I don't remember for sure, but it's on the police report."

"When did you make the police report?"

"I was shook up. I went home and called police from there. Two officers came and took my report."

"Did you go back to the currency exchange with them?"

"They didn't ask me to."

"Really?"

"That's right."

Cy paused. Penny Littleton had been pretty straight with him. Her confident demeanor and recollection of the facts was, for the most part, impressive. She looked him in the eye and answered his questions without hesitation. She displayed all of the nondeceptive attributes commonly observed with an innocent victim. In fact, the only reason she was even in the chair was because the investigating agents wanted her tested as a matter of routine just to satisfy themselves that she was not a coconspirator in the robbery. After all, the circumstances under which the robbery took place were a bit out of the ordinary.

"Okay, Penny, are you confident you've told investigators everything you know about this robbery?"

"Yes."

"And you're not withholding any information about the robbery?"

"No. Not that I can think of. I've really told everything that I remember."

"Very well. I'll be asking you these questions on the test, and if what you say is truthful, you should do just fine, okay?"

"Okay."

"Have you ever had a polygraph before?"

"As a matter of fact I have."

"Is that right? When would that have been?"

"Oh gee, let's see…um, thirty years ago maybe mid-sixties? Had to be tested because it was for employment with the bank."

"So you did all right with it or you wouldn't have been hired, right?"

"Apparently so, they never told me as I remember. I suppose there is more to it these days, huh?"

"In what way?"

"Well, equipment I mean. Your equipment looks a little different."

"Perhaps, but the theory is the same."

"I see."

"You remember these components?"

"Yes, not sure how it all works, but they look familiar."

"I am going to record changes in your respiration, perspiration, and pulse rate."

"That's right."

"Right. Breathe as you normally breathe. Everything else takes care of itself, okay?"

She nodded.

"All right, give me a moment while I make a few adjustments, and we'll get started." Cy sat down behind his instrument. While making a few corrections, he could not help but think of all of her nondeceptive demeanor and cooperation. He looked up at Littleton. She sat still as she was told. One thing bothered him, and the more he studied her, the more he noticed it. *Those jeans are really starched.*

Littleton was dressed too perfectly for the occasion. She wore a pair of Levi's with a crease down the center you could cut wood with. Her jacket was a matching Levi jean jacket also creased in the arms and breast pockets. Stiff as a board, she appeared.

Her hair looked like she had just come from the hairdresser. Her rosy red lipstick, gold dangling earrings, and a bright-red scarf set it all off. Was she attempting to disguise deception and perhaps influence him, or was she just a classy lady?

Cy began the test with the first chart rolling. His mind kept reverting back to her nondeceptive cooperation. He glanced up at her as he voiced the first relevant question. He failed to notice her climbing cardio tracing when she answered. A few seconds later, he read her the second relevant question.

"Are you withholding any information about the robbery?"

"No," she answered.

Cy didn't miss this reaction. Climbing cardio coupled with a six-chart division rise in her GSR. He quickly looked back at her previous reaction to the first relevant question and realized she had just failed her first chart. He concluded the questions and let the air disperse from the cardio cuff. In a couple of minutes, he would repeat the process. He reviewed the chart and set it aside.

"Okay, Penny, let's try it again, same questions," he announced. She nodded.

As he began chart 2, Cy couldn't help but study her again. *Look at that scarf.* By the number of creases and folds in it, I would guess it to be brand-new. Chart 2 rolled through with the same results—deception indicated in the relevant questions. This test was basically over, but he would run a third chart so as to comply with policy. During the running of this chart, he noticed her boots. *I believe she put a Kiwi shine to those boots. A spit-shine that would impress a drill sergeant.*

"Penny," Cy began as he moved around in front of her. "You failed this test."

"Really? I can't understand why."

Cy knew he had to be firm and trust in his charts. The most important principle in the interrogation would be his direct, positive confrontation. During the outset of interrogations, the guilty suspect will evaluate his or her opponent's own confidence in their allegation of guilt. If the suspect in the chair believes the investigator is not certain of their guilt, they are unlikely to confess. Although still unsure of her involvement, he would have to convey he was positive that Penny Littleton had something to hide regarding this robbery. Following her pause, Cy interjected "Penny, I have absolutely no doubt you had something to do with this robbery. You are withholding information of value, and I want to talk with you further. What are the circumstances that are causing you to be less than completely candid with me?"

Littleton retained her dignified persona. "But that is so untrue, Agent Donovan," she said. I have been completely honest with the police.

His mind was racing. Despite her deceptive polygraph, her calm demeanor and perfect attire added up to a well-thought out plan to deceive. Cy could feel it, and it had a way of energizing him.

"Penny, in my experience, there are two types of people who take money that does not belong to them. First of all, the greedy criminal excels in this type of crime and gives no thought to his actions. He cares only for number one. He is very selfish.

The other person is basically trustworthy but succumbs to outside pressures in his or her life. As such, this second type of person will act spontaneously and feel bad about it later.

"Penny, as I have said, there is absolutely no doubt you know something you are not telling us, and what I need to establish with you is whether you are the selfish individual who plans these type of robberies or are you simply someone who went along with the idea due to unforeseen pressures. Which is it, Penny?"

"Neither," Penny replied shaking her head no with a bit of a smile. "You're really mistaken here," she said.

Oh she is good, Cy thought. "The only mistake we have here, Penny, is the mistake you made in your cooperation with these guys."

"Now listen, I'm a sixty-year-old woman. What was I supposed to do? Two young hoodlums assault me at gunpoint, and now you want to accuse me of some sort of conspiracy? I didn't come here for this. This is not what I expected. You have been such a gentlemen, but now you accuse me of—"

"Yes, yes," Cy interrupted. "I do try to be a gentleman, but again, we both know there is more to it than what you allege. The more to it part is what we are missing."

"I am quite confident in my own mind you wouldn't deliberately do a thing like this. But many people in your situation would have acted as you did, Penny. I can understand that. Had I been in your situation, I may have acted likewise. However, there is something very wrong with what happened that night that you, Penny, seem very uncomfortable about disclosing."

"Perhaps you know these guys and you feel threatened? If that is the case, we can work with you on that. Is that what it is, Penny? Are you in fear of your life? Is there a family member caught up in this? Are the facts not quite accurate? Perhaps you left the currency exchange open and unalarmed? Perhaps there is more money missing than what has been reported?"

Cy threw many lines into the water hoping she would bite on one. Even if it was the wrong reason, he just wanted her off dead center. But it was to no avail.

Littleton was steadfast. She would not be induced or influenced in any way. She crossed her legs and fingered the seam in her starched Levi's. With a slight wiggle of her wrist to adjust her diamond bracelet, she again denied involvement in the caper.

Who is interrogating who? This would be a knee grinder, and Cy knew it wasn't likely to bear fruit, at least not on this day. But he would press on and fight the good fight. After all, she went out of her way to impress him with all her trumpery. There was a reason for it. Frauds do that sort of thing.

Cy went back for a moment and inquired about her upbringing. He knew by doing so he was taking the pressure off, but he hoped to find a sensitive chord with her that he could possibly use against her.

Responding very matter-of-factly, Littleton offered only a brief outline of her past. She had lost her mood to be very generous with frivolous information.

Cy asked about her own immediate family to include her personal life, the status of her children, and the status of her divorced husband.

With a long sigh indicative of boredom, she again offered very little. "I fail to see the relevance in your line of questioning," she stated.

"The more we know about you, Penny, the quicker we can clear you. Please?" he inquired rather subserviently.

"I suppose. Listen, I am divorced, and my children are grown. My only sibling, Joanna, died three years ago of cancer. I've never been in trouble with the law, and I don't have any significant health issues. Now, Agent, uh…"

"Donovan."

"Donovan, yes, I'm sorry. I'm really sorry, but you're boring me."

Cy paused for several moments.

"Oh, one other thing, I love cats."

Cy gave her a fake smile. He was beaten, and he knew it. But he would not be the one to quit. "How old did you say you're children were?"

"I didn't say. But I can tell you my son is twenty-one and my daughter is twenty-seven. Anything else?"

Cy failed to follow-up. He had touched on something but did not realize it. "You're withholding, Penny," is all he could come up with.

"Yes, you've said that, but again, you're mistaken, and you're machine is wrong also."

The mere mentioning that his machine was wrong caused him to reflect internally. Polygraph examiners know about false positives, but he refused to believe that is what he had. She was a fraud, but he had no leverage with which to combat her denials. He had no trump to play. In fact, she could get up and leave any time she wanted to, and he couldn't do a thing to stop her. That is exactly what she did.

"If you have nothing else for me other than allegations and accusations, I really need to leave," she said it very curtly but professionally. She uncrossed her legs and reached for her purse. "May I?"

"You're here voluntarily," Cy replied.

"Thank you."

Penny Littleton left the building. Disgusted, Cy sat back and reviewed his charts, which again looked clearly deceptive. *What is she holding back? She couldn't have planned this whole thing herself, but what was the full extent of her role?*

Nine months later, Cy got a telephone call. "Hey, Cy, how is life in Gary?"

"Well, if it isn't Dan Reburg, how have you been?"

"I'm doing great. What have you been doing in the steel city?"

"Oh, the steel mills around here have been closing up."

"Really?"

"Yeah, it's quite the depressed area, which bodes well for our line of work unfortunately."

"That's too bad. I don't know how it could get any more depressed than it was when I was up there."

"I don't think this town will ever recover."

"You're right. Hey, do you remember Penny Littleton?"

"Oh yeah, the woman in the starched jeans, sure, earlier in the year."

"Well, that was no false positive you had."

"Talk to me."

"Two perps were picked up in Arkansas last week. They were good for two bank robberies down there."

"Yeah, okay."

"As it turns out, they are pleading guilty. They've agreed to cooperate, and you'll like this."

"They gave up that currency exchange—said it was in March and gave all the details," Reburg said.

"And?"

"They said they paid a woman off who helped them into the place."

"Really? How much?" Cy asked.

"They said they gave her nine grand to keep her mouth shut. It was an after-the-fact sort of thing. They said she wasn't in on the planning. They were just being nice by giving her some loot to keep quiet."

"Bingo! That's what it was. Well, that conniving, shrewd—"

Dan stopped him. "Save it. We all know women are the best liars. We may still have the last laugh."

"How's that?"

"The one dude agreed to make a consensual call to her."

"Did she talk to him?"

"Just enough. Told him not to call her again and that she used the money to help pay for her son's college tuition."

"Wow! She's not as shrewd as she thought she was," Cy said.

"Right. We hope to indict her in the next grand jury."

"Keep me informed."

"Will do. Thanks for all your work on this case."

"Me? Hey, I was in and out of it."

"Yeah, but you were right. Now, stay safe up there."

"I plan to." Cy hung up the phone. It was Saturday. He took note of the jeans he was wearing—well-worn, overdue for the laundry basket, and his shoes…when was the last time he put polish to them? *Perhaps it's time to make some changes? Nah, wouldn't want to fool anybody.* He started to laugh and looked around to see if anyone was watching.

BARBIE DOLL

Much to the consternation of on-board special agents of the FBI, the drug use and sale policy as applied to all FBI applicants throughout the 1990s and well into the new millennium was far too liberal. In fact, it specifically allowed for as many as five uses of hard drugs—i.e., cocaine, LSD, heroin, and such so long as the applicant had not used any such drugs in a ten-year time preceding their application for employment.

It was Cy Donovan's perception, and the view of most Bureau polygraph examiners, that the amount of permissible usage prior to three years preceding an application for employment was a mystery, and continued to be a mystery as of the writing of this book.

Bureau polygraph examiners are told there is a limit but Human Resource Division (HRD) personnel have been skittish about formalizing a set standard. The problem is nurtured by the fact that in the new millennium, assistant directors (ADs) within

HRD and Security Division change about every two years and are often of the nonbadge-carrying variety. They lose sight of the fact that special agents of the FBI do have law enforcement responsibilities in the areas of drug use and sale.

Cy believed it was as though FBI special agents were confused with retailers, grocers, truck drivers, and insurance salesmen, when in fact, the only thing agents sold was jail time.

What they have recently adopted however is the "whole person" concept. Under the whole person concept, applicants were given conditional job offers (CJOs) even after admitting to over a thousand marijuana uses and/or hundreds of cocaine/hard drug uses so long as such uses are far enough back in their past!

FBI polygraph examiners are rarely impressed with what these "whole person" applicants bring to the table in addition to their illegal drug use expertise. Most will fail the polygraph, but some will and do pass. HRD is then left with an awkward predicament having already issued the CJO. Certainly, no one is considered for employment if they have ever used any drugs while employed in a sworn, law enforcement or prosecutorial position or a position of high public trust. No sale of illegal drugs whatsoever was permitted. Or was it?

Again, HRD personnel stepped in and said the applicant could have sold illegal drugs and still be considered for FBI employment so long as the sale was not for profit and the applicant admitted to it in his initial application. Certainly it was understood how they wanted to be forgiving to the poor kid who sold one joint at age sixteen and made no money on the deal. But Cy wondered how this logic was then applied to the thirty year old, who purchases a truckload of marijuana for thousands of dollars, and resells it for the same price? Would the Bureau give him a CJO? Again, an awkward decision for the AD.

As recently as 2009, one section chief involved in the hiring process indicated to this author that it would be very difficult to deny someone an opportunity with the FBI if they had a college education but had used marijuana one thousand times while growing up in the hood.

Cy could see the shine coming off the badge. In 2008, the Polygraph Unit in concert with HRD revised the applicant screening polygraph exam to include a serious crimes question. One of the standards adopted by HRD in the serious crimes profile specifies no theft over $500. You can walk off the dock at Best Buy with a television and apply to the FBI the next day so long as that television was valued at $499 and your application will still get serious consideration.

Cy had discovered that if the theft actually exceeded $500, that wasn't necessarily a problem either. One such incident took place as recently as 2010 when a special agent applicant admitted to a theft from Sears via fraudulent returns with a personal credit card totaling over $4,000. After being advised of the admission, HRD personnel compelled the examiner to administer the polygraph.

These are not uncommon occurrences in recent years. Nevertheless, just prior to this book going to publishing, that appears to be part of the underpinnings of the application process. Policies in the hiring process will teeter-totter back and forth depending on the flavor of preference for the current AD.

Suffice it to say however that the FBI, once and hopefully still, recognized as the world's foremost law enforcement organization, has placed itself in the position of allowing admitted users of hard drugs, cocaine sniffers, and needle poppers into their ranks so long as the uses were not within ten years of their application. You can be a dope pusher too and still get in so long as you're a poor salesman.

More and more people during tough economic times apply to the Bureau knowing they exceed the drug policy or at least tickle the limits. They throw their name in the hat knowing they have to pass a polygraph on these very issues.

Cy had digressed in thought long enough. It was time to get back to *Barbie Doll*. One very attractive young female attorney from the Oxford, Mississippi, area thought she fit into the FBI's drug guidelines, albeit, a snug fit.

Twenty-nine-year-old Leann Grigsby freely admitted on her application three cocaine uses and two LSD uses during high school. Additionally, she indicated numerous uses of marijuana but no uses in the last three years prior to her application. Not only was her admitted past drug usage a close call under the drug policy at that time, but her selection of clothing the day of her pre-employment polygraph was clearly a *snug fit* as well.

"Geez-o-Pete Carolyn, who is the gal in the lobby?" Cy asked.

"She's your 9:00 a.m. test, Cy."

"She's a real Barbie doll. A special agent applicant?"

"You got it."

"I tell you what, let's just give her a badge and put her on a squad."

"You don't want to do that, Cy. Take a look at her app. This one needs to take a poly."

"All right, let me get set up, then send her in."

"Fifteen minutes?"

"Yeah, that'll work."

He reviewed the application and took notice of the drug usage admissions. All within the guidelines but barely. Cy's rule of thumb was simple. Most people who have experimented with illegal drugs cannot recall a specific number of uses with true accuracy beyond five. Once the uses go beyond the number you can count on one hand, it gets difficult to be absolutely certain. They usually know they are not certain, and for that reason, they fail.

When confronted with the deceptive results, they may admit they are uncertain of the actual number, but frequently, they will insist they are still within the guidelines. Cy reasoned a problem existed if the examinee didn't know for certain and HRD personnel did not know for certain.

The Bureau is then stuck with the results of their polygraph for clarification. Without a further admission, it's the Bureau's decision to make regarding further processing of the applicant. A failed polygraph on drug issues is a no-go for the applicant. The Bureau simply cannot take the applicant's word for it, for the simple reason a security clearance is at stake. While it may be everyone's privilege to apply for FBI employment, no one has a constitutional right for a security clearance.

When it comes to national security, the US government must have safeguards or hurdles in place in their hiring process. It may not always seem fair. There may, in fact, be an occasional false positive when it comes to polygraph that eliminates a candidate; however, this occurs infrequently, if at all, and it is critically necessary that the government have such a barrier in place.

Certainly, the Bureau has eliminated some strong recruits along the way, but far more have been weeded out to the Bureau's advantage. Until another means of determining deception with even greater accuracy than polygraph comes along, polygraph will continue to carry the day.

Cy believed in the Bureau's use of polygraph with the hiring of applicants, but he, like all Bureau polygraph examiners, was annoyed by a policy that would leave an opening for someone who may have used hard, illegal drugs at some point in their life to obtain employment with the most respected law enforcement agency in the land. In fact, traditionally, at every annual polygraph conference, one or more examiners would debate this issue with a section chief or an assistant director. It always fell on deaf ears. Why, is anyone's guess.

After exchanging courtesies, Leann Grigsby took her seat across from Cy. Her smile was contagious coupled with an occasional giggle that was charming. Cy couldn't help but notice also that her navy blue skirt was too short and her button-popping blouse was too tight. She was definitely *in the game* to impress her opponent and *win the day* for herself.

"Leann, I've reviewed your application, and everything appears to be in order."

"Thank you. I spent a lot of time on it, Lord knows."

"I do need you to clarify one thing."

"Yes."

"You indicated numerous uses of marijuana as far back as high school, right?"

"That's right up until three years ago, yes."

"I see that. But how many is numerous?"

"The best I can recall is fourteen times."

"Fourteen?"

"Right."

"So you're aware of the FBI's guidelines regarding use and sale of illegal drugs?"

"Oh yes, and I'm quite sure I'm within them."

"Okay, and I see as many as five uses of cocaine and LSD eleven years ago?"

"Poor decisions on my part, I know, but that's all there is."

"Well, if what you're saying is true, you should do all right here today."

Leann only smiled. Cy could feel her eyes trying to drill a hole right through his.

"And one other thing, Leann, several speeding tickets, right?"

"Correct, most dismissed however."

I can only imagine why, Cy thought. "And a DUI?"

"Yes, I listed it. Another poor decision, but I paid the fine and took my thirty days suspension."

"Any use of alcohol in the last twenty-four hours?

"Other than a glass of wine last night, no."

"Do you habitually drive under the influence?"

"Oh no. That one time was all, and I was just barely over the legal limit then."

"Ever been asked to leave an establishment due to your condition?"

"Oh heavens no. Or at least not that I recall."

"You don't recall?"

"Pardon me?"

"Never mind. Is everything else accurate here?"

"Yes, I believe so."

"Understand, Leann, if I ask you a question today about your application, I'm not referring to trivial matters. In other words, if you're off slightly on a date, those are items that tend to get worked out in the background investigation. What I get concerned about here is when someone deliberately withholds something from their application that they know would hinder their employment. That's not the case with you, right?"

"Oh no, not at all."

"Good." Cy covered the remaining questions with her, then set about placing the components on her. Grigsby adjusted her long, flowing blonde hair and allowed her blue eyes to race ahead of every step he made as he went about preparing her for the test.

This girl is a firecracker waiting to ignite, thought Cy. He was quite careful in the instructions he gave her and the manner in which he conducted his business. *Light the wrong fuse on her, and this will blow up in my face real quick*, he figured.

Cy placed the Velcro of his fingerplates across her finely painted nails, attached the convoluted tubes very gingerly around her abdomen, and set the cardio cuff into place. He provided her a set of instructions and concluded by advising her to keep both feet flat on the floor for the duration of the test.

Grigsby uncrossed her legs, almost childlike as if to say, "Give me another instruction."

"All set?"

"I'm ready!"

He began his test and was able to conclude his first series of questions rather quickly. Grigsby clearly had no problem with national security issues at least as far as unauthorized foreign contacts were concerned. He had not expected a problem here anyway as Grigsby had never traveled far out of the mid-western United States. He prepared for the subsequent series dealing with lifestyle concerns. *This will be her nemesis*, he thought.

"Are you lying to me when you say you're only a social drinker?"

"No."

"Have you ever sold any illegal drugs?"

"No."

"Have you violated the FBI guidelines concerning the use of illegal drugs?"

"No."

Additional questions were asked; then, the test was concluded.

"You can relax," Cy advised.

Grigsby let out a sigh and began flexing her fingers restoring blood flow from the arm cuff.

"Just pretend you're squeezing a tennis ball," Cy advised. "It'll all come back to you quickly. He reviewed his charts but wasn't sure what he had. One thing he was sure of was she wasn't passing.

Of the ten questions he asked her, it was obvious she was troubled with drugs and drinking. *Typical*, he thought. *Reaction versus reaction, lying to both. We'll try it again*, he figured.

"Leann, one of these questions is bothering you more than the others. I'm not going to tell you which one, but we're going to repeat this series of questions and see how it all shakes out."

"Okay," Leann replied. "This is really stressful you know. I just really want this job. It's all I've ever thought about."

Cy took note of her comments. It wouldn't be the last time he would hear her say that. "Relax. I'm confident we'll get through this."

"I hope so."

"Okay, let's get started." He began another series. "Is your first name Leann?"

"Excuse me," she interrupted.

Frustrated, he shut down the test. "What is it, Leann?"

"I'm sorry, but will I know the results today?"

"Actually, you already know what the results are going to be, right?"

"Oh, well, sure, but..."

"Just relax. We'll talk about the results when we are finished."

"Okay."

As Cy continued on with a third series of questions, it wasn't long before Grigsby's real focus began to emerge. She may be more than a social drinker, but her real concern centered around drug-related issues. He was relieved he was able to make a call on this test after all. No inconclusive results today. He carefully removed the components from Grigsby. As he did so, she stared at him with anticipation. He broke the unfortunate news to her.

"I can't understand why I would fail this test. I just can't. Are you for real?" she asked.

Cy nodded as Grigsby's eyes watered up.

"I just don't understand. I mean, really! I've given up my inner-self on this application. I've listed all my speeding tickets, most of which were dismissed or amended due to faulty equipment. I was truthful about all of that."

"Leann," Cy began. "You and I both know your failure here today has nothing to do with speeding tickets. I asked you no such questions on this test. Now, having said that, tell me, are we talking about drug use in the neighborhood of one hundred times, or is it more than that?"

"Oh, no way. I'm absolutely certain I have not used marijuana more than fifteen times. I know I haven't. One hundred times? Are you kidding me?"

"No, Leann. You see, for most people, once the usage goes beyond the number of times you can count on one hand, it gets very difficult to remember with certainty the actual number of uses. Now, I have to say, we have a fairly lenient policy here, but you are beyond the guidelines. What we need to determine is how far beyond those guidelines you are."

"This is not happening to me. Does this mean I'm not going to get this job?" Leann began to sob.

"Do you have an explanation?" Cy asked.

"As to what? I've told you everything." Leann tugged at her skirt and closed her arms. She realized she wasn't going to influence Cy one way or another. She did have one card left to play. Play it, she did.

She began with alligator tears followed with the pleadings. "Please, Agent Donovan, I'll do anything to be a special agent, anything at all. It's all I've ever wanted to be, don't you see?" She paused while he listened.

She continued, "I know I've made some moral mistakes, but hasn't everyone? I believe I failed this test because I am embarrassed about my past, and that must have bothered me physiologically. I really am within the guidelines when it comes to drug use. Please, Agent Donovan. If you only knew how badly I want this job. I mean this is a career I've worked for since I graduated from law school."

"How many times have you used illegal drugs as a practicing attorney, Leann?"

"Never, I have not—"

Cy interrupted, "Now be honest about that, Leann. How many times?"

"Listen, there are a few guys in my firm who were passing joints around at a party in a hotel about three weeks ago. I was there. I shouldn't have been. But I showed up. I never used the stuff."

"Leann?"

"No, really. I admit I shouldn't have been there. I passed the joints around to everyone else, but I didn't use it."

"And you mean to tell me, Leann, as a twenty-nine-year-old attorney who has had her application in with the FBI for the last five months, you still go to a pot party just three weeks before your polygraph? With other attorneys no less? Wouldn't you say attorneys have positions of high public trust? Remind me to never seek assistance from your law firm."

"I know it was poor judgment," Leann continued. She reached for her purse and grabbed a tissue. "I should go, huh?"

"No further explanation?"

"I'm just really sorry I took up your time. I really would make a great agent. Will you please reconsider?"

"Listen. It's not my decision to make. I only administer the test. This will go to FBIHQ, and you will hear something soon."

"I'll do anything. Is there anything else I can do?"

Cy opened the door. "Drive carefully, Leann." He turned away. A moment later, he looked behind him. She was gone. *I don't need that today*, he thought.

He grabbed the paperwork for his next examinee and immersed himself in preparation. He was a bit behind schedule and wanted to get his next exam started quickly. Within about fifteen minutes, he had his next examinee in the chair. Just prior to beginning his test questions, he got a knock on the door. *This is unusual*, he thought. They never bother me during a test, must be something serious.

Cy paused and excused himself momentarily.

"Sorry to interrupt you, Cy."

"It was Carolyn Rocquet, the applicant coordinator."

"All right, what is it?" he asked.

"She's still here."

"Who, Leann?"

"Yes, she wants to talk to you."

"I'm testing and will be for the next two hours."

"I'll tell her."

"Please do, and thanks, Carolyn."

"Okay, sorry."

Leann Grigsby went away for that day. However, upon Cy's return from Mississippi on the following Monday, he was surprised to find a FedEx envelope sitting on his desk from Oxford. It was from none other than Leann Grigsby.

Cy opened it fully expecting a letter of disgruntlement riddled with false allegations designed to get him into hot water. It wasn't to be the case however. As he read through it, he discovered Leann was simply being herself.

"Agent Donovan, I will do anything to be..." he read on and chuckled. *This woman never stops*, he thought. He enclosed the letter, a diatribe of more sobs and pleading, with his own polygraph report and sent it on for quality control to review. As he thought back about her behavior, it became clear to him what he was dealing with. She was a histrionic female.

The histrionic female is frequently physically attractive and image-oriented. He remembered what he had learned through an advanced polygraph course. Typically, histrionic females often exhibit overly dramatic, manipulative behavior as was the case with Grigsby. Histrionic personalities tend to lie through distortion and exaggeration and make full use of manipulation in an effort to get their way. In retrospect, if he had considered a projection theme with her, he might have had more success. In other words, if he had described a situation for her where she acted in a similar manner because she was helpless to do otherwise, he may have had a different outcome than what he was to report. He had learned a lesson though. In the future, if, as an examiner, he gets a choice between testing a gorgeous young female or a homely one, he'll know to avoid the *Barbie doll*.

RED-STAINED MONEY

Some people are so fond of ill-luck that they run half-way to meet it!

—Douglas William Jerrold

BAD INTRODUCTION

A mid-November day in 1996 turned out to be a very bad day for a young teller at a bank just outside of Cincinnati, Ohio. A nineteen-year-old daughter of a pastor, Tammy Westfall, was happy to have a job at the bank and looked forward to doing well and proving herself as a reliable and trustworthy handler of bank funds. Tammy was intelligent, was well liked, and had a personality that brought cheer to everyone she came into contact with. Innocently naïve, but isn't everyone prior to age twenty-five? Her naïveté would not play a role however in what was about to unfold in front of her eyes on this day. A bulletproof vest may not have done her much good either.

The lone white male came walking into the bank with a purpose. He stood in front of Tammy almost before she had had a chance to look up. Armed with a loaded sawed-off shotgun in the sleeve of his right arm, he lifted his right arm toward her and demanded money.

"No dye packs, just all the money in your drawer and her drawer too," he demanded.

She opened her drawer and reached for some cash at which time he gestured to the teller to the left of Tammy and to his right. As he returned his right arm back to the front of Tammy, the shotgun fired…albeit accidentally, but the blast struck Tammy in her upper left arm and breast area. Tammy Westfall dropped to the floor. Any money stained on this day would not come from a dye pack.

Shocked and dismayed, the lone white male bolted immediately from the bank abandoning any further attempt to take any cash. This was not in his plan, and he was quite disgusted with himself over this botched robbery as investigators would learn later.

Fortunately, Tammy Westfall survived her nightmare as a bank teller that cold November afternoon. Due to the short distance between Tammy and the barrel of the gun, the round did not have the distance necessary to acquire the velocity to be fatal at the angle with which it struck her. Had she been standing more directly in front of his arm as the gun discharged, it undoubtedly would have been far more serious.

That's not to say it wasn't life-threatening. It most certainly was. Without the quick response from the local police and EMT service, she may not have lived to tell about it.

Others lived to tell about it also. In fact, six witnesses provided statements and or testimony to the events of that day. Of these six witnesses, most of whom were bank employees, not a single one recalled the would-be robber as wearing a ski mask nor did any of them describe the man as wearing a trench coat. The getaway vehicle eventually recovered by investigators was white in color. Other facts and testimony fit together well and lead to a quick apprehension of the subject. Prior to trial however, another witness volunteered what *he* saw that day.

Raymond Jay Dalligher, a driver for United Parcel Service, had observations of his own he wished to relate to the FBI. While sitting in his UPS delivery truck munching down on a sub sandwich, Dalligher stated a white male about 6'3" tall wearing a ski mask with a long trench coat came walking with a long gait right past the front of his truck. The individual pulled off the ski mask and hopped into a blue Pontiac, perhaps a 1979 to 1980 year model being driven by another heavy-set white male. The vehicle then sped westbound out of sight.

FBI Special Agent Chip Battle was perplexed by Dalligher's story. None of it corroborated the testimony from the other witnesses. Nevertheless, Battle initially saw no reason to doubt the man.

Dalligher had checked out. He was in fact a UPS driver, and he had no criminal history. He appeared honest with nothing to gain by fabricating anything. Battle scheduled a follow-up interview with Dalligher along with the aid of one of the local police detectives, a Lieutenant J. J. Rollins.

Dalligher appeared for his interview on time. Both SA Battle and Lieutenant Rollins questioned him at length, but little if anything changed in his account of what happened that fateful day.

A week or so later, Lieutenant Rollins and Agent Battle met up with Dalligher again in an effort to confirm his reason for being in the vicinity of the robbery that day and to tighten up some other details he previously provided.

Dalligher was cooperative and appeared genuine in his recollection of the facts. He advised the investigators he was on a UPS delivery route and had stopped for his lunch break at a Subway located in the same shopping strip as the bank. He was simply sitting in his truck eating when, in his words, "a tall man came walking past the front of my truck about a hundred feet away wearing a mask with a trench coat. He was walking fast from the direction of the bank and got into a blue Pontiac driven by another rather heavy man. Together, they drove off." Dalligher was insistent of what he saw and provided no further details.

Agent Battle and Lieutenant Rollins along with the US attorney's office were confused. Only Dalligher's account differed from the others. His rendition of the facts was discoverable as exculpatory evidence for the defendant. Was it going to be that Ms. Westfall would have no justice if her assailant were allowed to go free after nearly destroying her life? Such could very well be the case if Dalligher were to testify as to his recollection of the man in a mask.

Agent Battle had an idea. He proposed one more interview. "This time, we'll speak with him at our office. If his story doesn't change, we'll offer him a polygraph. If he can pass a polygraph on the issue, we'll have to live with his testimony unless we get a plea agreement before trial."

The US attorney's office agreed with the strategy, and yet another interview was scheduled with Dalligher at the Cincinnati office of the FBI. In the meantime, a trial date was set for mid-April 1997.

Once again, Dalligher cooperated. Like a good citizen doing his duty, he appeared for his interview with Agent Battle. This interview didn't last long. The result was the same. Same story, same identical set of facts as Dalligher related on his previous interviews. With a rather disconsolate sigh, Agent Battle offered him an opportunity to sit for a polygraph. Dalligher agreed.

"Hello, is this Cy Donovan?"

"Yes, speaking."

"This is Chip Battle, Cincinnati office."

"Hey, what's up?"

"The reason for my call concerns a polygraph I am looking to get done on a witness."

"Okay, well I know Norm recently retired. What did he do, throw you my name?" Cy said with a chuckle.

"Yep. He dimed you out, but that's a good thing, right?"

"Hopefully. Depends on what you've got."

"A rather bizarre case of facts, Cy. We have a bank robber who walked into a bank here just outside of Cincinnati with a sawed-off shotgun up his sleeve. As he made his demands on the teller, his shotgun went off severely wounding the teller. We believe the shooting was actually unintended because he bolted from the bank immediately with no effort to collect any money. You might say he made a *bad introduction*."

"Wow! Sad thing, huh?"

"Yeah. She survived physically, but psychologically, well, who knows?"

"I hear ya. Now, you said a witness?"

"Right. Here's the situation. We have the would-be robber in custody. In fact, we're set for trial in another week, and we've got a UPS driver who presents us with a different description of the perp than six other witnesses do."

"That's a problem."

"Sure is. We can't let this one get away from us. Tight case with that one exception, but it's enough to throw a jury into a tailspin, you know?"

"Understand. He's willing to sit for a polygraph?"

"Yes. He's been interviewed numerous times. Same story each time. He's lying, Cy. I've been in this business too long. I know he's lying. What I can't figure out is why. He has no reason to."

"Sure he's not involved?"

"No. I don't think so. Nothing adds up there. No connection at all. He came to us. I just can't figure him out, but he's apparently prepared to testify to a different sort of facts than what we already have."

"So you just need to know if he's deliberately misled you or lied about what he saw?"

"That's right. And what his motive is for doing this."

"We can get this done. You have a date in mind?"

"Tomorrow or the next day if possible. I just finished interviewing him for the last time this morning. I know he has Friday off."

"Well, Friday it is. I can drive in early in the morning. Could you set him up for 11 a.m.?"

"That would be great, Cy. I'll get back with you to confirm."

"Ten-four. In the meantime, could you fax me his statements along with a synopsis of the case?"

"You got it. Talk to you soon."

"Thanks."

Friday arrived quicker than usual, or so it seemed. Cy had managed to rearrange his schedule to accommodate Agent Battle. He pulled into the garage of the Cincinnati office eager to get going on this one in hopes of getting back on the road and home before anything else came undone as was often the case for Fridays.

Cy had managed to review Dalligher's statements along with the case facts, and it just didn't make sense to him. *Why would this guy go this far to subject himself to a polygraph when he is obviously providing false facts to begin with? Well, we'll just get to it,* he thought. There should be no need to go into this with a multiple set of themes in anticipation of a long-winded interrogation.

Cy had tested in Cincinnati before. The testing room was quiet and secluded, out of the way of employees and visitors coming in and out of the office. On this day, however, he would elect to try something different.

"Hey, Cy, Chip Battle."

"Nice to meet you, sir." Cy sat his instrument down and shook hands. It was readily apparent to him he was speaking with a veteran agent. Battle had the look of a seasoned investigator. With well-groomed, graying hair, a crisp white shirt, and weathered skin, he appeared as a man with integrity. When he shook hands, he kept eye contact with you as if to say, "You're as important to me as I will be to you." If Chip Battle thought Dalligher was lying, chances were he was correct.

"You know where the room is, right?"

"Yes, but you know, Chip, I've been thinking, would it be permissible if I set up my instrument in this interview room here? You see, it's just off the lobby and—"

"Busy traffic through here, Cy, you sure?"

"Yeah, I think so. Noise shouldn't be a factor."

"Whatever works. You're up to speed on his statements?"

"Yes, I am. Do you really think he's going to show?"

"He hasn't let me down yet. This guy will show. We just can't figure him out."

"I'll give him my best effort."

"Wouldn't expect anything else, you know?"

Cy set about setting up his polygraph instrument on the desk in the small eight-by-ten-foot interview room. This room was traditionally used to interview complainants who occasionally walked into the FBI to make an allegation or complaint all the while hoping to get the FBI involved in an issue that frequently was outside federal jurisdiction. Today, it would be used in a most unusual way.

Cy arranged all the components in a neat and visible fashion on and about the desk and chair. He then left the door open so that anyone who came in the lobby could see directly into the room. He moved a couple of chairs in the lobby over to the far wall where, if one were seated there, one would be looking straight into the room featuring the polygraph. As 11:00 a.m. neared, he left the room and went into the radio room where he could observe any visitors via a camera.

Cy didn't have to wait long. Raymond Jay Dalligher appeared as scheduled; although this time, he was nearly ten minutes late. After identifying himself to a desk clerk, he was asked to have a seat for a few moments until Agent Donovan could be summoned.

Cy was aware of his arrival but chose to allow him to remain in the lobby for another ten minutes. What he was about to observe would confirm what Agent Battle had told him. *This guy was lying, sure enough, but why?*

Without making a conscious effort, people generally have trouble controlling their nonverbal behaviors. They simply do not make a vigilant effort to control their body language at least not as much as they do their verbal cues. As Dalligher sat in the lobby chair, his chin dropped and remained resting on his sternum, but oddly enough, his eyes focused on what he observed in the room ahead of him.

Cy sat across from a monitor observing his potential examinee. Typically, the lowered chin often meant depression or acceptance. He needed more than that. He got it. It wasn't long before Dalligher glanced up to notice the camera lens in the corner of the lobby. Instinctively, his expression took on that of a *frozen face*. Cy recognized the look and understood it as a disguise to mislead anyone viewing from seeing a more meaningful expression that might show clarity as to what may be troubling him. Accompanying the lower chin and frozen face was yet another nonverbal that piqued his interest. Dalligher's hands were now protecting his groin.

"Textbook," Cy commented.

"Pardon me?" a young intern inquired who was monitoring the radio.

"Oh, never mind. Just thinking out loud." He continued looking for a few moments longer. He surmised that Dalligher's frozen face was, in all likelihood, an opposite expression internally. Dalligher was certainly attempting to monitor his own kinesic activity by inhibiting his facial expressions, but in so doing, he lost awareness of what his hands were doing. Suppression of his groin was protective in nature and inconsistent with the frozen face. It all added up to a cluster of deception in Cy's opinion.

What made it all so fascinating was that Dalligher had yet to be asked a single question in today's interview. In fact, he had yet to meet Cy. But he had met the polygraph, sort of, and that is all he needed to see.

"Raymond? Cy Donovan."

Dalligher stood up to shake Cy's hand. Cy had just come out from the radio room in a roundabout fashion and entered through the front door somewhat surprising him. "Nice to meet you," he offered before Raymond had found any words. "Stay seated." Cy wasted no time as he pulled up another lobby chair and sat down directly in front of him. For a moment, it was just he and Raymond in the lobby while the desk clerk looked on rather curiously from behind a glass window.

Cy wasted no time. With all celerity, he opened. "Listen, Raymond, you came here today to sit for a polygraph, right?"

Dalligher nodded.

"Well, let me tell you something. We don't have to go into that room, and you don't have to take this test." Raymond Dalligher glanced over Cy's shoulder at the room he was referring to; then, he reacquired with his frozen face looking straight at Cy.

"I've reviewed your previous statements to Agent Battle and Lieutenant Rollins. You need to understand one thing, Raymond, and you need to see it very clearly. You are not the subject of this investigation. We have a young woman whose life has been shattered by an evil act perpetrated by some goon we're trying to prosecute and keep off the street. Now, if you think your statements are going to advance the cause of justice for this young gal who is likely to need some sort of therapy for a few years to come, then by all means come forth, and we'll eventually have you testify in federal court. If however, you feel, for any reason, you need to change any part of your statement to ensure that what your saying is the truth, then now is the time to do it. What's it going to be?"

Dalligher looked away and paused.

Cy maneuvered so as to catch his line of sight.

Dalligher looked the other way.

Cy maneuvered again.

Raymond Dalligher retained his frozen face but spoke, "I didn't see a mask."

After a continued pause, Cy intervened. "What else needs correcting?" he asked, careful not to use the word *lie*. It certainly didn't bother him to call anyone a liar, but this wasn't the time.

"I can't tell you what he was wearing," Dalligher continued.

"And you can't tell us the color of the car he got in either, I presume?"

"Right, I can't be sure," he whispered.

"Can't be sure?"

He nodded.

"Why put us through a goose chase, Raymond?"

Raymond just sat there with no response.

"Actually, Raymond, I don't think you saw anything, did you?"

"I was there," Raymond replied, looking up at Cy.

"I know you were there, but you didn't see what happened, did you?"

"Well, I was there."

"Okay, fine, but listen to me. I'm going to need another statement from you. It will be a short one. I'll get it prepared. You can read it and sign it if you agree to it. Then you can get out of here, okay?"

Dalligher nodded again.

A short statement was prepared making it very clear that Raymond Dalligher's previous statements were falsehoods. He was very apologetic and wanted that put in his statement as well. It was inserted, and Dalligher signed it.

"Now tell me," Cy asked, "I know you've got a DUI in your background. We're you somewhere that day in the UPS truck you shouldn't have been?"

"I was off my route."

"How far off?"

"Too far."

"And UPS knew it, right?"

Dalligher nodded.

"And one more violation might have meant you losing your job unless of course you could sort of justify it be telling them you witnessed a bank robbery, saw a getaway car. This led you hither and yon so to speak, right? In a bogus attempt to get a license plate or some story you may have told your superiors, you can probably hold onto your job. After all, you're fulfilling some sort of civic duty here, right? Am I going in the right direction here, Raymond?"

Dalligher looked over his shoulder again into the room with the polygraph instrument. "Well, I was there."

"Right, you were there, but I'm on the right track, am I not?"

Dalligher looked again into the room. "Does that thing really work?"

"There's one way to find out," Cy said as he got up from his chair.

Raymond got up from his chair also and said, "Maybe another time."

Cy chuckled and opened the door. *There comes a time when you have to let someone save a little face for themselves. This would be one of those times*, he figured. "Stay on your route now, okay?"

"Sure thing."

Cy watched as Raymond Dalligher exited through the elevator. He went back to the room and rang Chip Battle.

"I just knew it I knew it," Chip said. "Man, what a waste of our time." Battle let out a long sigh. Well, at least we can move forward now. I want to thank you, Cy. The US attorney's office will be grateful too.

"That's all right. It's what we do."

"And you do it well. He must have failed his test pretty bad, huh?"

"Well, um, I guess that would be one way to put it."

TOLL THE STATUTE

The snot had rolled down his mustache one too many times. Cy relented and provided a tissue. It had been nearly four hours since Joey Fuentes had failed his polygraph, but nonetheless, he didn't want to leave. He couldn't leave. The burden was too heavy to carry any longer, and he needed to relieve himself of the worry. Finding the strength to convey his transgressions to Cy Donovan had taken some time, but Cy was patient. It took a lot of patience to sit across from this man.

Joey Fuentes was a self-employed, thirty-two-year-old remodeler addicted to painkillers and fond of his marijuana. He struggled to support a wife and three kids with nothing more than a high school education, a general equivalency diploma at that.

Five years earlier, in July of 2003, Fuentes got mixed up with another individual by the name of Phillip Enrico. For over a year, Joey looked up to Phillip in an avuncular way almost as though he were related to him. Fuentes would live to regret ever knowing Enrico as it was Enrico who introduced Fuentes to life on the run, life on the run from robbing banks.

This guy's hygiene is wearing me out, Cy thought. He never had to spend this much time with anyone in a polygraph setting where a man's body odor was so overwhelming. Joey Fuentes's facial features depicted unclean and disheveled hair resting over an unshaven gaunt face. His eyes were bloodshot, but he did well to disguise his sobriety or lack thereof. To say that his jeans and T-shirt needed laundering would be an understatement.

Despite his appearance, Fuentes's overall deportment was one of cooperation. A few days prior to his scheduled polygraph, Fuentes had been interviewed by special agents of the FBI in

Tennessee. When shown photographs taken from a surveillance camera at a carwash in Kentucky in the summer of 2003, he freely admitted the photos were of he and Enrico.

In the photos, Enrico was observed inserting red-stained money into a change machine. When queried about this money, Fuentes remembered the money as being red-stained but denied it was money from a bank robbery. In fact, Fuentes clarified with the agents that he had specifically asked Enrico where he had gotten the money and Enrico advised him a friend had given it to him and for Fuentes not to worry about it.

When asked about his whereabouts the day of the bank robbery, Fuentes offered that he had been asked to drive Phillip Enrico to Wal-Mart, a Dollar Store, a Laundromat, and a carwash in Tennessee but not Kentucky. He assisted Enrico only in running him around to take care of errands. The vehicle driven was a 1991 Pontiac Grand Prix owned by Fuentes's girlfriend.

Fuentes vehemently denied any involvement in a bank robbery nor did he acknowledge the true origin of the red-stained money in Enrico's possession. Fuentes was asked if he would submit to a polygraph, and he agreed to do so.

The agents scheduled Joey for the polygraph with Cy Donovan on a Saturday morning in May, less than ninety days from the five-year anniversary of the bank robbery. Although the agents had identified the probable perpetrators, they had little to take into court for a successful prosecution. In fact, this case was about to be placed in a pending inactive file due to the fact that the statute of limitations would peremptorily dictate its course.

Fuentes's polygraph charts were indicative of someone who was tired. The fact of the matter was Joey had been up most of the night debating whether he should even appear for such a test. Although he advised Donovan he had had about seven hours of sleep, such was not the case. Fuentes was physiologically spent.

There was however enough juice left in his galvanic skin response to record clear and consistent reactions to one relevant question. "Did you know for sure the red-stained money had come from a bank robbery?" This question would prove to be the stimulus that Fuentes had a problem with. He failed his test on that issue and voluntarily remained in the chair facing off with Cy in a classic interrogation exercise.

Cy chose his themes carefully. He did not expect to have to exhaust all of them, but he did. What he didn't realize was that Fuentes was prepared to confess his involvement, but he wasn't listening to Donovan's textbook approach.

Initially, Cy attempted to minimize the seriousness of what Fuentes and Enrico had done. He reminded Joey that no one was hurt in the robbery. This was a one-time event, an error in judgment, simply an impulse action as opposed to a premeditated plan. Certainly, he believed otherwise, but this would be his approach. Cy minimized the amount taken in the robbery, less than $5,000. He emphasized Joey's need to provide for his family, and if it weren't for that necessity, he wouldn't have done it.

Joey Fuentes never heard the pitch. He seemed oblivious to the man sitting across from him. Fuentes was in a state of contemplation.

Cy resorted to another strategy. He blamed external factors for causing Fuentes to act as he did the day of the robbery. "Listen, Joey," he implored. "Robbing banks is not in your character. If you're not framing houses, you're not bringing in any money. It's not your fault the economy is down, the building trades are in a slump, and you cannot maintain consistent work. In fact, this wasn't even your idea to begin with, was it?"

Fuentes failed to respond. But he didn't deny involvement any longer. He did however portray a blank screen for Cy that was becoming more and more frustrating to interpret. He's not listening to me. Cy figured. It's like he was listening to another drummer. Cy was perplexed. He offered up another theme that he was pretty sure wouldn't carry the day either, but he proceeded with style. "Joey, you're not an arrogant man, but I've got to believe Phillip has a whole different approach to things right?"

There was no response.

"I mean he's cocky. Thinks he can do whatever he wants and he can direct others to do the same. Isn't that the case? Isn't it?"

Fuentes shrugged his shoulders but remained silent. He reached down to the floor to pick up his empty can of Mountain Dew he had brought in with him. He drooled a bit of tobacco or dip he had stored under his gum. It was his own physiological way of coming to resolution with his decision.

"Look at it this way, Joey. Were it not for Enrico, you wouldn't be here today. He put you in a bad position." Cy wasn't clear what that position was, but he gambled that Fuentes would educate him. He watched patiently as Joey took a deep breath but said nothing and reached for his can again to spit.

Cy stood up a moment with his clipboard in hand. He walked about the room a bit studying his information. He came back in front of Joey and asked a question that struck a chord. "How many kids do you have?"

Fuentes was about to spit but paused. He looked up at Cy and gestured with his right hand, three fingers.

Cy sat down. "And what are their ages?"

"Three, six, and nine."

"Listen, Phillip Enrico is going to do some serious time for this job. Don't let him put you in this position. You need to be available for your kids. You need—"

"There's more to it than that." Joey sobbed.

Cy listened.

Joey sobbed and spit; he sobbed and spit some more. It got to be sort of a mess, but Cy leaned in.

"Talk to me, Joey. Help yourself. You need to get this behind you because it isn't going to go away soon."

"You don't know. There's more to it than that."

Cy gave him a small box of tissues and moved a trash can to within his reach. Are you in fear of your life, Joey?"

"He'll kill my wife. He'll kill my kids. He's already tried."

"How?"

"After I moved to Kentucky, two men whom I don't know came to the house. I do believe they were both meth users."

"How do you know that?"

"I seen one before with Phillip. I just don't know what they do. I've heard Phillip talk about it."

"Go on."

"They knocked at the front door, then just walked in. I was sitting in a chair with a gun under a pillow so they could see part of it. My dog was next to me."

"What kind of dog?"

"Pit."

"Did they have guns?"

"Don't know, but I assumed so. I know they had come to harm Leslie and maybe the kids too. I know that because Phillip had told me something would to happen to her." Joey spit.

"And what happened?"

"They told me Phillip had sent them and that they had something to talk to me about. But I think they saw my gun 'cuz they didn't stay long."

"I'm missing something, Joey. Why did Phillip tell you something would happen to Leslie? There has to be a reason."

"He didn't trust her. He figured I had told her about the robbery, and she would run her mouth."

"And he wanted her out of the way?"

"That's it."

"What happened after the two men left your house?"

"We left Kentucky within a couple of weeks and came back to Tennessee."

"Does Enrico know where you live now?"

"Probably, but I'm not sure. He knows I'm not in Kentucky anymore."

"Still in touch?"

"Yeah, we talk occasionally."

"Where is he now?"

"Cincinnati area."

"Where in Cincinnati?"

"Around there somewhere, not certain exactly. It's a Cincinnati number that I call when I talk to him I know that."

"When did you talk to him last?"

"A week ago."

"What did he do in the robbery?" Cy figured it would be easier for Joey to talk about Enrico's role first.

"All I know is that when he came back to the car, he had a paper bag with him. I noticed it was red-stained. He had red stain on him too. He got down in the backseat and told me to drive on."

"All right, Joey, but what car, and where were you parked?"

"I drove my 1984 Ford Granada and pulled into a driveway of a white house. This is where Phillip told me to park."

"Where exactly was this house?"

"A block or so from the bank. He got out and said he was going to borrow some money and a bag of smoke from a friend. He walked up by the side of the house, and I could not see where he went from there."

"How long was he gone?"

"About ten minutes or so. He came running back with the bag."

"Did you know at that time he had robbed a bank?"

"I drove him."

Cy interrupted. "You didn't answer, Joey."

"When I drove him back to his house, he showed me the money, and he told me I was an accessory because I took him down there. I asked him what he had done, and he said he had robbed a bank."

"Keep going."

"Phillip and his wife, Cindy, took me home. They picked up Leslie, and she took them back home. I stayed home the rest of the night. A day or two later, Phillip and I went to a car wash. Phillip said he was going to put some of the red-stained money into the coin machine. I washed the car. A couple days later, I borrowed some of the money he had received in the bank robbery. Some of the money I borrowed was red-stained."

"How much did you borrow?"

"About $250."

"Where was the car wash?"

"Not sure somewhere around town."

"Then what?"

"About six months later, I moved to Kentucky."

"So what you're telling me, Joey, is that you only drove the getaway car, right?"

"Well, yeah."

"And you didn't know Phillip was going to rob a bank that day?"

"No. Like I said, I didn't know until we got back to his house."

"You didn't plan this robbery ahead of time with Phillip?"

"No, I didn't know about it."

"And his wife didn't know about it either?"

"I can't say what he may have told her, but he didn't tell me."

"Let me see if I have this right, Joey. Number one, you didn't know he was going to rob the bank ahead of time, right?"

"That's right."

"Number two, the first time you knew he had, in fact, robbed the bank was after you drove him back to his house and he showed you the money and told you what he had done?"

"Right. We didn't plan this together. He told me later I was an accessory."

"And number three, you saw him put red-stained money in the coin machine at a local car wash?"

"Yeah."

"Finally, you borrowed about $250 of the red-stained money from him?"

"About that much, yeah."

Cy paused while he quickly evaluated the subject sitting in front of him. He would stop short of putting him in the same category as a homeless person. *There are a host of psychological problems associated with those folks*, he thought. However, he was fairly certain Fuentes suffered from substance abuse issues.

Joey's own admitted close association with Enrico, who, in turn, had an affiliation with methamphetamine users was one clue. Additionally, he had admitted to the case agent he had smoked pot the day prior to this test. At age thirty-two, he was more likely a habitual user as opposed to an occasional experimenter of the euphoric hemp. Any maladaptive pattern of substance use would likely lead to a significant impairment of judgment or distress.

Fuentes's lifestyle was certainly indicative of one with such a problem. He had failed to fulfill major role obligations at work or at home. He had recurrent legal problems. He also suffered from recurrent social and interpersonal problems exacerbated by the effects of drug use. This was evidenced by his ongoing marital difficulties colored with domestic abuse complaints.

Nonetheless, Fuentes had some nerve. He had elected to show up for his polygraph and had now come forth with crucial information. But he wasn't completely forthright, and Cy chose to tell him so.

"Listen, Joey, I can appreciate what you're telling me. If what you're saying is the complete truth, you wouldn't have any problem giving me a signed sworn statement, would you?"

Joey reached for the can. "Yeah, I can do that."

Cy pulled out a notepad of lined paper. He reached for a pen from the inside of his suit jacket pocket, one that he knew had plenty of ink left in it.

"Joey, I will prepare a statement for you, one sentence at a time. Together, we'll read it. If it reads as you would have it read,

I'll ask you to sign it and swear to it. If there is anything in the statement you don't agree with, we'll strike it and revise it. I won't ask you to sign anything you don't agree with nor will I write anything you didn't tell me. Fair enough?"

"Yeah, sounds fair to me."

Cy began to write. It was a painstaking process but a critical one. Cy taught statement taking in his own course on interview and interrogation. He practiced what he preached. His principle for getting confessions that held water was simple: get it verbally, get it in writing, get it signed, sworn, and witnessed, and you've got them. A confession received one time is on weak legs. It must be reduced to a signed sworn statement and witnessed.

After about thirty minutes, Cy reached the point where he thought he could finish. He was bothered, however, by the changing demeanor of Fuentes. Although he had agreed with Cy throughout the draft, he had stepped up his use of the can. He was definitely working the juice out of his dip. Quite annoyed by it all, Cy elected to confront his examinee one more time.

"Joey, we've reached the point where I would normally ask you to sign and swear to this statement. Before we do that, I want you to understand something."

Fuentes nodded.

"If there is anything you are deliberately withholding from me regarding your involvement or Enrico's involvement in this robbery, tell me now. Otherwise, if you sign this knowing you've given me false information, it's a felony, and I'll have you charged with that. Do you understand?"

"Yeah." Fuentes nodded and reached for the can.

Cy grabbed the can and set it aside before Joey could get his hand on it. "Joey, you haven't told me everything today. Now I need the truth."

"But I've told you—"

"No," he interrupted. Listen to me. I'm not in the business of looking for ways to fit you into a federal lockup. You're the one who came forward today Joey, not Enrico. You're the one with a family. You're the one with responsibilities. I am here to work with you, not against you. Now, you can help yourself or you can fuck yourself. Which is it going to be?"

Fuentes paused for what seemed like an eternity. Cy had taken a chance. He knew he may never get this into writing now. He may, in fact, walk out with verbal admissions that he could testify to, but he needed more, and he was well aware of it. He pressed Fuentes again with another question.

"How much of this did you know ahead of time, and at what point did you know it?"

Joey turned his head away from Cy and dropped it into his hands.

Cy gave him a few moments, then moved in closer setting his statement aside. "Give yourself a chance here, Joey. No one got hurt. No one's going to get hurt. You're cooperation is important at this point. I don't want to have to testify against you, so don't put me in that position. Don't put yourself in this position any longer. Move it along, Joey. Talk to me."

Fuentes was embarrassed that his tears were tracking into his mustache once again.

Cy grabbed him the tissue box.

Joey made full use of it.

"He had this, this, uh…this make-believe bomb," Joey said.

"Phillip did?"

"Yes. He strapped it to his stomach so he could show it to a teller. It was just a stupid thing."

"Right. Go on."

"It was stupid. Just stupid, you know? Like an alarm clock backward."

"I know. What else do we need to talk about?"

"That's really it. Really."

"You'll have to own up to it, you know?"

"That's it though."

"This makes it clear you knew of this robbery before it was going to happen, Joey."

"But I didn't rob the bank."

"Yeah, I know. You just drove him there and picked him up after the fact."

"That's all there was to it."

"And you're willing to sign a statement to that effect?"

Fuentes nodded.

Cy got his statement. Fuentes signed it with a clear conscience and dry eyes. The case agent was brought into the room to witness Joey's signature as Cy swore him to it.

"I think you need another can."

"Yeah."

"Okay, Joey, we're going to need you to work with us now, you know. Regarding Enrico, that is. You're up for it, right?"

Fuentes nodded again. "He knows about this five-year thing. He told me that come this summer, I wouldn't need to worry about it any longer."

"Funny you would say that. You came in here anyway, why?"

"Dunno. I didn't believe him I guess. He's not one to trust."

"We appreciate your cooperation, Joey, and the fact you volunteered to—"

With his right hand holding his can, Joey motioned negatively for Cy to stop. Then he spoke, "Save it, sir, I don't need any more of your self-help lecture."

Cy obliged and just looked at Joey.

Joey squinted back at him and let loose a long drool into the can.

The deed was signed, and the day was done.

THUGS AND THIEVES

In this world there are only two tragedies; one is not getting what one wants and the other is getting it. The last is much the worst.

—Oscar Wilde

FOR NO GOOD REASON

The old rusty water tower stood like a sentry against a cold and gray swollen sky. February in Hammond, Indiana, is rude and unwelcoming. Cy loved it, but he didn't know why. It was the evening hour, and he stood looking out the window of the second floor witness room of the federal courthouse hoping a jury would bring back a verdict soon.

In the distance, the whistle of a train could be heard and jarred Cy's memory back to his youth. He loved train whistles. As a child, they kept him awake at night but in a good way. Raised on the wrong side of the tracks, he always yearned to hop a train just to see where it would take him. But he never did.

Hammond of 1996 was ugly, especially in winter. The roads were potholed and full of slush. Cars well beyond their useful life limped along streets with a taillight out or a muffler hanging too low. Business signs were outdated and only half-lit or half-hung. For every well-kept building on the city streets, there were at least ten that were, well, you get the picture. Suffice it say however that Hammond was and always has been a step or two ahead of its neighbor to the east, Gary.

Its blue-collar pride kept it that way. *Call it nitty-gritty America*, Cy thought. Perhaps that is the draw, the attraction. People here are too proud to take a handout. People who are used to tough times become tough themselves. They don't take kindly to being bullied. Northwest Indiana and the south side of Chicago have plenty of folks who like to do just that. Plenty of thugs and thieves.

Nineteen ninety-six and ninety-seven saw a series of home invasions throughout the Hammond area. At the forefront of these home marauders were a group commonly known as the Latin Kings. The Bureau had been looking into them for some time. Gang task forces were set up, and some inroads had been made through the use of informants, albeit cautiously. The gangs almost always dabbled in the drug trade, and they would not hesitate to use force to acquire their share of illegal narcotics. Drugs and guns were the feature story behind most Bureau investigations in this part of the country. Throw in some prostitution and public corruption, and you have a full Easter basket of rotten eggs.

Cracking these eggs usually required the use of a snitch. Enter Puleo Prince, a.k.a. Pug. Pug was short and pudgy without much of a future. He had managed to graduate Hammond high school, but by age twenty, he already had two convictions for something known in Hammond as House Common Nuisance. Being the unruly soul that he was, it was only a matter of time before he found common ground with a notorious group of Hammond troublemakers.

At 9:30 p.m., Cy suspected the jury was undecided and deliberations would likely be suspended—soon to continue tomorrow. After all, federal district court judge Andy Brewster wasn't known for keeping juries past 10:00 p.m. on a Friday night. However, he just might in this case in hopes of avoiding sequestering the jury throughout the weekend.

A few yawns later, Cy found a position of comfort on the worn-out leather sofa and dozed off. Twenty minutes later, he was startled by a knock on the door.

"The jury is in, Cy."

He looked up to see one of the court security officers (CSOs) staring at him with a grin on his face.

"You know something?" Cy asked.

"I know nothing," the CSO responded.

The jury foreman handed the verdict to a bailiff who, in turn, handed it to Judge Brewster. After the verdict was read, Cy was relieved. The last subject of a gang of six had just been found guilty on six of nine counts of violent criminal offenses for his role in a series of armored car robberies over the course of two years. At age forty-two, six of nine counts would get his subject forty-five years, which was essentially a death sentence.

Cy could ask no more. Perhaps now he could focus his attention on perfecting his craft as a polygraph examiner as opposed to managing a burdensome caseload. It had been a month since his last polygraph. Once a case goes to trial, all other duties get put on hold until the trial is over. He would soon discover he was about to get reacquainted with his lie detector.

On Monday morning, Cy met with his old partner, Special Agent Johnny Keill for a quick breakfast at a diner not far from the office. Following the usual chitchat and Monday morning quarterbacking about Cy's trial, Keill mentioned he would like to have Pug put on the box. Keill was responsible for the case on the Latin Kings, and before he went any further, he wanted to rule out Pug's involvement in a home invasion in Hammond a couple of weeks earlier.

"So how long have you been working this guy?" Cy asked.

"Not long. He came to Hammond PD and offered some information. He's been jammed up before and wants to avoid any more jail time. Actually, I shouldn't say he came to Hammond. What happened was Hammond interviewed him regarding a shooting adjacent to Magoun Street. He denied any involvement. The next day, he called Detective Jill Ambrose and offered information on the Magoun Street home invasion."

"Was he in on that?"

"Says he wasn't, but he claims to know who was," Keill said.

"So you want to know if he's involved or not?"

"Right. I'm sure he's not telling us everything."

"I'm sure he's not. Thieves always hold something back."

"We need to get to the bottom of it because these assholes are dangerous. They won't hesitate to whack anyone, especially if there is dope involved."

"I can test him this week."

"Let me reach out to him and see about getting him in. You have to read him his rights?"

"Yep. You know the drill."

"Well, that shouldn't be a problem. I'll talk to him."

Pug was very slow and deliberate as he signed the Advice of Rights form, Puleo Prince. Much the way Cy had him pictured, Pug was African American although probably not pure. He wore a button-down short-sleeved cream-colored shirt that needed laundered. You could see his belly as the bottom four buttons barely came together in a desperate attempt to hide his gut. The shirt was not tucked into his Irish green warm-up trousers that would have looked great on a true-to-life basketball player. But Pug was no athlete.

He sat at the end of Cy's desk breathing a little harder than someone should be, almost as though he had asthma, but he did not have asthma. No, Pug was just an out-of-shape, well, Pug. He was likeable with his chubby face and nonthreatening demeanor. Not real bright and from a broken home, one could almost understand how he came to be a player of sorts with the Latin Kings.

Pug had put himself in a dangerous position, and he knew it. If any of his buddies even suspected him as a snitch, his life would be short-lived.

Cy understood Pug's plight and attributed his concern as a reason for his nervous demeanor. Perhaps that was the primary reason, or perhaps there would be more to the tale. In any event he hoped to find out. As he made his way through the pretest interview, one thing became clear. Cy would do most of the talking on this day. Or so he thought. Fortunately however, staying focused was not a problem for Pug.

He appeared fully occupied in his thoughts. As Cy reviewed the case facts with Pug, Pug nodded right along whether he said anything or not. He appeared to be in a daze from time to time. Cy was concerned at first but soon realized that Pug had a whole lot of information he had yet to reveal. Initially, he had no problem reconfirming for Cy what he had already told police.

Pug had given up the players, namely the ring leader Eddie Merdecai, Merdecai's cousin known only as Jamie, Jamie's girlfriend, Regina Sheef, and her friend Maggie Timson. Pug had also named Yogi Schult whom he believed to be Hispanic, another unknown Mexican male and Pug's buddy, Hurly Miller.

Pug named the ones he knew had entered the house on Magoun Street for the purpose of stealing marijuana, which Merdecai thought was owed him for a deal gone bad. Pug had implied to police they had not gotten anything, and no one was home. Pug had also denied he had participated. He had only previously admitted to overhearing the others making their plans at Merdecai's home from Merdecai's bedroom.

Satisfied that Pug wasn't yet prepared to divulge anything further, Cy reviewed the test questions with him. When asked, "Were you present in the house on Magoun Street when the robbery took place?"

Pug answered, "No."

When asked, "Did you participate in the robbery on Magoun Street?" Pug again answered no.

He ensured that Pug understood the questions, and Pug acknowledged he understood and would he please get the test started.

Cy wasted no further time.

As Pug packed his overweight 5'6" frame into the polygraph chair, Cy picked up a scent of marijuana. It was the first he had smelled it, and it aroused his curiosity. He had covered drug use and medications with Pug in the pretest and got no indication from Pug that he had smoked any dope or used any illegal narcotics in the last twenty-four hours. In fact, Pug had denied being on any prescription drugs or drinking any alcohol either.

One thing was certain—he had at least been around some pot smokers if the scent was still on his clothes. In any event, Cy would watch his charts closely.

When it comes to drugs, the degree of increase or decrease in physiological activity depends on the dosage or use of the drug as well as the amount of food in the person's stomach when the drug was taken.

The person's tolerance also comes into play. Whatever physiological change is seen should be consistent throughout the chart and therefore can be disregarded as a norm. More particularly, when it comes to marijuana, any increase or decrease in the cardio, pneumograph, or galvanic skin response tracings will be unpredictable.

With that in mind, Cy needed to be comfortable with what Pug had told him regarding prior drug usage. Hence, prior to commencing with the test, Cy asked him one more time if he had used any marijuana in the last twenty-four hours. Pug's response was an immediate "absolutely not."

Satisfied, Cy moved on.

Like a good soldier, Pug sat up straight and followed his instructions. After the first chart had been run however, his posture had changed. His shoulders were slumped, and his head was tilted slightly to the left. Prior to the running of chart number 2, Cy reminded Pug to sit straight, and Pug had responded well. Asleep, he was not—defeated but not asleep. Cy ran the second chart and a third. There was no unpredictability in the tracings. Puleo Prince was deceptive times three.

"Well, well, well." Cy uttered loud enough for Pug to hear.

"What's that mean?"

"What do you think it means?"

"I dunno. You're the expert."

"And you're the fibber."

"*What?*"

"Sure, you know you failed this test." Surprisingly, there was no comeback denial. There was just silence.

"Listen," Cy said. "You don't strike me as some sort of thug or thief for that matter. I've got to believe you just got cajoled along on this thing, and it wasn't your intent to—"

"Whatchya mean when you say cajole?" Pug interrupted.

"Persuaded, Pug. You know. They talked you into coming along, right?"

"Right, okay, but I didn't hurt no one."

Cy nearly dropped his pen. He had gotten his first admission without much effort at all. He remembered what Rudy once told him, "Some guys will fall right into your lap because they just need to talk. Just show them you're interested and that you care, then listen to them sing."

"Let's talk about this thing. We need to separate fact from fiction. You know? Truth from lie, okay?"

"I ain't told no lie, man. What I told the detectives is the truth."

"Except for the fact that you were at the house too."

"Okay, but it's like you said. I was just there, you know? I didn't do nothin', which is why I didn't mention that earlier. I can't be going to jail, man. I just can't."

Cy watched as Pug fought off some tears. "Listen now, work with me, and I'll work with you. I can't promise you anything, but you're cooperation will go a long way to keeping you out of jail. Understand me?"

Pug nodded.

"I need details. Tell me what really happened."

"Look, man, what I told police is true. It's what I didn't tell them, you know? They didn't ask."

"I'm not buying that, Pug. What matters is that I get the whole story now. It's a matter of being forthright. Do you know what that means?"

"Yeah, I think so."

"What?"

"Just tellin' all I know."

"Right. Without being asked. You have an obligation to tell us everything if you expect any leniency in this mess."

Pug paused and looked away.

"You with me?"

"Yeah, I'm with you, man. What I told police is true as far as what we did before we went into the house."

"You mean the planning of this thing at Merdecai's house?"

"Yeah, that's right."

"Okay, as I understand from the detective's report, you, Merdecai, Merdecai's cousin—Jamie, Jamie's girlfriend—Regina, and Regina's friend—Maggie were at Merdecai's house, right?"

"Uh, yeah and others."

"Right. Also present was Yogi Schult, an unknown Mexican, and you're buddy, Hurly Miller."

"That's it. Merdecai, Yogi, Hurly, and the unknown dude went into Merdecai's bedroom while I sat and watched TV. They made their plans to go into this house on Magoun Street and get pounds and pounds of marijuana."

"How do you know that's what they talked about?"

"'Cuz I could hear 'em. I don't think they much cared that I could hear 'em 'cuz I was going to be along. But they were the heavies, you know?"

"You were going to be a minor player?"

"That's it. Merdecai, he's the heavy dude in this along with Yogi."

"Got it. Keep going."

"They came out of the bedroom see, and about twenty minutes later, we started to leave. I got into Maggie's burgundy Chevrolet with Merdecai, Miller, and Maggie. She drove us over by Woodmar Mall in Hammond. I did not see what car the Mex'n and Yogi were in. When we got over by the mall, we parked near the department stores on 167th and Indianapolis Boulevard. When Yogi arrived, he and the Mex'n dude came over to our car and started arguing about who was going to carry the gun."

"What kind of gun?"

"It was a long-barreled chrome nine."

"Who had it?"

"It was in Maggie's trunk. Merdecai got the chrome piece, and the unknown Mex'n gave Yogi a black gun."

"So there were two guns?"

"Yes."

"Any more?"

"No."

"Go on."

"Yogi and the Mex'n dude walked away for a few minutes and came back. They talked a bit. Then they left while Maggie, Miller, Merdecai, and I drove in her car over to another street. I think it was Baring Street where we parked. Then Miller, Merdecai, and I got out of the car. Maggie stayed in the car. We met Yogi and the Mex'n dude at the house on Magoun Street."

Pug paused.

Cy sensed he was about to get into the core of the matter and chose not to press him.

After a couple of minutes, Pug took a deep breath, clenched his fist, then unclenched it, and continued, "You see Merdecai knocked on the door. A woman answered. Before she could say anything, Merdecai kicked the door through and yelled in the woman's face, 'Where the weed?' He then grabbed the woman around her head with his left hand over her chin and jabbed a finger into her mouth. I really wasn't expecting this, you know?"

"Okay, keep going."

"Merdecai took that chrome nine and jabbed it into her spine so hard she yelped. The rest of us followed him into the house."

"The rest of you being yourself, Yogi, the unknown Mexican, and Hurly Miller?"

"Yes, we all went in. I stood by the door watching while the others started rummaging through the house. I was acting as a lookout."

"Okay, that's different than what you told police before."

"I know. I know I denied being in the house, but I was."

"Was that your only involvement, as a lookout?"

"That's all I did."

"You're sure?"

"Okay, I did pull the telephone cord out of the wall after Merdecai told me to."

"Go on."

"Merdecai kept yelling at the woman, but she couldn't speak."

"Why?"

"He wouldn't let her, man."

Cy could see the tears welling up in Pug's eyes.

"Merdecai just kept his hand up under her chin and pushed her neck back, and then he pushed her backward over to the couch. He shoved her into the couch and stuck that gun under her chin demanding to know where the weed was. She was terrified and started shaking her head."

"As if to say she didn't know, or was she just not going to tell him where it was?"

"I don't think she knew, man. In fact, we didn't get no weed at all. I don't think there was any weed in that house."

"Was it the wrong house?"

"You know, I hadn't thought about it, maybe it was. I really don't know even today."

"Was anyone else in the house?"

"Just a little girl, that's it."

"Was she harmed?"

"No. Merdecai threatened to jack her up, but Yogi talked him down from it. Yogi is the only one he will listen to. Merdecai is cold, you know? He's brutal. This woman didn't have much. She was just trying to get by, and we came in and tore her life up."

"What else happened?"

"Well, she was scared, and she couldn't talk even after he took that gun away. He left her on the couch expecting me to watch her. I didn't really have to. She wasn't going anywhere.

Pug sighed and took another deep breath. Merdecai and Yogi went upstairs. The Mex'n dude started tearing up the place. More like vandalism, you know?"

"You didn't participate in that?"

"No, I just stood there and didn't say a word."

"Regret that?"

"I regret the whole thing, man. It didn't have to happen this way."

"The little girl and the woman, Pug, not seriously hurt?"

"No. But that little girl started crying, like out of control, and I think the Mex'n couldn't take that, so he stopped being such a jerk. He had already broken some stuff and flipped over the furniture. No reason to, not really."

"How long were you all in the house?"

"Not that long. About fifteen minutes later, Merdecai and Yogi came down from upstairs. Merdecai had a television, and Yogi had a VCR, which he gave to me and told me to hold it. Merdecai was very upset about not finding any weed and threatened to come back. He left with the TV. We all left. The TV got put in the trunk of Maggie's car, and I put the VCR into the backseat. She drove. I still can't say what car Yogi and the Mex'n dude got into 'cuz I really didn't pay any attention to it."

"Anything else you can remember?"

Pug sat in the polygraph chair with a dazed look on his face.

"What is it, Pug?"

"Nothin' really. Just the look on that woman's face. Merdecai, man, I believe he would have shot her had we not all been there."

"You think so?"

"Definitely. He got nose to nose with her. Showed her all his ugly teeth. He was foamin' at the mouth, man. He would have at least beat her. All for no good reason. I don't want to be a part of this. I don't want to be a…a…"

"A thug?"

Pug nodded.

"Is this all there is to it?"

"That's it, man, that's everything."

"Are you willing to give me a signed, sworn statement to this?"

"Anything you need."

"Let's get it done and hope that the next chapter in your life will be a better one."

"I hope so. We've been here a long time. Is it still cold out?"

"It's always cold in Hammond."

COUNTERMEASURES

The greatest part of our faults are more excusable than the methods that are commonly taken to conceal them.

—Francois Duc de la Rochefoucauld

CRUSHED FINGERPLATES

Clarksburg, West Virginia, is rich in history. Named for the Revolutionary War Colonel George Rogers Clark, it is also the birthplace of Confederate General Thomas "Stonewall" Jackson.

In the early to mid-twentieth century, Clarksburg had a reputation as the hub of West Virginia with a census reaching over thirty-two thousand in 1950. Since then however, industry and business took on a trend not unlike other areas of the country and moved away to outlying areas. As such, population dwindled to half that number by the turn of the new millennium. Nevertheless, Clarksburg remained very typical of the heart and soul of America with its many parks, strong work ethic, and family values.

Perhaps for these reasons, the FBI took note, and in the mid-1990s, they moved their fingerprint examiners there and built a fabulous complex now known as the Criminal Justice Information Services (CJIS) division.

Staffing CJIS would be a long and arduous task. To get the necessary compliment of employees on board to have it function like a well-oiled machine would take a couple of years. Not everyone assigned to the division was able or willing to transfer from FBIHQ in Washington, DC, to this less than robust and largely rural community in West Virginia. As such, area residents were sought out through an aggressive hiring initiative.

Although the core values of the surrounding community were strong, all those who applied to CJIS still needed to be carefully screened as a security clearance was necessary. As part of the application process, all candidates for employment would need to consent to a preemployment polygraph focusing on foreign counterintelligence, use and sale of illegal drugs, and overall honesty as to their application.

Like all communities throughout America, Clarksburg wasn't immune to the influence of illegal narcotics. One in five who applied to CJIS throughout 1996 and 1997 would fail their polygraph, and most of the time, use of illegal drugs would be the culprit.

During a two- to three-year time frame, hundreds of individuals came forth for their *voluntary* polygraphs, sometimes as many as thirty per day for weeks at a time would challenge the lie detector. Although the Bureau had been polygraph testing all applicants since March 1994, these testing specials were a real task for the Polygraph Program and necessitated the training of additional examiners.

What was once a compliment of forty well-trained polygraph examiners became a cadre of about ninety examiners coast to coast. In conjunction with the staffing of CJIS, it was important to note that word was beginning to spread throughout the antipolygraph community about the Bureau's use of polygraph in all-applicant testing.

Timing could not have been better with the burgeoning use of the Internet to assist the naysayers in promulgating their antipolygraph propaganda and agendas. A big part of the antipolygraph movement would soon fester like a cancer through *online* discussions with would-be polygraph takers and former or recently trained polygraph examiners who were, for whatever reason, nonbelievers in the science.

Prospective examinees were and are today educated, encouraged, and trained in the use of countermeasures in an effort to beat their opponent, the US government polygraph examiner. Some of these antipolygraph activists were victims themselves of a false positive and some just cannot accept or tolerate the US government using a less than perfect science to screen federal job applicants.

Their argument is heard and understood. Quite frankly, most active examiners would cherish the opportunity to utilize a more accurate method of separating truth from deception, if it existed.

The pursuit of such a technology, i.e., brain fingerprinting, is admirable and will continue to be studied by federal agencies to ascertain reliability and validity from time to time.

Those who oppose the use of polygraph would do well to channel their energies toward a technology that supersedes polygraph rather than to publish literature and share secrets on how to defeat a methodology designed to, in essence, make their lives and the lives of all Americans more secure.

Failure to utilize a technology as accurate as polygraph to screen for a security clearance is foolish. Having said that, failure to pursue an advanced technology that might render polygraph outdated is even more foolish. Any effort to thwart either is at least shameful neglect and a careless lack of patriotism.

Webster defines a countermeasure as a measure taken to oppose another measure. In terms of polygraph, a countermeasure is an attempt by an examinee to create a false negative outcome or at least interfere with a correct outcome. The false negative result refers to an outcome whereby the examiner determines that deception was not apparent on the polygraph charts when, in fact, the examinee was indeed being deceptive in his responses.

Countermeasures come in several different forms, most of which are easily detected by an experienced examiner looking for such an attempt. Some attempts are more blatant than others. One of the more bizarre acts of countermeasures was perpetrated by an applicant for CJIS on a July afternoon in 1996 in a Clarksburg hotel room.

Charles Biedick was a mail clerk applicant. Other than the fact that he owned a federal firearms license, there was nothing terribly unusual about his application. Certainly, if he passed his polygraph, he would be subject to as thorough a background investigation as anyone else. He showed up in the hotel lobby in a timely manner and was escorted to a room for his test. Cy Donovan met him in the hallway.

"Cy Donovan's my name."

"Chuck Biedick."

"Nice to meet you, Chuck. We're right in here." Biedick was shown a chair to sit in. This was a straight back desk chair with strong wooden legs.

Cy sat in another chair with a swivel.

Biedick was cooperative but unemotional, uninspiring in his dialogue. Cy recognized his lack of personality, but then again how much personality does a prospective mail clerk need? After all, it wasn't his job to select or deny anyone a job. He would however grant him a polygraph, which would or would not take Mr. Biedick to the next step in the hiring process. It wasn't long before Cy was ready to go.

"Do you understand all these questions?"

"Yes," Biedick acknowledged.

"Do you need me to repeat any questions?"

"Nope."

"Okay, we're all set." Cy set the pressure in the cardio cuff and rolled through the first chart. The second and third chart followed as a matter of routine. "This concludes the first series," Cy announced. "Give me a few moments to look things over, and we'll get started on the second series."

"All right," Biedick mumbled.

After a close review, Cy was bothered by what he observed in the pneumograph tracing. Biedick's respiration, although steady, was slower than what it should have been. In fact, Cy looked at his watch and tried to mimic what he was seeing on Biedick's charts. He knew it wasn't normal to take eight to ten seconds to cycle a breath.

Before proceeding to the lifestyle series, Cy decided to seek the opinion of his quality control supervisor located in another room down the hall.

"Chuck," he announced, "I'm going to leave you here for just a few moments. I've got an opinion on these charts, and I just want to get that confirmed, okay?"

"Sure."

Cy walked to the door. As he left the room, he was careful to place the upper locking hook of the door into the doorjamb so the door wouldn't lock shut behind him but rather leave a slight opening in the door. His only purpose in doing so was to be able to avoid inserting his card key when he returned. Card keys sometimes fail in hotel rooms, and he did not want his examinee left alone any longer than necessary. To do so would be rather unprofessional and awkward for the examinee.

"Hey, Jim, take a look at these. Did well on the test, but I'm concerned with the breathing," Cy said.

Jim Kimmestor was a supervisory special agent with over eight years in quality control. He knew countermeasures when he saw them. He flipped through the charts rather quickly, then offered his opinion.

"You know, Cy, the breathing isn't right. However, there is little to no reaction in the GSR or cardio on the relevant questions. I would admonish him on the breathing, then proceed to the lifestyle series. Chances are he is prepping himself for the lifestyle questions he knows are coming, and you'll see real reactions in that series. If he wants to continue to play games with you on the lifestyle series, we'll call it inconclusive and make him come back a second time."

"Works for me, Jim," Cy replied.

"He's all yours."

Cy made his way back to the room. The locking hook was still in the doorjamb so he was able to enter without making much noise although that was not his intention. Good thing however as he was able to observe Biedick concluding an act he would not believe.

Chuck Biedick's back was to the door, so he did not see Cy enter. He very quickly adjusted his chair as he sat back down. His fingerplates lay on the floor. He was about to pick them up when Cy spoke.

"I've got 'em, Chuck. Relax, you doing all right?"

"Uh, yeah, fine," Biedick answered somewhat surprised. His face blushed.

Cy tossed his clipboard onto the desk and stood looking down at Biedick. He would choose his words carefully as he examined his *crushed fingerplates*.

Fingerplates by design were made of steel and had a curve to them so as to cradle the fingers. They do not bend easily. In fact, they cannot be bent without the use of a tool or outside force pressing down upon them. The fingerplates Cy picked up off the floor next to the leg of the chair were no longer curved. He was shocked to discover both plates were bent completely flat rendering them less than completely functional. Holding the fingerplates in the palm of his hand, Cy looked at Biedick.

"What is this all about?" Cy asked.

"Um, well, I don't know. They fell on the floor."

"No, Chuck, they didn't just fall on the floor. They were attached to your fingers with Velcro. You removed them, dropped them to the floor, and crushed them with the leg of the chair. What was your purpose here today?"

"Well, that was accidental."

"No, they're both bent. Again, Chuck, why?"

"Well, I don't know, I guess I stepped on them."

"No, you didn't step on them. You deliberately crushed them, and you know it."

Biedick had no further response.

Cy removed the other components from him. He pointed to the door. "There's the door. Don't even think about coming back."

Without a word, Biedick got up and left.

Cy sat down a moment to gather his thoughts. *I can't believe anyone would have the audacity to do such a thing.* He collected the crushed fingerplates and took them back down the hall to show Kimmestor.

"I can't believe it either. Now I've seen it all, the ultimate countermeasure attempt. No security clearance for Mr. Biedick."

"Right, now who's next?"

APPLICATION DISCONTINUED

When speaking to groups unfamiliar with polygraph, Cy Donovan never believed any good social purpose was served by getting into a full educational discourse on the use or effectiveness of countermeasures as applied to a polygraph examination. He preferred to stick with short discussions. A short discussion here will suffice.

There are a few different categories of the type of acts employed by examinees to alter the outcome of their examination. Generally, they fall into mental and physical countermeasures, employment of chemicals or pharmaceuticals, and miscellaneous, i.e., the fingerplate crusher discussed earlier.

The problem most subjects have who are determined to engage in countermeasures is their inability to suppress deceptive reactions to the relevant questions. Certainly, with a little bit of training, it isn't difficult to create realistic-looking reactions to noncritical questions. But how does one diminish or eliminate physiological responses to those questions deemed to be most threatening to their well-being? There is really only one way, and that is through aggressive, blatant efforts to initiate physiology in the noncritical questions.

Ill-intentioned examinees realize that once sitting in a chair, they cannot make their heart beat faster or slower, and they cannot make themselves perspire, but what they can do is alter their breathing. They also occupy their thoughts through dissociation.

Occasionally, they will attempt to inflict pain on themselves by placing a tack in their shoe or biting their tongue at a particular time during a test. Some will even attempt to contract their anal sphincter muscle at periodic intervals. Such movements can and will cause a distortion in the cardio tracing on the polygraph chart. A significant attempt of this nature was employed by a special agent applicant to the FBI in the summer of 2006.

George Smythe III was granted an appeal to sit for his third preemployment polygraph examination in Birmingham, Alabama. Smythe had been deemed inconclusive on his first exam and was automatically rescheduled for a follow-up test. Unfortunately for Smythe, he failed his second test primarily due to physiological responses to questions concerning his violation of the FBI's guidelines concerning drug use and sale.

Smythe made no admissions but promptly sent forth a letter requesting a retest. Despite a prior arrest for attempted auto theft and now a failed preemployment polygraph, the human resources division at FBIHQ once again felt it only proper to offer Mr.

Smythe a *third* exam, a third opportunity to squirrel his way into the FBI.

Cy Donovan was handed the task of testing Smythe this time. His experience taught him that applicants who come in on appeal are normally very cautious and forthcoming in their demeanor. *Respectful* and *obedient* are adjectives that normally describe these applicants as they are so thankful to have the opportunity to seek redemption. Such wasn't the case however with Mr. Smythe.

Smythe was timely with his appointment but rather cavalier and supercilious in his attitude. Smythe had a strong sense of pride. He was dressed professionally, and Cy opined that Smythe was more accurately putting on an act to get himself psyched up for the big game.

Prior to running any polygraph charts, Cy elected to get right to business in his pretest discussions with Smythe. He was eager to get to know his examinee, to get a flavor for what made this man tick. He soon discovered Smythe to be someone who would play his cards close to his chest. He answered Donovan's questions but certainly wasn't offering anything further. In other words, any information Cy wanted from George would only come after additional and continuous follow-up. This has a way of wearing out an interviewer.

After about twenty minutes of a less than successful attempt at rapport building, Cy would settle for Smythe's minimal cooperation and begin testing. He concluded the first chart with his typical announcement, "This test is over. Please remain still." He then let the cuff pressure out and announced, "You can relax."

No longer using an analog instrument, Cy pulled the first chart off the printer and compared it to the screen on his notebook computer. He really couldn't believe what he was seeing.

Across the top of the chart were the pneumograph or respiration tracings. These tracings were textbook perfect except for the momentous increases in inhalation/exhalation as each tracing left the baseline and climbed skyward before returning to homeostasis. This occurred three times throughout the chart, which was abnormal and an immediate red flag for countermeasures.

Adding to the aggravated rise in the respiration channel were abrupt changes in the cardio channel. These significant distortions in the pulse rate timely with the respiration changes were a clear indicator that Smythe was deliberately attempting to alter the outcome of this test. It appeared he needed to do this due to the significant reaction to one of the relevant questions as well.

Cy pondered for a moment, then decided to run chart 2 using the same format with the same order of questions to see if his examinee would be so brazen as to repeat what he had done on the first chart.

This time, Cy would watch him carefully from head to toe looking for unnecessary movements. Chart 2 was run and concluded without any peculiar movements observed. However, upon reviewing the chart, the tracings were once again indicative of countermeasures on the part of Smythe. This time, Cy also noticed a huge GSR reaction to one of the relevant questions. *Now is the time for a little something different.*

Cy would counter the countermeasure with a proactive question sequence to see if he could catch his examinee off guard. He began the third chart in the same manner as he had begun the first two. Halfway through the question sequence, he changed the order placing two relevant questions back to back. As suspected, another effort was attempted by Smythe to alter, if not artifact, the pulse rate tracing. This time, however, the pulse rate tracing reverted back to normal too quickly as Smythe's timing had been thrown off by the order of the questions. Chart 3 concluded, and Cy had seen enough.

Placing all three charts on the desk in view of Smythe, he called his attention to the abnormal tracings. "You're not so naïve, are you?" Cy asked.

"What do you mean?"

"Listen, one doesn't need to be an experienced polygraph examiner to be able to look at these charts and know that they look unusual."

Smythe looked over the charts and looked back at Cy and then stated, "You shouldn't be seeing any reactions in the drug questions."

"What would you call this?" Cy responded as he pointed to an eight-chart division rise in the GSR tracing on one of the charts. He then pointed at the abrupt changes in the respiration and cardio channels on each chart and commented as to how they were repeated on all three charts. He then pulled the charts away and got knee to knee with Smythe.

He began, "George, you can provide an explanation or leave the room, your choice."

"I'm not sure I understand."

"Sure you do. Do you want to talk to me about the research you've done on polygraph or abstain?"

"I don't have anything to say. I mean I've done no research if that's what you—"

Cy interrupted, "Listen, I've been in the business too long. Your deliberate attempts here today were so blatant it's comical. Now, you can be candid and forthright or you can stand in denial, and I'll have to ask you to leave. Which is it?"

Smythe sat back in his chair and took a deep breath. "I went online, discovered a book that discussed various ways to beat a polygraph test."

"And?"

"I didn't attempt to alter the first two tests before today."

"Okay, fine," Cy said. "But you had something going on here today. It is one of three things, George. Either you're biting your tongue, squeezing your rear end, or you have something going on in your shoe."

"You don't see consistent reactions in those drug questions," Smythe blurted out, not answering Cy's question.

"If I recall correctly, George, we've already addressed that. So you're choosing not to answer the question?"

"I've told you all I know. I'm not a drug user, and I'm not going any further with this."

"And we're not going any further with you."

With that announcement, George Smythe III immediately raised out of the chair. He gathered his suit coat and asked, "Where's the door?"

"Just down the hall, first door on your left."

In bombastic fashion, Smythe left down the hall walking right past the exit door to the end of the hallway. Frustrated, he made his way back to the door and was gone.

Application discontinued.

BIBLE CODE DECIPHERER

The cardio tracing jumped every time Cy asked the relevant questions to Archibald Budge a.k.a. "Hard Core." Not only was there a jump in the cardio channel, but he also observed a corresponding drop in the galvanic skin response. They were not the type of reactions he had seen before and certainly were not indicative of a genuine response normally associated with deceptive reactions during a polygraph test. Budge's reactions to the nonrelevant questions were not significant or out of the ordinary. Puzzled at first, Cy thought he had the cardio cuff on too tight, and Budge was unconsciously flinching as a way to combat a cuff too snug. Could this simultaneously influence the GSR tracing as well? His experience as an examiner was being challenged and his patience tried.

Archibald "Hard Core" Budge had found his way into the polygraph chair following his disclosure to local and federal law enforcement officials of a plot to kill a federal judge. Budge had escaped state custody in Louisiana during hurricane Katrina but was recaptured and found himself in a county jail in east Tennessee.

While in the slammer, Budge became acquainted with a few other choice citizens by the names of Buford "Tiny" Stichens, Brock "Shorty" Hollister, and Adam "Lil Nuts" Beacons. All four, to include Budge, were reportedly members of a street gang known as the Imperial Insane Vice-Lords. Members of the Vice-Lords often found themselves incarcerated for violent crimes and drug offenses.

In July 2006, Tiny Stichens found himself looking at a life sentence for his role in a robbery-gone-bad-to-murder incident in East St. Louis. The sentence handed down by a senior district court judge was appealed successfully, and Stichens was awaiting an opportunity to return to East St. Louis for resentencing.

Members of the Vice-Lords had plenty in common little of which was anything honorable. As such, it was certainly not out of the ordinary for these characters to commiserate and communicate with one another during their time together in the joint. It was during their time together in the county lockup that Archibald Budge saw a chance to help himself, or so he thought.

Budge, like other informants sometimes do, came forth with information concerning the hatching of a scheme by Tiny, Shorty, and Lil Nuts to have the judge killed who originally sentenced Tiny. As one might expect, this got the attention of the feds real quick.

Unbeknown to Shorty and Lil Nuts, Hard Core Budge was brought out of his cell one morning to reiterate his story to special agents from the FBI. Budge had a way of selling himself much the way a shyster of a low-budget car dealership might do. A thin man, he spoke with his hands, had an answer to every question, and he toyed with a handlebar mustache that had a long way to go before it was a handlebar.

According to Budge, Vice-Lords members Tiny, Shorty, and Lil Nuts were communicating with each other from cell to cell via a numerical code they had devised. This code, also known as a Bible code, consisted of a sequence of numbers only known by Vice-Lords members. Budge inferred to the agents that he had overheard the other members relating to each other with the use of these numbers. He insisted he was able to decipher these numbers and, as such, was confident that a plan was being put together by Tiny to have a judge taken out.

Threats on the lives of federal officials move swiftly through the investigatory process. Subsequent investigation following the Budge interview led investigators to doubt the authenticity of Budge's story. However, as is often the case with informant allegations, Budge's information had to be vetted and soon. The question the agents had to resolve was whether or not Budge was making up this plot in an effort to help his own cause and possibly reduce his own sentence. Hard Core had become a prime candidate for a polygraph exam.

Archibald "Hard Core" Budge appeared, in custody, for his polygraph session. Cy had been briefed well by his fellow agents regarding the facts and story perpetuated by Budge. He was also enlightened by Budge's demeanor and slightly overzealous cooperation during his interviews with the agents.

On the day of his polygraph, Budge held true to form. Although still cuffed, he stood right up, held out his hand, introduced himself as Cy entered the room. Before Cy could speak, Budge said, "Nice to meet you, sir. Always like to meet a real expert in his trade."

He didn't have to say another word. Cy knew exactly how this test was going to go. The verbal cue put forth by Budge set off the alarm clock for him. He immediately thought of another tidbit of advice given to him by his retired colleague, Rudy Mahovolich. *Watch out for the guy who stands right up when you walk in, the guy who is overly courteous or unnecessarily respectful. He is your phony. He is your crook.*

Cy had him uncuffed. The escorting agents left the room. He told Budge to have a seat while he sat down across from him. "As I understand it, they call you Hard Core, is that right?"

"Yeah, I guess I picked that up somewhere. For time served I suppose."

"And you're getting ready to serve some more time, right?"

"Uh, yeah."

"What do you prefer to be called?"

"The name is Arch-ee-bald Lee 'Hard Core' Budge."

"I see. How about I call you Archie?"

"Whatever works."

"Okay, fine. Archie, have you ever had a polygraph before?"

"No, have not."

"Do you know how it works?"

He chuckled and spoke, "I make it my business to know a little something about everything I get involved in."

"What do you know then about polygraph?"

"I know it's not always right."

"How do you know it's not?"

"I've been around the block a few times, sir. I'm a con, remember?"

Cy looked Budge straight in the eye as Budge displayed a pencil thin grin.

"Got a motive?"

"Motive? I can tell you this. If you all want to keep a judge alive, you better take heed of what I've been tellin' you guys."

Cy noted how he failed to answer the question directly. "Got it," he acknowledged. He would allow Budge to draw him into his story, then let the polygraph charts dictate his next course of action.

"So tell me about these Bible codes."

"What do you want to know?"

"Whatever you have to tell me."

"That's a bit loaded, you know? Listen," Budge leaned forward, "these are numerical codes you see. You wouldn't understand them if you're not, shall we say, in the club? What I'm saying is, Tiny speaks to the others through a series of numbers. He's determined to get revenge on this judge. I guess he didn't like the way the judge spoke to him or somethin'. But anyway, he's looking for help on the outside, you see?"

Cy nodded with interest. "It must be complicated."

"You adjust to it, you know? When you ain't got nothin' but time, you take interest in things you know somethin' 'bout."

"I'll bet you do."

Budge sat back in his chair.

Cy sensed he didn't really want to explain anything further. He cut to the quick. "You didn't make up any information about those codes, right?"

"No, no."

"And you're saying you certainly didn't make up any plot to harm the judge either?"

"No, no, no, no, no, no, no!"

"Good, good, Archie. We'll cover that on the polygraph, you know?"

"Right, right."

Cy spent a little time reviewing Archie's background with him and discussing some additional issues of concern to him. It wasn't long however before he knew it was time to put Mr. Budge on the box. He was anxious to get confirmation of what he already suspected. Budge sat straight up in the chair as Cy affixed the components to him.

In a most cooperative fashion, Budge took no issue with any of the questions posed by Donovan. His government issue V-neck shirt displayed a chest and neck that blushed when Cy reviewed the questions with him one more time. The room was quiet and warm, almost too warm. Deception was thick in the air, and Cy thought he could cut through it with a knife. But he wouldn't need it. Deception on this day was handed to him in the form of countermeasures.

"Did you deliberately make up any information about those codes?"

"No."

Cy was troubled as he saw the abnormal jump in the cardio tracing. He suspected a movement but saw nothing. It was difficult to observe the examinee and the chart tracing at the same time. "Have you made up any information regarding a plot to harm a judge?"

"No."

This time, a corresponding dip in the GSR was timely with another jump in the cardio tracing. Cy again observed nothing and checked his sphygmomanometer. The cuff pressure was proper, but his examinee was doing something improper. Rather than continue testing, he opted to address the matter immediately. The polygraph of Hard Core was essentially over.

"Archie, we have a problem here today, don't we?"

"What? Already?"

"Does Hard Core want to play hardball, or does Archie want to cooperate?"

"I don't understand. What more do you want from me?"

"You're flinching and moving unnecessarily during the test, and you know it. Now I don't have time to sit here and counsel you like a father preaching to a ten-year-old. We're both adults. You're incarcerated, and you don't care to be. But you made some poor judgments in the past, and you're paying for it. If you think you can reduce your sentence by creating a future event that isn't going to happen, you're very, very wrong. In fact, if this goes any further, you may very well lengthen your sentence because we'll press charges for providing false information to federal agents."

"But these guys are serious. I'm tellin' you, man, these—"

Cy reached for his cell phone and dialed up the case agent. "Come and get this joker, and call the US attorney. This event is not going to happen. He failed this test. He monkeyed with it. He's a phony."

"Dude!"

"Listen, Archie, I'm not your dude. You've had—"

"Okay, okay, okay, Mr. Don…?"

"Donovan."

"Right, Donovan. Okay, listen. These codes, you know, they're real. They consist of twenty-six variables. Once you know one word, you can decipher the rest."

"But you can't tell me exactly what you deciphered, can you?"

"Tiny got into the New Testament. There are too many variables in the New Testament, and it became too difficult for me to be sure of what I was hearing."

"Archie, you're trying, but you're not being forthright."

"Whaddya mean?"

"The complete truth, Archie, quit trying to make yourself look good. The game is over. Quit the charades."

"These guys speak in code."

"So what? You can't tell me we need to ramp up to protect a judge, can you?"

Archie was motionless.

"Can you?"

No response was forthcoming.

"Just as I figured. Game over."

"Are you gonna charge me?"

"Not my call. I will tell you this much. I need a statement from you, and it needs to be very clear and very truthful. Do you understand?"

Archie sighed and nodded.

"One more thing."

Archie looked up at Cy in a morose sort of way.

"I'll need an explanation as to what you were doing during this test."

Budge reached with his right hand and fingered his mustache. For the slightest instant, his eyes rolled up to the right.

Cy caught it. He reached for Archie's hand and placed it back down on the arm of the chair. "Nonsense, Archie. Just tell me."

Budge let out a long quiet sigh, then spoke, "Well, I have a problem, you know?"

"No, I don't know. You need to tell me just what that problem might be."

"I have to flinch my bicep muscle on occasion. Old injur—"

"Just bothers you when certain questions are asked, right?"

"Well…"

"And the finger movements?"

Budge reached for his mustache again then put his hand down quickly. He said nothing. He just grinned.

The door opened as the case Agent walked in to re-escort his prisoner down the hall to finalize his revised statement.

Hard Core looked over his shoulder. He saw the handcuffs in the case agent's hand. His grin was replaced with gloom as he realized his scheme bore no fruit.

STRAIGHT TALK ABOUT LIARS

Getting the confession requires practice and luck; practice often and hope you're lucky.

"It comes down to interpersonal skills boss. The agent who has them stands a good chance to develop into a decent interviewer or interrogator. The gruff, hard-nosed guy rarely gets it in the end. However, if you can couple his perseverance with the guy who relates well with people, you will have a winning combination. Our new agents need to understand that."

"Couldn't agree with you more, Cy, which is precisely why I called," the unit chief replied.

"Really?"

"That's right. I need someone from the polygraph unit to go to Quantico and speak at a new agent's class. Can you do it?"

"Sure. We normally have a thirty-minute block of instruction down there. As you probably know, I've done this in the past. Our previous unit chiefs have always supported the new agents classes this way."

"This one is going about it a little differently."

"Okay."

"You've got a two-hour block."

"Two hours? I can't go on about what we do for two hours! That's just not practical. It's just not something we discuss for—"

"Don't get excited. Listen to me. I need you to educate them on post-test work. Interview and interrogation. They simply never get enough of it in the other classes. You gotta script, right?"

"Yes. It's a rather formal discussion called 'Straight Talk About—"

"Yeah, yeah, that's it. Great! I'll count on you for the first Monday in August. Get with Donna Betts. She's one of the class coordinators, and she's got the curriculum. She'll have a time for you."

"Right, I know Donna. We'll get it done."

"Thanks, Cy."

"Any time, boss."

The class settled in quickly after the midmorning break. Cy had met several of the new agents in the hallway and as always, was quite impressed with how they carried themselves. They addressed him as sir, and their questions were logical and to the point. What he had to say to them this morning would also be logical but blunt, no psychobabble. They would get enough of that in the other classes. He spent the first twenty minutes discussing the uses of the polygraph within the FBI. Following a few questions, he began his lecture in earnest—"Straight Talk About Liars With or Without a Polygraph."

Ladies and gentlemen, what I have to say to you today is useful with or without a polygraph. This information has been absorbed from literature I have received over the years and from my experiences in law enforcement over the last twenty-five years.

I have provided you with handouts of my PowerPoint presentation, which highlights what I am about to say. Retain it, review it, and practice it. Once a month or so, take an hour out of your workday, pull this information off your shelf, and review it. Understand one thing: interview and interrogation (I & I) is a practice. If you don't strive to improve, if you don't practice, you will flounder when the game starts. If you don't want to excel at the practice of I & I, then you're wasting the time of those who rely on you to include fellow agents, supervisors, the general public, and yourself.

The information I am providing you is reliable, but understand there are exceptions to every rule or situation. That is why I & I is a practice. Suspects often confess following an interrogation that is done professionally with due consideration for their well-being. In other words treat them the way you would want to be treated, and they will be more likely to trust you.

Retain your authority without being arrogant, and they will talk to you. They will talk to you if you are good at your practice because they can't handle the guilt. But you must prove you are a competent interviewer. You must have good interpersonal skills. You have reviewed your material and practiced it with real subjects time and time again. In actuality, most of you won't do this, and you will find yourself depending on luck. Practice often, and hope you're lucky!

Now, when you bring the mope into your room, you sit him down, and you maintain a nonadversarial demeanor. You allow just one denial. After that, you calmly put your hand up, convincingly accuse him, get knee to knee with him, and interrupt him when he tries to deny. "You've already said that, Jimmy, tell me what happened after she got into your car."

Continue on with open-ended-type questions that will compel him to elaborate on the issue. Try not to challenge him by telling him his behavior shows he is lying. He will challenge you back, argue with you about it, and suppress that behavior throughout the remainder of your time with him.

One student raised his hand and inquired, "Do you normally have notes with you during your interview?"

Cy responded, "Yes, but be subtle in how you refer to them so as not to allow them to become a distraction. For instance, you might have a note that says 'rpm.'"

"Which stands for?" the student asked.

Rationalize, project, and minimize. Rationalize with him by giving him a self-satisfying, although incorrect, reason for his behavior. "Ernie, any woman who has treated you the way she treated you deserves to be punished. You just hit her harder than you intended."

Project the blame onto someone else. "Greg, I know that George had no reason to meddle in your affairs, and if it wasn't for him coming on to your wife like he did, I know you would have never struck your wife, am I correct?"

Minimize his actions. "Okay, Kenny, we know you struck her, but let's look at this. You had no intention to hit her as hard as you did, and you certainly did not kill her or put her in the hospital. She's not going to have any long-term problems because of this. It's really not that big of a deal, is it?"

Beware of personal space. Position yourself in a subtle fashion in front of him and between him and the door. If you hear talk about wanting to leave, advise him that he is here voluntarily. Most guilty subjects will sit for you if you treat them the way you would like to be treated. They want to convince you. They can't do that by leaving, so they sit and concoct a tale.

The innocent person will not stand for being accused of something he did not do. Within the first thirty minutes or so, he will tell you to pound sand if not immediately. The guilty will often sit for hours. Although he tries to convince you, his conscience wants him to talk about it. He will talk to someone in authority if he trusts the person.

Cy paused for a sip of water. His class had taken an interest. No one was dozing. In fact, they appeared quite attentive. He made an adjustment or two with his PowerPoint and continued.

Let's talk a bit about verbal cues. If you're subject says any of the following, rest assured he is being less than honest with you.

Q: "Frank, did you remove the cargo out of those gondolas over at the rail yard?"

A: "That's not possible. You can't take things out of there because guards log everyone in and out."

Now this question called for a direct response. However, he chose to spin a yarn without really answering the question. He *fails to answer the question directly*. He's hedging to buy time. Here's another involving cartage theft:

Q: "Jerry, did you leave that trailer load of meat in the alley for your brother to unload?"

A: "Well, if I did that, that would make me a thief, wouldn't it? And how could I retain my license if I were a thief? If I'm guilty of that, prove it."

Again, he *fails to answer the question directly*, and he *challenges you* for asking the question. Another example:

Q: "Dr. Morris, I have to ask you, did you inject Elizabeth with poison?"

A: Chuckling, Dr. Morris responds, "Just the other day, I was talking with some nurses on the floor about a pending lawsuit going on against the hospital across the street from ours because of the wrong medicine that was administered to a patient causing the patient to go into a seizure. Perhaps you read about it in the newspaper? Fortunately, I have a wonderful staff and a hospital that supplies me with state-of-the-art equipment that really prevents that kind of thing from happening. I certainly wouldn't jeopardize my career by trying to engage in an activity harmful to a patient."

He gives *overly specific answers* about irrelevant things but again never answers the question as asked. If you have to prod him to answer specific things about a crime, you can be sure he will struggle with the answer. You may get a shake of the head or a soft no followed up immediately by more rambling. If you prod him some more, he may say, "Look, I gave you my word. If I say I didn't do it, then I didn't do it." Still not the direct response you're looking for, is it? Here's another one concerning larceny from a bank:

Q: "Terri, did you take the $989?"

A: "I didn't take $989. I have been down this road before with the officer on Monday. As I told him, I lost money one time about two years ago, and I owned up to it, and the bank knows about it. Besides, that money came from the petty cash fund, and we've never had that much in that fund before, so something is wrong. Somebody has their figures wrong."

A couple points to consider here. When they tell you they have already answered that question, they do not want to answer it again because they are uncomfortable having to repeat the previous lie. Secondly, she may be right about the amount. Financial institutions notoriously error in the amounts they report missing, but there is money missing, and she took it!

The innocent person says, "Look, I didn't steal $989, and I didn't steal any money from this bank whatsoever, and I never have. Find the person who did it, and lock them up." The guilty person rarely suggests a jail sentence, but she will spar with you with a clever tongue and suggest you have the wrong amount and the wrong person.

Another: Joe has been brought in to be interrogated about an awful crime, and he comes prancing into your room rather nonchalantly addressing you as sir and commenting on your attractive necktie. In a polygraph pretest interview, he may say,

"Yes, sir, you're the expert, sir, whatever you say." Don't let his charades sway you. This is *manufactured inappropriate behavior*. Beware of this guy. He'll tell you about all the people he knows who could be responsible. He'll stand right up when you walk into the room.

Now how about the guy who uses *selective memory* when you interview him? You probably know the type. It may go something like this:

> Q: "Donny, were you in the warehouse yesterday at ten o'clock?"
>
> A: "Well, not that I can remember."

Okay, the event just happened yesterday and he has the gall to tell you he can't remember. Of course, this is baloney. People know where they were the day before. Furthermore, this question called for another yes or no answer. When they choose not to remember, close in time, rest assured they do remember. In fact, even if it was a year ago, if they committed a crime, they know what you're talking about. They may not remember precisely the calendar day, but they know they did the deed. They will buy time by responding with a memory lapse. Here's one of my favorites:

> Q: "Tony, did you harm that little girl?"
>
> A: "With God as my witness…" or, "Sir, I am a Christian."

Now I ask you, why does he have to *invoke religion* into the interview? Because he did it. That's why. I would fear God too if I knew I was going to hell for what I did, wouldn't you?

He is simply trying to make you think he is someone he is not. The guilty person has no alliance with the almighty. Therefore he just blurts it out without thinking that he is offending God by lying in his name, and he's insulting your intelligence.

I once gave a polygraph to a guy suspected of sabotaging parts at a lab. Just before I started running charts, he asked if I would share in a prayer with him. I held his hand most sincerely while he prayed he would pass my test, and I prayed for a conclusive result followed by a confession. He failed. I got most of it out of him. Although, he held back some as well. They always hold back about 25 percent of the complete truth. It is their way of retaining an ounce of dignity.

Cy paused again. "Any questions so far?" One raised his hand as Cy removed his suit jacket.

"Sure, go ahead."

"How would you handle the belligerent person who chooses to get harsh with you?"

"Look at it this way. You're on a ladder, and he's on a ladder. You need to stay one step above him in terms of civility. If he wants to take the conversation into the gutter, don't follow along. Don't get personal. Retain your professionalism. There will come a time when they try to take control of the interview. You cannot let that happen. Some of these clowns need to be woken up with an obscenity or two, and yes, I'm guilty of taking it that way but not for long. They need to know you're not just a lump of Jell-O. Once you put your mean streak on display, you generally won't have to do it twice. They will see you are for real and very capable of playing hardball. Some are too stubborn to face the facts, and neither you nor anyone else will be able to educate them. They will not be worth your time, but they will soon have plenty of time to do. On the other hand, you run into some mopes who will deny they did the deed, but they never get too upset at your accusations. They just sit there.

Now let's talk about guilt. Your mopes are eaten up with it, and they're concerned about what you know. They just don't know how much you know.

I've got to tell you, if you put me in this position and I'm innocent, I'm going to tell you that you're wrong in so many words. "No, I didn't do it, you can go pound sand because I'm outta' here." That is what I expect to see from an innocent person. The innocent person will not stand to be humiliated for very long.

As an investigator, if I think I have to get accusatory with someone to get that innocent response, I will do it regardless if I offend an innocent person. I have to feel good that what they're telling me is truthful. You can always go back to them later when the case is resolved and apologize. Make a special effort to do that, and a good citizen will respect you for it. Or you may get cussed out! It's not an easy profession—if it was, more people would be doing it, and your caseload would be a lot less.

Okay, you will sometimes get this guy, who, on occasion, will agree to sit for your polygraph without hesitation. So you make the arrangement with the polygraph examiner and the date and time comes and goes, but he doesn't appear. You may or may not have trouble getting in touch with him. When you do reach him, you get any number of excuses from the simple "I forgot" to "My employer had too much work for me to do," "My brother advised me not to go through with it," or "I hear it's not always accurate," or of course some just lawyer up. This is all a good clue you are looking at the likely perpetrator.

How about the *shrewd liar* who *throws you a bone*? This guy comes in and after a couple hours of interviewing, tells you he took a screwdriver from the hardware store, but this was when he worked there, and he denies being part of the burglary that netted some thieves four toolboxes, three power drills, and a generator. He claims to know one of the thieves but doesn't associate with him anymore. He swears this is the truth, and the only reason he is telling you this is because he trusts you.

This guy is hoping you bite off on this bone and leave him alone. He's given you something because he knows you're not likely to prosecute on such a small matter if he wasn't actually at the scene of the burglary. He fits our shrewd liar category.

"He gives you a bit here, a bone there, and hopes you'll drop the matter. He may even try to call your bluff and say, 'Okay, if you want me to say I did, fine, but I didn't really do it.' A sort of, pseudoadmission, if you will. He is banking on you not taking him seriously. In actuality, he is just a half step away from giving up the full story. Don't let this guy off the hook. What about the people who come in with the *qualified responses*? Examples of qualified responses include "basically," "sort of," "I believe," "possibly," "fundamentally," "perhaps," "I'm not trying to evade the question, but," "I know you're looking at me like I'm lying, but," "You may not believe this but…"

> Q: "Jackie, were you part of that crew that stole the SUV from behind the grocery store last Saturday night?"
>
> A: "Well, you see, *basically*, I was just standing on the corner while Jimbo and his brother scoped out the alley."
>
> Q: "Did you know they were going to steal a car?"
>
> A: "Well, *I believe* they were looking for Jimbo's girlfriend. She *probably* gave them permission to use the car because I don't really *think* they would just take the car, you know, I mean I *sort of* just figured it was cool, you know."

Jackie is just a simple liar. He knows why they went into the alley, he knows how the SUV was stolen and where it was taken. And if it was taken to a chop shop, he knows where that is too!

Cy paused momentarily. A student in the front row took advantage and asked, "But, sir, you can't always assume the mope in fact knows the entire scheme of his cohorts."

That's a good point—you can't. But you need to know the vast majority of the time he will know more than he tells you. Count on it. You will learn these lessons after you start believing the person in the mope chair, and later you find you have egg on your face because you thought you had the truth.

Now here's an example of someone not being *forthright*. These too are shrewd liars. I personally think these are the worst liars because they think they are getting away with something by hanging their hat on a crooked nail—a nail they think you don't know is crooked.

Q: "Jason, were you there when Ben was shot?"

A: "I was at Eddie's house, and I didn't shoot Ben."

Well, it's true. He was at Eddie's house, and you already know someone else shot Ben, but he's not being forthright with you by not telling you he dropped off the killer at Ben's house on his way over to Eddie's, and he knows who the killer is and what the killer was going to do. This is the guy who fails the polygraph on the issue of "who shot who" because he chooses to withhold key information from investigators.

Beware of the *intelligent liar*. You will come to recognize this joker from such comments as "You have no comprehension of how my company works" or "You wouldn't have any knowledge or understand what we do." This is the guy who will question you about your understanding of their business.

I once had an attorney that I got indicted on a bankruptcy fraud matter. During my interview of him, he told me that if I knew how to interpret the US bankruptcy code, I would understand that what he did was perfectly right and ethical to do. For some reason, a judge didn't see it that way, and he lost his law license for five years.

Okay, let's talk about understanding nonverbal behavior and how it relates to verbal cues. One thing you have to understand about nonverbals or body language is the word *clusters*. It is no secret in the industry that a good interrogator looks for body language in clusters, and he incorporates those deceptive nonverbal movements with the deceptive verbals to form the clusters. Now let's get down to it.

When we talk about nonverbal deceptive behavior we are talking about behaviors that occur in clusters of at least two or more. They can be two nonverbals simultaneously, a verbal with a nonverbal simultaneously, or two verbals simultaneously. This is one area where rookie investigators often error.

Listen carefully when I say this. None of the following nonverbals mean anything during an interview unless you see them in clusters. Let me add that I like to see clusters more than once during the same interview session. We are talking about grooming gestures such as inspecting fingernails, picking lint, scratching, wiping sweat, adjusting glasses or jewelry, or protecting the groin. Additionally, you will often see them covering their mouth, coughing, clearing their throat, or rubbing their eyes. This list is not all-inclusive as there are others.

Let's up the ante a bit. When you see them shifting their feet, their hips, or their elbows simultaneously with another movement or verbal cue, your antenna should go way up. When it comes to shifting those joints that "fix" one to the chair, you need to be concerned especially when these movements come in a timely fashion with the asking of the question, presentation of a photo or evidence. These are not micromovements.

A few more peculiar nonverbals commonly associated with deception include the open-palms in a bargaining gesture, the tilted head at an angle while looking you in the eye with his fist covering his mouth, the cold, hard stare as if to intimidate you, or the guy who moves backward in the chair more often than he should. Let's not forget the guy who comes in wearing shades and a hat daring you to ask him to remove them.

Of course you also have the unusually neat dresser who is a bit too well manicured for his profession. Finally, you will see the crutch-bearers. These are the characters that bring a file with them to the interview or another person, an alibi if you will or someone who will testify to their integrity. They want to take you on psychologically two to one.

Watch for the verbal/nonverbal disconnect. You'll know it when you see it. It may look something like this: You confront your subject, accuse him of the murder, and he nods in agreement with you, then denies he did it. Or you accuse your subject, and he sobs on your shoulder, gathers himself and his tears, looks away from you, and cold-heartedly denies the killing. Of course there is also the guy who can't get his words right after you accuse him: "Yes, I did, din't, didn't, I mean it's up to the courts deci… um, to decide." All the while his head is in his hands. Remember, you won't see the verbal/nonverbal disconnect from the innocent person. The reason is they are confident in what they are telling you. They're confident because they're not telling lies.

When it comes to basic kinesics, understand that human behaviors are learned during childhood and often are passed on from one generation to the next through genetics. A person's gestures may give us a clue, but no one truly knows the vocabulary of kinesiology as it applies to body language communication.

To sum up nonverbal behavior, remember that single behaviors mean nothing. Think *clusters*. Behavior must be timely with the stimulus—i.e., when the question is asked during an interview. Also, these behaviors should be consistent when the stimulus or question is repeated. Don't forget that your subject is watching you as you are watching him. Therefore, don't look at your watch! He'll size you up in a heartbeat and wait you out.

Cy paused. "Does anyone need a break before I get into individual crimes and who perpetrates them?"

A couple new agents shifted in their seats, but no one left the room. "I'll keep going. If anyone needs to take a break feel free to do so."

A difficult person to break down is this twisted character who seeks out children for his own sexual gratification. I would argue that he cannot be cured regardless of how long he is treated. He has to be contained, out of reach of potential victims. This of course is not real practical once they get out of prison.

In actuality, a child molester is offended by his behavior, but he will find it quite difficult to acknowledge the immorality of it. Hence, he maintains his innocence. You will see these perverts affiliated with jobs related to children. He may work as a magician or clown. He may involve himself with youth groups or be heavily involved with young people at a church. He may be an umpire, referee, or scoutmaster. He is intimidated by adults. Therefore, he surrounds himself with the activities of the youth.

If I may be so bold, I can tell you with confidence if a child of minor years reports that Uncle Charley touched his peepee, you can wager a month's pay it is no fairy tale. Young children do not have a reason or a strategy in mind to make this up. You can bet another month's pay that Uncle Charley has diddled around with other young peepees in his day. In fact, he will likely have a network of young boys he goes back to time and again.

Now you ask, "How do you break these guys?"

Oftentimes, child predators prey on dysfunctional families. This gives them an edge if the father is no longer part of the family unit or seldom around. Uncle Charley provides an outlet for the boy whose mother perceives a need for fatherly guidance or the mother is derelict in her duties.

It may be useful to approach Uncle Charley in this manner: "Charley, you know the boy needs an adult male presence in his life, and your motive was good by offering to take him fishing, or whatever. It wasn't your intent to do anything immoral with him, but you just lost site of yourself here. As you're sitting on the blanket with him along the riverbank, you recognize an opportunity to satisfy your own sexual needs. Certainly, you love children. And soon you and he begin to talk. Pretty soon, you offer him a stick of gum that drops down between his legs. Together, Charley, you, and he look for it. And you accidentally put your hand on his thing."

Now it isn't long before Charley tells you he has these inclinations to do this sort of thing with boys, and he can't help himself.

You may have to work another theme on him such as revenge against the mother for being a poor mother or some such angle, but you bring him around if you show you care about his well-being. You keep the pressure on, keep him focused, don't get off on a tangent. You have to get into the weeds with these people. It is most disgusting, but you have to get into their world.

You have to explore with Uncle Charley just what he sees when he's looking for that stick of gum, what he hears the boy say, what he says, how he feels, what his state of arousal is, etcetera. If you can't get into his world, you won't get the confession. Quite frankly, most of us can't. Our moral upbringing won't allow it, and we carry a badge, which attests to an even more elevated status of morality we try to live with. But the fact of the matter is the badge compels you to pursue his world for the sake of the children and for justice. Questions?

The class was too busy with note-taking. Cy moved off the PowerPoint and spoke from memory. He had their attention. He continued.

Hopefully you get the general idea with these people. Every situation is different, but the bottom line is that you have to understand how they think, visualize with them, and they in turn will visualize you as someone they can trust.

Let's talk a bit about the rapist. Most of you will find your rape suspect has a criminal history. First-time offenders are rare. Work with your local departments to conduct searches within their archives. You may find a subject with a criminal history indicative of a rape suspect.

Once you have someone in your room and you've reached a point where you know you are going to interrogate him, it will become important for you to get his acknowledgement that he placed his penis into her vagina. All you really need here is an admission to some sort of penetration.

At this point, I don't care if she consented or not. It's not important how he got it done so long as he admits to some sort of penetration. Oh sure, it is important to get a precise truthful account of things, but you will get that eventually. You have to get to first base before you can get all the way around. You do that by establishing penetration. You may have conflicting stories as your case reaches the halls of the courthouse. That is fine. Her story will normally prevail over his. If her story isn't compelling, most prosecutors won't take it to trial.

At this juncture Cy got the attention of another student, who offered up an experience she had as a local cop interviewing a rapist.

Cy responded and thanked her for sharing this with the class. He then added, "Please share stories like this with one another while here at the academy, not just in class. This is how we all learn in this business."

You will find themes dealing with seduction also work well with these monsters. The *common act* approach will have success from time to time. What you want to try to do here is keep your subject from looking at himself like he's the scum of the earth. Even though that is what he is. If he believes that what he did is something guys do on a routine basis or because he was the victim of seduction, you will find he will listen to you. Like the child molester, you have to get him to admit to a sexual act. Whether it is penetration or attempted penetration, you must establish sexual contact. Once you have established sexual contact, then you have him in a position of compromise.

One thing you can be sure of is that these guys abhor the thought of going to prison. They will talk in a circle over and over. The more they talk, the more concentric their circle becomes. Keep them talking. Eventually you will be discussing rehabilitation opportunities they will envision as they ride the bus all the way to the federal lockup.

"I've had enough sex. How about you?" Cy got his share of chuckles from the class. "Let's get violent now and talk about the armed robber."

You will find that many of these jokers aren't nearly the bullies they portend to be out in the street. They're actually cowards hiding behind a gun. Pardon the expression, but they're frequently just scared little shits. There are exceptions, and we'll talk about them too.

Oftentimes these guys are affiliated with a gang of sorts. They have a fear of someone in their little click talking. You discuss with your subject the cold, hard fact that eventually someone in the group gets jammed up and starts talking to save his own ass. He will understand that.

You stress how important it is that he isn't the one who gets jammed up. And for him to avoid any such predicament, it is imperative he cooperates with you to get the best deal he can early in the game. Let's face it, you're selling jail time, and selling time in the slammer is the same as selling anything else. The early birds get the best deal. Be sure he understands he can be the force that penalizes the others instead of being the victim that gets penalized. He will surely be the victim if he fails to act.

Another approach with an armed robbery suspect is the *stop before you ruin your life* argument. "Sammy, you have probably come close to shooting someone in the past. You may have started with juvenile pranks such as stealing purses and such, but you've graduated now to armed robbery. Eventually, you're going to hurt someone. You're going to kill someone when you have no intent to do such a thing, Sammy." Focus on getting him to understand that he is getting gradually worse with his criminal acts.

You also have the theme dealing with the fact that some robberies are not *premeditated*. "Listen, Jeremy, you didn't intend to threaten anyone or to use a gun. You only wanted the money, right? Problem is, someone came along whom you didn't expect so you just acted without thinking this thing through."

You're trying to get him to cough up something. Get him to acknowledge he was there, and you will steamroll from that point on. He will give you some self-serving story initially. This is fine. Now you have him talking. He will deny the dastardly act, but you will have his acknowledgement that he was there.

There is no let up on your part. You're knee to knee now, and you persist. You don't look at your watch, you don't look at the door or your partner if he is in the room. You look at your subject. Your eyes will bore a hole into his soul. You tell him as much, "Jeremy, I'm going down the ladder into the depths of your soul. Together, you and I are going to kick up a few skeletons, and then we're coming back up. You with me, Jeremy? Now let's get it resolved. You didn't intend for this to turn out like it did, did you?"

And of course you may have the *drugs and alcohol excuse* to work with. This is a theme that essentially gives him a way out. You are telling him people don't do these things if they are sober, and he wouldn't have either. Emphasize with him he will have to come clean—that it was drugs or alcohol that clouded his judgment. You tell him he is as decent of a citizen as anyone else and if it weren't for the awkward pressure of his peers, he wouldn't have been under the influence of any drugs or alcohol at the time. Stress upon him if he expects to sway the court to seeing his side of it, he will have to be honest regardless of how embarrassing it may be to him.

Of course, there is more to it than this, you are simply trying to give him an excuse to latch onto temporarily. Let him give you the horseshit, and then you can dig around in it to find the golden gem of truth you know is there.

"Okay, four more to go. We have auto theft, terrorism, espionage, and the murderer. Are you all still with me?" Cy got his share of affirmative nods and moved on.

Stealing cars. *Just taking a car for a pleasure trip* is a common theme often used with these thugs. You plant in his mind that you sincerely believe he only intended to borrow the car and that he would return it. Press upon him if he doesn't come clean, the court will get the idea he did intend to steal it for himself and will try him for auto theft. However, if he cooperates with investigators in a truthful manner, he will have a good chance of being tagged with a far lesser charge depending on which state you are in. It will be his choice. He can play hardball and take his chances, or he can get a burden off his shoulders.

Of course you never promise him anything. You're simply giving him an education on how things work based on your experience. Sometimes, cars are stolen on a dare or the spur of the moment. You can drive this into his mind as a way of saving face also. "Actually, Lejuan, the owner is at fault here. He should never have left his car running when he went back into the apartment. We know you didn't wake up with a plan to steal a car that day. You only wanted to borrow it long enough to see how it rides. Now, if you make it look like you're into grand auto theft when all you really wanted to do was take it out for a trial run and return it, the court may burn you for it. What would you rather be identified as, Lejuan, a petty larcenist or a grand thief?"

Again, what you want to do is get him to acknowledge he took the car. Once you have that admission, your foot is in the door. Soon you and he will be climbing the ladder of justice. Do it right, do it professionally, and he'll actually thank you for it in the end. He'll actually thank you for setting him on a straight course even though he's going to prison for three years.

When you can get mopes to actually thank you for ruining their day, then you know you've earned the title of special agent. That is what we do, folks. We ruin the lives of the criminal mind for ruining the lives of the honest citizen. They do it illegally, but you will do it legally. Therein lies the justice.

The terrorist. Unfortunately, unlike years past, this is a subject who is finding himself on our radar screen more often than we would like. Whether your subject is domestic or international, many of the same rules apply. However, while you may be undaunted in approaching your domestic terrorist, you will find it necessary to do a little homework prior to entering the room of the subject who is of Arab descent. Due to recent world events, for our purposes here today, we will focus on the interrogation of those people who are of various Islamic extremist/terrorist groups. Please take the time to educate yourself on the particulars of Islam, Al-Qaeda, and the Taliban. The handouts provided will give you at least a thumbnail sketch of what you should be aware of before interviewing these people.

It is not my intention here today to get into a diatribe with you on which religion is the right religion. I frankly don't care what your persuasion is, but if you're going into an interview with someone of Arab culture, you had better care about his or her beliefs or at least have some understanding of them if you wish to have any success at all.

You should know that an Arab named Muhammad founded Islam over six hundred years after the death of Christ and that Muhammad was born in Saudi Arabia, Mecca to be precise. You should know that the Quran or Koran is the Muslim's Bible that contains the so-called supernatural revelations of Muhammad he received from God through an angel, Gabriel. And you should know that Islam is comprised of both the Sunnis who make up the majority of all Muslims and the Shiites, a minority. This separation came about as a result of no named successor after Muhammad died. This is not all you should know.

Be aware that Muslims worship in a mosque. Mosques are growing exponentially now throughout the US. While there are certainly legitimate Muslims who proclaim their faith in these mosques, there are also radical Muslims who attend these mosques and get their inspiration for terror through meetings with others who are of the terrorist mindset. Whereas the Catholic church has a priest, the mosque is lead by a mullah or imam. Don't presume that the mullah is the instigator of a terrorist element. Most are legitimate but unfortunately, some will turn a deaf ear to those conspiring ill will. You may have an informant one day who is a mullah, and it is important you establish the right relationship with him.

It is important you are familiar with Ramadan. Ramadan is observed by Muslims as it is a commemoration of the first revelation of the Quran to Muhammad. As part of this commemoration, Muslims will fast dawn to dusk for about thirty days during Ramadan. If you are considering a polygraph of a Muslim during Ramadan, be aware that his physiological responses may be at a minimum due to lack of food, water, and sleep.

You will acquire more information on Arab culture as your career grows. You should already know that Al-Qaeda is one international terrorist network founded by the late and misguided Osama bin Laden. It is through Al-Qaeda that bin-Laden sought to rid Muslim countries of US influence by inciting a holy war or Jihad.

Finally, have an understanding of the Taliban who are comprised of primarily ethnic Pashtuns. Taliban are harsh Islamic fundamentalists who controlled Afghanistan in the late 1990s and into the new millennium. The desire of the Taliban has been to install a regime based on their fundamentalist understanding of Islam. It was through the Taliban that a protective umbrella, so to speak, was provided for bin Laden and Al-Qaeda.

When it comes to these terrorists, these demons from hell, remember to keep some key elements in place for your interrogation. Like any other serious crime, your interview should be conducted in an environment you control. It should be just you and the subject, and your initial approach with this guy is nonaccusatory. You will bridge from your nonaccusatory interview to questions which will be more behavior-provoking.

As with other crimes, you will provide him with a moral justification of his action. He will deny, and you will forestall those denials by not allowing them to come forth. You are the one in control.

One option here is to offer him a choice—i.e., "Has this been your idea for some time, or did you just act spontaneously to something that upset you?" If your subject opts for the less threatening choice, then you proceed with questions that are nonleading in an effort to get the full story.

Certainly, you have the religion theme to work with here. You sit square with him and probe as to whether his actions were due to his own personal beliefs or were they a result of religious teachings and persuasions from others. Again, you give him choices always assuming it is one or the other.

As has been discussed earlier, rationalize, project, and minimize with him. He can rationalize his behavior if, in his mind, it was based on fundamentalist beliefs. Allow him that rationale even though it is evil and misguided. He will have time to correct his thinking when the jury returns.

Suggest someone for him to blame. It is always easy to blame our own government for his heinous acts. Take that position with him for a while. After all, we do make mistakes around the globe. Make him believe that you too are disgruntled with the US's "oppressive" influence in Third World countries. You may not believe this, but by taking this position, you offer him an entity to blame.

You can actually minimize a terrorist's act. "Obviously the financial loss could have been much greater. In comparison to other such acts in the past this one pales in comparison. Not nearly as many people died." You may even suggest that he really only intended property damage, and he had no intent to harm people. Now of course any property damage and any death is unacceptable, but you will let him believe as long as the disaster was minimal in comparison to others, his efforts succeeded in bringing attention to a serious issue. Certainly not the right way to go about it, but all you are trying to do here is get an admission. Get your foot in the door with this monster, and eventually, you can introduce him to the world of a US penitentiary.

I would like to move off the terrorism subject now and spend a few minutes in discussion of espionage before we close it with the murderer. You will not have the opportunity to interview or interrogate many spies. However, I would be remiss if I didn't address this with you.

For those of you who find yourself working in the counterintelligence arena for very long, you will need to be keenly aware of a few things. Let's talk about their motives. Money. Money is a big carrot that is often dangled in front of them especially if they are in bad financial shape, i.e., near bankruptcy, two mortgages, kids in college, skyrocketing credit card balances, etcetera.

So the need for cash to offset these issues and support a family will be a theme you will explore with your subject. As with themes in other crimes, you are projecting blame for the deed to something other than the subject's own direct irresponsibility. You're helping him find a palatable excuse. After all, no one is perfect. Most of us have mismanaged our money at least a little bit along the way in life. You will share that with him and help him see that.

Another hand went up for Cy, however, he deflected the question for after class, due to the fact he was past allotted time, and pressed on.

Another argument that often applies is the *passed over for promotion* or the *low pay* theme. You will see many times throughout your career where the more qualified person gets screwed out of a promotion because the lesser qualified individual either knows someone on the career board, gets more face-time with superiors, or just plain looks better in a suit. We all know one, a blue-flamer in an empty suit.

Unfortunately, the government is good for these slights, and many have had to shoulder a biased selection process throughout a career because of it. You can share this argument with your subject and watch his nonverbals as you go along. Chances are you will already know if this theme is a likely motive after having done some preliminary investigation.

When it comes to disgruntlement, we sometimes get the person who wants to teach the organization a lesson for poor security. This is a great theme to work into because you can make the argument that by engaging in espionage, your subject is actually benefitting the organization in the long run by revealing their security weaknesses. Your subject becomes a *martyr* for a good cause. Of course, this is poppycock, but you make him see the value of his actions in so many words. In essence, the organization becomes stronger and more secure due to his efforts.

"Robert Hanssen," voiced a student from the back of the class.

"Good example," Cy chuckled.

Your sincere belief and effort in conveying this to him is critical. He will know he is looking at prison time, but in the end, you find a way for him to see how good things can come out of it if he cooperates with you. He can be regarded throughout history as a man who brought about positive change to an outfit that in the long run saved a country! A good investigator with sound and sincere interpersonal skills can convey that baloney to the downtrodden fool who made a horrendous decision in his life.

You may also encounter the left or right wing extremist who, for political reasons, sees fit to bring harm to a country he sees as a sinking ship. This will be the guy who has lost hope that his own political beliefs will ever prevail. As such, he has latched onto a cause or an ideology he subscribes to as the only way for a society to function. Now his patience has worn thin, so he makes the decision to bring about change another way. This poor, pitiful soul needs a partner who shares his concerns. You become that partner throughout your interview with him and sympathize with his misguided ideological philosophy. Much the way you partner-up with the child molester you become someone he can trust.

You may find the person who has gone the espionage route for political reasons may belch out his admissions very quickly, but on the other hand, he can also be quite reluctant and not trust anyone with the government. It will be a roll of the dice as to which personality you have the pleasure of dealing with. If it is the former, consider yourself lucky. If it is the latter, well, you tried. You won't get them all.

Finally, you may have an opportunity that provides you some leverage if your subject was caught with damaging classified material at home or elsewhere. Here you may employ the argument that someone else in the organization failed to do their job, and you were only safeguarding the material until you could get back to the office. If he has been caught with it, chances are he has thought of this excuse already but is unsure if he should try his luck with it. By opening it up with him, he may become more comfortable with that excuse because quite frankly, what else is there?

Allow him to go this route as a way of prolonging the interview so that he will have time to measure you as someone he can trust to look out for his well-being. You will likely be able to unravel this excuse for him depending on what else the investigation has revealed. If he has a habit or pattern of taking the crap out of secure space, his goose may be cooked.

Your skills will be tested regardless of which theme you pursue with the espionage character. They know they are drowning in hot soup, and many will lawyer up before you get a chance to practice. But you will have your opportunities the longer you work these violations. Make the most of them. Exhaust your themes and never give up too soon.

As we discuss the murderer, I want you all to listen very carefully now. We're in the homestretch, and this is important. You will all come face-to-face with killers more often than you care to. The bright side of the picture I am about to paint for you however is the fact that the killer is an easy person to interrogate.

Yes, that's right. The murderer is easier than the thief, robber, or the spy, and some will argue even easier than the child molester.

Why is that you may ask?

Emotionality. Murder shocks the conscience. Emotions flow with the event more so than other crimes. There is simply more on the line here and your subject knows it. He is caught up in these emotions and you must take advantage of that. Society will condemn him for the act, and as such, he will have trouble devising a self-satisfying but incorrect reason for what he did.

Your approach with this demon is to hit him head-on by making it clear to him all the evidence you have against him even if it is only circumstantial. Like the others, you settle for only one denial, and you move forward. You are knee to knee, eye to eye. Wherever his eyes go, yours follow. You are persistent but professional.

He will need to be clear his remorse is critical, especially as this thing moves in front of a Judge and jury. If he is seen as some arrogant prick, his future will be in serious jeopardy. It is your job to be sure he understands this.

Traditionally, the courts look for a willingness to repent on the part of the defendant. Without it, he is doomed. It takes courage to admit to a wrongdoing. Be sure he finds that courage.

Cy pressed on.

You will be prepared for this interview as you may only get one shot at him. You will have a number of themes in your pocket. Frequently, you can start out with putting the blame on the victim. "Benjamin, you had no intention of hurting anyone, but under the circumstances, you had no choice because your own life was on the line. If that homeowner had not threatened you and had not reached for that gun, you never would have shot him." You're assuming he did it. You know he did it, and you convey that to him. To do otherwise is to show lack of confidence on your part, and he will see through that. "Now, Rick, I've got to believe you would never have beaten your wife to death had she not been threatening to hurt your little girl. I'll bet she's done this before, hasn't she?"

You also have the drug and alcohol theme available. This is the lack of responsibility due to an unclean mind approach. It's similar to placing the blame on the victim. "Karen, you have no criminal history to speak of, and if it hadn't been for the fact you were drinking all night, you would not have done this." Courts are sympathetic in these cases as they have a problem with handing out long sentences to people who weren't thinking with a clear head.

The killer must understand the big picture. You must make him see it. Again, you make no promises, no threats, no coercion, and you never speak or appear to speak on behalf of any judge or prosecutor. Be straightforward, and he will respect you for that.

Occasionally, you will have multiple suspects involved. This works out because it allows you *the use of another* argument. "You're not the one who actually fired the gun, are you? Ferdie, now listen to me. You may be a victim of circumstances here if you're not the one pulling the trigger. You are only hurting yourself by lying about it. I mean if you two went in that house to get your dope back and your buddy lost control and did something you guys didn't plan, then why are you taking the hit? It wasn't your intention to hurt anyone, right? Or are you the one who shot him? Perhaps you tried to stop him from doing this thing. No one will know, Ferdie, unless you clear the air. Now help us out here before all the wrong people get the wrong idea."

You are simply trying to get him to admit some form of participation in the act. It's like loosening carpet. Once you have it loose, it's a lot easier to roll up. You will roll him up with the facts, but to do so, you must understand the emotions of the moment and apply the pressure.

Study his nonverbals. You must pursue because I guarantee you that murder works on the soul. Sometimes his ego will get in the way of telling you the truth. Point out to him that a court of inquiry has more sympathy for a humble person who has remorse but very little sympathy for arrogance. You will hear him say many times, "How can I admit to something I didn't do?" If he didn't do it, then why is he still sitting there listening to you work your themes? The innocent person doesn't stand for that, would you?

He may also say, "If I told you I did it, I'd by lying." If they want to take that position, get them to theorize how they would have done it if they had the propensity to do such a thing. Get them to relive the act. Sometimes you discover that your suspect has already relived the act with an inmate. Strange how often this sort of information gets back to you, and when it does, the game is half over.

Remember this when it comes to killers—most will eventually tell someone the truth at some point in their life. They will also confess to someone in authority whom they respect and trust. That someone can and will be you. You have to earn their respect and trust.

Here is something else very important I have discovered over the years that I refer to as the polygrapher's paradox...if your subject truly believes you care about his well-being, he will talk to you. The trick is getting him to believe you truly care when in fact, most of us really don't care. The paradox being that you really must care in order to convey your concern for him effectively. Think about that one, class. We care about our loved ones, but can we find it in us to genuinely care about the mope sitting in front of you who has just killed someone or brought serious harm to someone or their property?

Again, I & I is a practice. Work at it. Don't leave this job up to some prison chaplain ten years down the road while the mope is rotting away on another charge. See to it that it is *you* who brings justice to the victim and the victim's family.

Take pride in developing a reputation as a bulldog, a persistent competitor for the truth. You will not get them all. However, if you believe in yourself, hone your skills, and practice often, you will get your share. You will roast your share of liars.

Class, I am past my allotted time. It's been my pleasure to speak with you this morning. I wish you all the very best in your careers. I'll be around through lunch, so if any of you have any questions, feel free.

As Cy started for the door, he heard some vigorous handclapping from a gentleman standing in the doorway of the classroom. This, in turn, brought on a nice applause from the class. He was surprised to see his old friend Rudy Mahovolich.

"Cy, I believe you're blushing," Rudy said as he held out his hand.

"Rudy, great to see you! What brings you down here?"

"You know since retiring last month, I have a little time to kill, so I came down to the academy to see a few people one last time."

"Well, I'm glad you looked me up. How have you and the family been?"

"I'm doing just great, thanks for asking. Family's fine also. And you?"

"Doing great. Got detailed here to do this little talk on I & I."

"Yeah, I know."

"Really, how?"

"The unit knew I was down here, so they hit me up on my new cell and asked me to look you up and pass along a message."

"And what might that be?" Cy asked suspiciously.

"Knoxville has a source living in a tree house they want tested."

"What?"

Rudy laughed as the two of them walked down the hallway. "I'm serious, Cy, you can't make this stuff up!"

EPILOGUE

Polygraph testing in the criminal arena has long been the bread and butter of the FBI's Polygraph Program. Whether it be suspects, informants, or actual subjects involved in criminal offenses, it has been through the testing of these people that the Bureau's polygraph examiners established their reputations.

From the mid-1970s all the way to the new millennium, stories like Cy Donovan's were commonplace and common chatter among Bureau examiners at annual polygraph conferences. We learned from each other's experiences and became better interviewers and interrogators as a result. Although we had no quota, no agenda, we took tremendous pride in gaining confessions and admissions from the deviants in our society seeking to hide the truth. As we entered into the twenty-first century however, two key events would play a dramatic role in altering the course of the FBI's polygraph program.

First and foremost, the arrest of Robert Hanssen on February 18, 2001, had a devastating affect on the Bureau. The mere thought that one of their own special agents had become a turncoat for the communists was inconceivable. Not only had he violated his sworn oath to "support and defend the Constitution of the United States against all enemies, foreign and domestic" and to "bear true faith and allegiance to the same," but he had done so since 1979.

A thorough and complete understanding of his wrongdoings in the area of espionage will not be attempted here. Enough has already been written concerning the exploits of Bob Hanssen and more will likely be written in the future. Suffice it to say he appeared to have no concern for compromising the American citizenry.

What is germane to the focus of this book is the influence the Hanssen tragedy had on the Bureau's polygraph program. One could certainly argue that Bob Hanssen singlehandedly redirected the goals and objectives of the Bureau's polygraph unit. Without question, his activities set into motion a transition from how the FBI would utilize polygraph in the future. In less than thirty days following Hanssen's arrest, Director Louis Freeh ordered an enhancement to the personnel security polygraph program (PSPP) within the FBI. The affect of this enhancement, although necessary and critical to establishing a counterintelligence safety net against potentially treasonous employees in the future, was a serious blow to criminal investigative polygraph testing.

One may ask, how can this be? The answer lies in the restructuring of the Bureau and a titanic shift in focus from criminal investigative priorities to an emphasis on counterintelligence and counterterrorism.

Part and parcel to this shift would be the PSPP. This program was reinvigorated, and authority was granted for testing Bureau employees periodically, where before, authority had been severely limited in the days of Bob Hanssen. Without this authority, Hanssen was never obliged to sit for a polygraph prior to his arrest.

Sitting at the core of the PSPP resurgence was this author, albeit grudgingly so. No examiner worth his salt enjoys screening fellow employees. This is akin to asking the linebacker on a football team to be the referee. Examiners thrive on the confrontation with the crook, the wrongdoer, the deceiver. That is where they excel—in the exam room, reading someone their rights, reading their polygraph charts, reading their verbal and nonverbal cues. Honing one's interview and interrogation (I & I) skills in the testing of employees in a PSPP setting is a far cry from the experience one gets in routine criminal testing.

Now certainly it goes without saying we are very fortunate our fellow Bureau employees are candid and forthright when it comes to issues of national security. But having said that, a strong focus in this realm of testing at the expense of criminal testing has had an adverse affect on Bureau polygraph examiners. There is no compelling need to develop one's I & I skills when the need to have those skills is so infrequent.

This is not to say the PSPP is detrimental to the FBI—quite the contrary. What has been injurious for the Bureau and its core of polygraph examiners is the dramatic shift from an emphasis on criminal casework to posturing for counterintelligence and counterterrorism. Contributing to this shift was the second key event of the new millennium, 9/11.

During the aftermath of 9/11, the Bureau's polygraph program was inundated with agent's requesting immediate polygraph exams of subjects suspected, in some way, of terrorist affiliation. All field offices were affected with an onslaught of leads to be covered. Many of these leads erupted into additional follow-up polygraph testing in an effort to separate a person of interest from a real suspect or otherwise. Polygraph exams were sought seven days a week at any time of the day or night for four months following 9/11. In fact, over four hundred terrorism-related polygraph examinations were conducted Bureau-wide from September 11, 2001, to the end of the year.

Now certainly terrorism is criminal in nature, but polygraphs dealing with terrorism tend to be more like "fishing expeditions" in that we "screen" more folks in this area. That is not to belittle terrorism testing. In fact, it is critically important we become skilled artisans in the interview and interrogation aspect of the terrorism polygraph exam because we often lack the leverage we enjoy in a criminal test, leverage meaning evidence. Hence, the terrorism polygraph tends to be a *hybrid* of the criminal test in its correlation. More specifically, it is the post-test interrogation that often becomes problematic if a translator is necessary. With the use of a translator, the flow of conversing confrontationally has a way of losing momentum. It is somewhat akin to driving a screw into a small hole without grease. The head of the screw becomes distorted in short order. The whole effort becomes an aberration of its intended course. The point is, I & I as it relates to polygraph, would lose momentum in the years ahead with a decline in criminal testing.

The FBI became obsessed in preventing another Bob Hanssen affair and, God forbid, another 9/11. They simply had no choice in the matter. Congressional pressure mandated a new direction for the Bureau. The agency's existence was at stake. Something had to give, and unfortunately, what gave was criminal testing.

Typically, a polygraph examiner's sphere of expertise is in theme development. It is through theme development that confessions are obtained and cases are made. When an examiner is redirected to an activity where getting the confession is but a rare necessity, his or her interrogation skills erode. This is, in essence, the problem the FBI polygraph program currently faces and will continue to face in the years ahead.

The two aforementioned shifts in priorities for 2001 brought with them an additional change that continues to be problematic for smooth management of the FBI polygraph program. Prior to 2001, the polygraph unit fell under the oversight of the laboratory division. Understandably so given the fact that polygraph is both a science and an art. FBI examiners are trained by forensic psychophysiologists and must meet continuing education requirements as established and mandated by the National Center for Credibility Assessment (NCCA), formerly the Defense Academy for Credibility Assessment (DACA) and prior to that the Department of Defense Polygraph Institute (DoDPI). However, scientific nexus notwithstanding, the Bureau saw fit to place the polygraph unit under the umbrella of the now expanded security division following the Hanssen debacle.

There was an advantage for the unit to sit within the structure of Security. That advantage amounted to a much larger budget for the polygraph program, which has always been burdened by heavy travel expenses. Having said that, the benefit of the deep pocket was soon superseded by an overwhelming disadvantage.

The paralyzing oversight of security division executive management who lack the scientific understanding of how and why polygraph exams are administered the way they are, is a repetitious dilemma for unit managers. Senior executive service personnel change every two years or so, and with the change comes the burden of reeducating newly positioned executives who want nothing more than to change something so that they can say they thought outside the box and that made all the difference. When in fact, the changes they often propose would be troubling if not disastrous for polygraph.

For example, one such change pursued on more than one occasion was for an HRD employee, untrained in polygraph, to sit in on an appeal board with a voting position for applicants who fail their polygraph and appeal for another shot at it. One can only imagine the frustration of polygraph unit managers having to constantly educate and advise the untrained employee what is meant by such terms as question onset, artifact, pneumograph tracing, habituation, orienting response, homeostasis, galvanic skin response, and preventricular contraction.

Another recurring hurdle unit managers have to deal with every other year is this notion from some senior executives that we should have nonagent polygraph examiners conducting our exams. I could fill a chapter on the number of position papers our unit chiefs have had to write, rewrite, or reconstruct in support of special agent examiners as opposed to support employees in the pole position of our program.

First of all, support employee examiners do not carry a badge and do not have arrest powers. As such, they lack the authority, power of persuasion, and respect necessary for success in criminal testing.

Criminal exams can get rather confrontational. Consider for a moment what would happen if a support employee got into a tussle with a belligerent examinee, and someone got hurt. The FBI would be very foolish to allow a support examiner to be placed into this setting. Yet it gets considered.

Once the unit reminds the powers that be who are frequently of the nonbadge-carrying variety we are a law enforcement agency, a fallback position is taken whereby it is proposed that support examiners run applicant screening exams only. The problem with this idea is that special agent examiners have had years of experience with investigating cases and, as such, have acquired the necessary elicitation and interrogation skills, which serve them so well in the polygraph suite. The interpersonal skill of the trained and experienced special agent examiner leads to resolution of cases. Likewise, these same skills result in pretest and post-test admissions in preemployment testing of failed applicants, which greatly aid HRD in their hiring decisions.

When criminal testing is slow or inactive, applicant screening is a means for special agent examiners to hone their skills in the discipline of polygraph. If special agent examiners were deprived of the opportunity to conduct preemployment exams, their effectiveness would diminish over time in operational testing. And let's not forget how our experience has shown that applicants do from time to time intentionally withhold information they believe would hinder their opportunities at employment. An experienced special agent examiner will have a greater likelihood of identifying these issues prior to any conditional job offer being extended inappropriately.

Finally, it should have become clear in 2008 with the introduction of a serious crime question in the applicant-screening format, a sworn law enforcement professional is really the only option that makes sense in the preemployment testing arena. Since the serious crimes issue was brought into the equation, it has not been too uncommon wherein an applicant brings to light an act he or she may have done, which necessitates an Advice of Rights waiver being issued and a criminal investigation opened.

No, support examiners are not a good fit the FBI. Fortunately, over the last ten years, the unit has prevailed more often than not with sound articulation and reasoning to thwart misguided or poorly thought out motives for constant change.

The FBI has always responded when pushed into a corner. That is what champions do, and the Bureau has a long-demonstrated history of rising for the bell. If I may be so bold as to ring that bell, now is the time for our cadre of special agents to answer the call to become seasoned interviewers and skilled interrogators.

The Bureau will always have a need for a true people person, an agent who can combine his understanding of verbal and nonverbal behavior with good interpersonal skills to go out and get his fair share of signed, sworn statements. Whether polygraph is or is not employed, in the end it all comes down to people skills.

The art of persuasion, when employed well, will almost always involve convincing your subject that you *truly care*. If your subject believes you care, you stand a better than 50 percent chance of getting his confession. The only true way for the interrogator to convey to the subject that he cares for him is to actually care for him with all sincerity. To do otherwise, to disguise sincerity, is to invite failure. As discussed in the last chapter, this is the potential paradox the interrogator, the polygraph examiner faces when he or she goes into the room in a criminal setting.

The efforts of this story emanated from the days of analog polygraph instrumentation, as Cy Donovan referred to in his use of "old reliable." The FBI was perhaps the last, if not the last, federal agency to transition to computerized testing. That transition began around the turn of the new millennium by one examiner who subsequently left the program after a gallant effort. The transition was completed in 2006 thanks to a tremendous effort by one man, one examiner from the Portland division who was subsequently highly decorated for the achievement and rightfully so.

As with the Hanssen matter, the Bureau frequently learns the hard way. In actuality however by being last in the club with the new toys, the Bureau did not have to endure the pitfalls, the trial and error, and the glitches and problems associated with the early introductions of computerized polygraph instruments (CPSs).

As this book comes to a close, there is a trend in the Bureau for agents to become wizards of the shared drive, database gurus, mouse-clicking drones, and electro-geeks. However, push eventually comes to shove, and someone will need to have the ability, desire, and competency to go knee to knee.

The incriminating statement, the admission of guilt or full confession does not come via WinZip, e-mail, or sitting behind the latest version of a new laptop, iPad, or some such electronic gadget. It does come through mixing it up with society's derelicts through controlled confrontation. Having said that, consider polygraph.

Polygraph will always be an effective tool, a means to an end. Any technological device whether it is polygraph, the voice stress analyzer, or perhaps brain wave technology (still undergoing research), can be a good tool if employed ethically and legally and can provide you information not previously known.

Regardless of the reliability or validity of the tool, it is the *utility* of the tool that matters most. The agent who recognizes this will do well. The Cy Donovans who are willing to peer into the soul of their examinees and rattle a few skeletons will carry the day more often than not. When the day is done and the score is spun, the ledger will show how you answered the bell. You answer the bell by going knee to knee.

AFTERWORD

It was with great trepidation that I ventured into this book. The stories unfolded in this reading pale in comparison to the work done by some of the FBI's finest polygraph examiners. The real artists in this profession are the men and women who traveled near and far at a moment's notice to come face-to-face with some of society's most demented people. They faced them, they reached deep into their soul for hours on end, and they came out with confessions or admissions quite frequently. When they failed, when the disclosure was not forthcoming, they almost always came away with information of lead value.

This is the essence of why we use polygraph in law enforcement. It is an invaluable tool to investigators especially when utilized by an experienced interrogator. A skilled craftsman like a few I will mention here.

First of all, my former colleague from Detroit pulled off a trifecta, a feat not likely to ever be equaled. You, sir, are the only examiner who traveled to three different cities in one day in 2000 and got three bona fide confessions from criminal subjects! Now that is a real hat trick.

Secondly, who can forget the request that came down from the director's office for our esteemed Atlanta examiner to go to

Ghana. This was a rare occurrence whereby government officials in Ghana sought the help of the FBI in a serial murder case. The right examiner was selected, and the right examiner went to Ghana and obtained the right results. You were Atlanta's best and the Bureau's best at the time. Your test results and subsequent confession to eight murders by your subject confirmed what we, in the polygraph program, already knew. You were the best. You were the one we could always count on. You are to be commended.

Let's not forget our examiner from Dallas. A kidnapping/murder suspect who not only confessed to you but accompanied you to the body! Without question a gut-wrenching day for you and your career but a hallmark day for you from an interview and interrogation standpoint. You practiced your craft well and brought closure to a case where others may have floundered. People confess to those whom they trust. You secured his trust and, in turn, became one of the Bureau's go-to guys when the situation called for a top-shelf examiner.

Similar cases to the one in Dallas were solved in both New York and New Haven divisions. Being long-time examiners with the FBI and two of the finest, you will both remember your day with each of your subjects. As a result of your efforts, hard-nosed, lengthy interrogations resulted in finding the victims of these horrendous crimes and brought justice to matters, which may have gone unsolved were it not for the both of you. Neither of you were afraid to call a liar a liar and arouse a few truth-tellers along the way.

The true pillars of the program were the long-term quality control reviewers who moved to Washington and served at FBIHQ. They fought the administrative battles with Department of Justice officials, FBIHQ front office executives, DoDPI, DACA, NCCA academicians, and the occasional whiner who got their feelings hurt during a polygraph exam. One of you in particular served thirteen years "in the kitchen" during the earliest years of the program while another did the quality control review of over thirty-two thousand polygraph exams before retiring and then came back and did some more! If there were a hall of fame for Bureau examiners, you two would go in on the first ballot.

There were others who excelled beyond their call of duty in FBI divisions across the country. From Honolulu, Los Angeles, San Francisco, Seattle, Phoenix, Las Vegas, and San Antonio in the west to Miami, Jacksonville, Tampa, Columbia, Washington, Newark, Richmond, Norfolk, Mobile, Philadelphia, Baltimore, Pittsburgh, and Boston in the east. Breadbasket America had its share of top-shelf examiners as well from Milwaukee to Chicago, Indianapolis to Omaha, and Little Rock to Knoxville. They have all had the privilege of employing one of the Bureau's finest I & I agents at one time or another including Memphis.

Did I say Memphis? Oh, yes indeed. I will leave you with this one as it breaks my heart but uplifts me with pride all the same. In July of 2006, Jackson, Mississippi, was in need of a polygraph examiner to assist in yet another kidnapping matter. A young girl had been abducted, shot in the head, and left for dead near a wood line. The subject at the time whom local authorities believed to be involved was detained for further questioning.

Our Jackson examiner was out of the division at the time and unavailable. As such, the Jackson office reached out to a veteran examiner from Memphis. The Memphis examiner responded and soon found himself face-to-face with a very troubled individual. This person consented to the polygraph and subsequently failed the test on the issue of his involvement in the disappearance of the young girl. The Memphis examiner knew he had the probable killer in his chair. What he didn't have was the girl.

Upon completion of the test, he immediately pressed his subject for the whereabouts of the girl. Fighting off denial after denial, he eventually persuaded the subject to take him to the body. The examiner was shocked to find out, as was the subject, that the girl was still alive! She had a bleeding open head wound from a gunshot and had survived nearly a full day lying in the woods. She indeed recovered from this ordeal thanks to the heroic efforts of one of the Bureau's finest polygraph examiners. The local authorities took all the kudos in the case. The Memphis examiner, however, will forever be the owner of the FBI polygraph program's finest hour.

ABOUT THE AUTHOR

William J. Warner retired as a special agent from the FBI in 2012 with over twenty-two years of service. He spent sixteen of those years conducting polygraph examinations and/or managing within the FBI's polygraph program. Warner entered the FBI with a law degree and picked up a master of arts in forensic psychology along the way. Prior to his service with the FBI, Warner served as an internal investigator for the Metropolitan Atlanta Rapid Transit Authority Police and did a three-year hitch with the 82nd Airborne Division. He was born and raised in Bryan, Ohio.